LOVE ON THE RUN

Bree suddenly felt a swell of emotion from the pit of her belly spread throughout her body. She remembered their kiss and the moments since then when she had felt an attraction to him. She felt a little dizzy.

"Graham." His name came like a whisper from her mouth.

The sound of her whispering his name and the sight of her soft lips created a sense of urgency in Graham. His body reacted without warning or reason. His lips came down on hers with tender affection. All he wanted in this world was to comfort her.

Bree felt a flame light inside her at the touch of his lips. They were tender, but possessive and seductive. She heard herself let out a quiet sigh as she kissed him back. Her arms reached for his neck, pulling him closer to her as their lips explored each other. Bree was cloaked with a feeling of comfort and security.

The softness turned to a demand as Graham's body wanted more. A desire to comfort had turned simply to desire as he grabbed at her shoulders, pulling her to him. He was heating up like a volcano as his lips parted hers. Slowly his tongue entered her mouth, and he let out a moan.

The urgent feeling of his hands on her skin and his mouth on hers sent Bree from a flame to a fire. She ran her fingers over the back of his head, bringing her body even closer to his. Her tongue responded to his, exploring his mouth, feeling the excitement of the unexpected fueling her own.

"Bree," he whispered as his mouth left hers and went to her cheek, her chin, and settled in her neck. His tongue teased at her neck in between warm kisses. She was so soft and smelled so good.

Bree heard her own breathing heavy and fast as his tongue felt like lava on her neck. Her hands grabbed at his shirt, wanting him to be closer. Wanting him to take more. Wanting more for herself.

BOOK YOUR PLACE ON OUR WEBSITE AND MAKE THE ARABESQUE ROMANCE CONNECTION!

We've created a customized website just for our very special Arabesque readers, where you can get the inside scoop on everything that's going on with Arabesque romance novels.

When you come online, you'll have the exciting opportunity to:

- View covers of upcoming books

- Learn about our future publishing schedule (listed by publication month and author)

- Find out when your favorite authors will be visiting a city near you

- Search for and order backlist books

- Check out author bios and background information

- Send e-mail to your favorite authors

- Join us in weekly chats with authors, readers and other guests

- Get writing guidelines

- AND MUCH MORE!

Visit our website at
http://www.arabesquebooks.com

LOVE ON THE RUN

Angela Winters

BET Publications, LLC
http://www.bet.com
http://www.arabesquebooks.com

ARABESQUE BOOKS are published by

BET Publications, LLC
c/o BET BOOKS
One BET Plaza
1900 W Place NE
Washington, DC 20018-1211

All Kensington Titles, Imprints, and Distributed Lines are available at special quantity discounts for bulk purchases for sales promotions, premiums, fund-raising, and educational or institutional use. Special book excerpts or customized printings can also be created to fit specific needs. For details, write or phone the office of the Kensington special sales manager: Kensington Publishing Corp., 850 Third Avenue, New York, NY 10022, attn: Special Sales Department, Phone: 1-800-221-2647.

First Printing: January 2002
10 9 8 7 6 5 4 3 2 1

Printed in the United States of America

LOVE ON THE RUN brings back many of the characters first introduced in my novel A FOREVER PASSION. A FOREVER PASSION provoked countless letters from readers and fans who fell in love (and hate) with members of the Hart family, the dynamic relationships, and the interesting possibilities of the supporting characters. The recurring theme of those letters was ''Bring them back!'' It's because of that that I dedicate this novel to my readers and thank them for their inspiration.

Chapter One

This was beyond incredible timing. It defied coincidence. The only explanation was that the powers that be were determined never to let Bree Hart escape her family.

Her manager was nowhere in sight, so her tired arms placed a dirty plate on the counter behind her for a quick five-minute break and leaned back. The television was placed in the nook between the bar and the kitchen. It was where everyone took a breather before facing the crowds. The television was always turned to *Courtroom Television*.

Bree studied the image of her brother as it filled the screen. His face very handsome, his smile as smooth as silk. If they only knew what lay beneath.

"In Manhattan today," a newscaster in the foreground said, "an ever-increasing force in the legal industry, Keith Hart, won another hot one. In a case that began with a bang six months ago, but lost a little of its glitter recently, Keith Hart was successful in acquitting his client, Sophia Lane, an administrative assistant charged in the insider trading scandal at Trotter Securities.''

"Keith defending a secretary?'' Bree asked out loud with a smirk. "Doesn't sound glamorous enough for him. Admins are generally not in the tax bracket of his usual clients. There's got to be something else to it.''

The newscaster continued. "The investment banking industry scandal began almost a year ago, when hotshot broker Robert Barber was accused of using his high-level connections to illegally advise his clients on upcoming mergers, product placements, layoffs, and megadeals that would effect stock while the information was still deemed confidential and not released to the financial industry. Barber's clients rank among the most powerful and influential men and women in New York, Los Angeles, and Europe.''

"Sounds more like Keith,'' Bree said with a nod. She folded her arms across her chest and settled in to hear more. If there was no escaping the Hart clan, she might as well get a laugh out of them.

"Barber was arrested and charged, along with his assistant, Sophia Lane, a thirty-year-old former elementary school teacher. The state of New York, along with the securities exchange commission, charged them both with using illegal information to help Barber's clients get the edge on the rest of the firm's investors and the investment community as a whole. In this world of technology, E-mails sent via computers and cell phones composed most of the evidence. Personal accounts and testimony were weak at best.''

Bree's eyes widened for a moment when Howard Staley rushed by with at least three hot plates laid across his arms and hands. She calmed down when she realized it wasn't her boss. Still, she was nervous about people connecting her to her family. That was the last thing she needed. Nervous that her picture would come up and then the rest of the story. Then she'd be in trouble.

"Hey, Ebony," he said without glancing at her. "Nice to see you working hard."

She rolled her eyes at him even though he was long gone by now. Howard was a jerk. Because he was a Columbia law student, he seemed to think he was above all the rest of the lowly waiters. He took it upon himself to give advice to everyone about how they should be living their lives. Right down to how they should talk.

She turned her attention back to the screen.

"This was a major victory for the working man and woman in America," Keith said as the microphones stretched toward him on the steps of the courtroom. He was all charm and charisma. His demeanor, his dress, everything about him said he had it all, and would win at all costs. Made for the camera.

Emotion tugged at Bree at the sight of him. She hadn't seen her older brother face-to-face since she left Baltimore eight months ago, and she missed him. As much as she couldn't stand him, she missed him. He'd had a lot to overcome, as had all of them, in the past two years. He had emerged a more confident and successful man. He had also emerged a more controlling and tenacious man.

She was floored six months ago when she heard he had opened up a New York branch of his new law firm. But Bree wasn't scared. She knew how much of a snob her brother was and never expected their paths to cross. He was an Upper East Side man, and she was a Harlem girl. She was now, at least.

Even if they would happen to run into each other in this city of eight million, she was smarter than he. She could see past any of his power plays.

"... we have seen today is an attempt by a powerful firm and a powerful government agency with endless legal resources try to find a scapegoat in someone that they assumed could never match them." Keith paused for effect. There was complete silence around him. "But they lost. They lost because all of the power and money in the world can't make up for the truth."

Bree laughed. The truth. What was this about? Keith had never been one to really care about the truth. It was more of an afterthought for him.

As the camera followed Keith and his client toward a limousine, the reporter's voice was heard. "No doubt Keith Hart has emerged as one of the most powerful lawyers on the East coast. With a New York presence for only six months, his notoriety has been exceptional. And it certainly hasn't hurt that he comes from one of the most prominent African-American families on the East Coast. Still, many observers say the key to Ms. Lane's acquittal was the lack of strong testimony and the inability of the experts to corroborate evidence. It was an unusual case, which began months ago with the plea bargain of Robert Barber, who later testified against Sophia Lane. Well, thanks to Keith Hart and the justice system, Sophia Lane is now on her way home for good."

Bree was touched by the story, seeing the woman as emotional as she was when the camera faced her. Still, she wondered why Keith was involved. It was more his nature to represent the likes of Robert Barber, not Sophia Lane. Bree wasn't going to let her curiosity get the best of her. She had to stay away from her family. For her own sanity.

"Hey, you! I know you."

Bree turned with a jump. It was Nabb! Her stomach tightened as she looked around.

"Where's Robin?" he asked, stepping to only a foot away from her.

He looked intimidating, well over six feet and at least 250 pounds. He had a short, unkempt afro and a scraggly goatee. The ring in his nose glittered almost as brightly as the gold caps in his teeth. And there were so many of them.

Bree stood her ground even though her stomach was a mess. She lifted her head, sticking her chin out. "You better get out of here, Nabb. Only employees can be back here. I'll yell for the manager."

"Don't threaten me, you little . . ." He looked around, backing off a bit. "I'll go where I damn well please. Now, where is that lying roommate of yours?"

"I don't know where Robin is," she lied. Robin was hiding out at a friend's house in Queens. Hiding from Nabb. "She just gave you two grand. Why don't you leave her alone?"

"That's not how it works." He made a gnarling sound, raising the left side of his mouth. "Maybe I need to explain to you."

Bree refused to back down. He couldn't possibly hurt her. Could he? "Stay away from me. I don't have anything to do with you."

"The hell you don't." He grabbed her arm just as she turned to go. "Don't walk away from me when I'm talking to you."

"Get your hands off me!" She jerked her arm free and pushed him. He didn't move. After all, she was only five feet, two inches and 115 pounds. But the gesture itself was all she needed. He backed off again. "I didn't borrow anything from you. Your problem is not with me."

"My problem is with whoever I say it's with. You're Robin's roommate, so you probably spent that money too.

Therefore, the both of you owe me another two grand and I want it now."

"Well, she's not here and I don't have your money." Bree's mind was already racing. She had to get him out of here. She didn't want to lose her job. She needed this job, as much as she hated it. "I'll tell her you stopped by."

"I could save you the trouble if you just tell me where she is."

"Not a chance, Nabb." She placed her hands on her hips, if only to keep them from shaking.

Nabb looked her up and down. The expression on his face told her he was borderline impressed or amused. One or the other. Either way, she knew it wouldn't last long.

"You tell her I want that money in twenty-four hours or I'm coming after both of you." He reached under his shirt and pulled it up, revealing a small pistol. "You see this, whatever your name is?"

Bree didn't nod. She just stared at him, defiant and stubborn as she always was. In her mind, she was screaming, *A gun! A gun! A gun!*

"It means I mean business," Nabb said, covering up the pistol. "No more playing with you giggly little girls. I'm a businessman. Twenty-four hours. I know where you both live. I know where you both work. Don't tempt me."

"Fine, just get out of here," Bree said. "Get out of here before I yell. Everyone will come running. This is a classy place. They won't tolerate nonsense."

He shrugged. "Let 'em come. I don't care. I don't care about nothin'. That's what you and your little girlfriend need to know. I don't care about no one or nothing. So don't mess with me. I want my money."

Bree let out a heavy breath as soon as he was gone. She leaned against the wall. What in God's name had Robin gotten her into? At first it seemed exciting, but now . . .

wasn't this how it always was? Exciting at first, then reality sets in. Would she ever learn?

Bree had always found a way to get out of anything some way or another. But this time, it wouldn't be that simple. She needed to get in contact with Robin. But right now she needed some air.

"Where do you think you're going?"

Just as she reached the door to the alley behind the kitchen, Bree was halted by the familiar voice. Restaurant manager Jackson Ballard was eyeing her with both hands on his hips. His short, stocky figure was dressed in a soft blue business suit that, although not fitting him well, perfectly matched his eyes, which stood out as the only attractive quality on his whiter-than-snow face. His blond hair was always in a ponytail with a few strands purposefully hanging at the sides.

Bree put on the charm by instinct since she knew she was doing something she shouldn't. She was good at this, especially with men. Even the ones that didn't particularly find women attractive.

"Jack, I was just looking for you. Where have you been?"

"Working," he said. "Like you should be. Did you think I was taking a break out back? I never take a break, Ebony. Breaks are for losers."

He signed a sheet of paper presented to him by one of the cooks, who quickly ran away.

"I'm getting a little bit of a headache," she said, squinting her oval-shaped, dark brown eyes. "I just thought a little fresh air would—"

"Not a chance, kid." He rolled his eyes. "I'm not in the mood for your antics tonight. It's Thursday. You know how crazy it gets on Thursdays. And your flaky friend Robin bailed on me, so you owe me double the work."

"How do you figure that?"

"Sick, my rear end. She's probably off for the weekend

somewhere with some guy she just met yesterday. And you're covering for her.''

"I'm vouching for her, Jack. She's really, really sick. She can barely move.''

He rolled his eyes. "It doesn't matter either way. You got two more hours before your break. Get back to work. And do it now.''

Bree's lips pursed together in anger as he walked off. Her eyes sent darts to the back of his head as she contemplated taking a break anyway. She hated being told what to do. Absolutely hated it.

She glanced around the busy kitchen. No one was paying attention to her. It was crazy here around dinnertime. Logan's was a neighborhood regulars' type of restaurant that served Irish and Italian meals from old Boston recipes right in Manhattan's Upper West Side. The clientele were mostly twenty- and thirty-somethings making a boatload of money that would be willing to fork over thirty bucks for osco busco and sausage links and walk away considering themselves more cultured than before.

Bree laughed at them, but she envied them as well. She used to be one of them. She used to have all the money she needed to eat wherever she wanted to. And she did too. Weekends on the harbor in Baltimore or downtown D.C., the nicest restaurants, drinks on her at the hottest nightclubs.

She could live in the Upper West Side, or East Side for that matter. If she wanted to. But it all came with strings attached, strings that were beginning to choke her. And her mother's latest stunt was the last straw.

So she left that life behind in Baltimore and "ran away" to New York. Ran away, because no one ever left her mother, Victoria Hart, without her permission. In New York, she was building a life for herself the way so many others had to. From scratch. And it was harder than she had imagined. Especially when she did it under a false identity.

But she would do it, Bree thought as she took a breath and headed back to the dining room. She didn't need a break. She wasn't a quitter and she would never let Victoria say I told you so. That alone was enough motivation to keep going.

"Can I get you a drink or a snack, Mr. Lane?"

Graham took his usual seat in Keith Hart's office, next to the door. He smiled at Keith's attractive Native American assistant. "No thanks, Seta. I just had lunch before coming over here. My appointment is at two, right? When is Keith showing up?"

She bit her lower lip before blowing strands of black hair out of her face. She looked up at the large clock encased in cherry wood against the wall.

"He should be here now. He came back from lunch over a half hour ago, but he stepped out. I asked him where he was going, but when he's on the cell phone, there's no getting to him. I have your appointment on his palm pilot schedule and he usually sticks to it like glue. I'll beep him again."

"Thanks."

He smiled at her, sensing an awkward moment as she stared at him with a dazed look. She blinked and smiled, as if she suddenly realized she was staring at him. She blushed, lowering her head as she hurried out.

Graham was filled with mixed emotions right now. He'd been on an emotional high since yesterday thanks to Keith Hart, but he never really cared for the man and was annoyed with the thought of meeting with him. Every meeting was the same. Ten percent substance, 90 percent Keith patting himself on the back.

Graham found him pompous, arrogant, and self-centered. The kind of guy who would do anything for a slice of fame and the right amount of money. The kind of guy who valued everything Graham felt was wrong with the world.

Much to Keith's dismay, Graham hadn't heard of Keith Hart, or the Hart clan, for that matter, until six months ago when Keith called his home, asking to represent his sister, Sophia, in court. Keith explained his background, his Ivy League degrees, his family connections, his successful Baltimore law firm, which was opening an office in New York as they spoke.

Graham wasn't prepared to fool around with Sophia's future. He had been looking for the best lawyers in New York, despite what they would cost. As with the others, Graham did his research. Being a professor at Columbia University had several advantages. The law school was prestigious and the contacts were at his fingertips.

Graham was impressed, and that wasn't an easy thing for him. In the end, Keith was the best choice, and he was Sophia's choice, so Graham agreed. Every interaction he'd had with Keith over the last six months ending in an argument or with Graham doing everything he could to keep from cursing the guy out. His tactics were less than ethical, his manner abrasive at best. When it came down to it, Graham respected Keith's abilities, but he wasn't in awe of the man only four years his senior, and Keith didn't like that. Graham assumed that Keith had spent many years in the shadow of his older, more successful brother Marcus, and exacted his revenge on everyone else.

But despite Keith's tactics and ethics, because of him, Sophia was a free woman. He could never thank Keith enough for that.

But now came the issue of payment. The issue Graham knew would come eventually, and it was tearing at him. Keith was one of the best lawyers in New York, but also one of the most expensive. Graham did well as an economics professor for an Ivy League school. Better than most. Columbia wanted him badly enough to fork over more than they ever had for such a young professor. Still, he was a college professor, not a titan of industry. And now that he was not just supporting himself, but Sophia, paying Keith Hart was more of an issue than ever.

But, as Graham leaned back in the leather chair and glanced around the office that was a granite marble model for power deals, paying Keith wasn't the most important thing on his mind. Trotter Securities tried to frame his sister. Sophia did none of the things she was accused of. Now that the school season was over, number one on Graham's agenda was getting to the bottom of who exactly set out to frame his sister to take the fall for their own deeds.

Not just who, but how and why. Why Sophia Lane, a harmless secretary? The thought of it all filled him with rage as fresh today as when it first began. So angry, Graham didn't even notice the door to Keith's midtown Manhattan office being opened and a beautiful woman walking in.

"Who are you?"

Graham looked up. Just the sight of her made him feel a little dirty and unkempt in his jeans and crew shirt. She was a striking woman, probably in her sixties, although she wore her age better than any woman Graham had ever seen. The familiarity of her milk-chocolate skin, the soft peach, silk pantsuit, the auburn hair tied back in a conservative bun jogged his memory. He had seen her small, fine features in Keith's face. In his face, and in the pictures of the articles Graham had read when he was researching Keith Hart six months ago.

"I'm Graham Lane," he said, standing up. She had to be tall. In heels she gave him a run for his money and he was six feet, two inches. He held out his hand to her. "And you're Victoria Hart."

The look on her face amused him. She was torn. She was flattered that he knew her, but not at all interested in actually touching him. But she did, briefly shaking his hand. Very briefly.

Victoria looked him up and down slowly. "Are lawyers dressing down these days?"

He smiled a charming smile. "I'm not a lawyer, Mrs. Hart. I'm your son's client."

Her expression said she didn't believe that at first. Graham knew Keith's other clients were all wealthy people. He didn't look that bad. Just a little rugged.

Her head went back, her sparkling earrings moving gently. She smiled and laughed an emotionless laugh. "Oh yes. You're Mr. Lane, Sophia Lane's brother."

"Yes, I am."

She took a seat on the client side of Keith's desk and placed a small black purse on the desk. But not before glancing the space over to make sure it was clean enough for her belongings. "You owe my son quite a lot of gratitude."

"Yes, I do." Graham didn't care that she said it this way. It was true. "You wouldn't happen to know where he is? We have an appointment."

"My son will show up when he can." She looked down at her pants, wiping away something that wasn't there. "You won't take long, I hope."

How can I know how long it will take if the guy won't show up? "Actually, it's a pretty detailed conversation we need to have."

"About what?" Victoria seemed disappointed to hear this.

Graham sat back down in his chair. "That's confidential, Mrs. Hart."

She shrugged. "Well, I want him this afternoon. I'll only be here today. You see, I attended a showing at Sak's. On Fifth Avenue."

Did she think he didn't know where Sak's was? He was born in Brooklyn, for Pete's sake.

"And," she continued, "I'll only be here for a few more hours before my flight back to Baltimore. My baby has been spending too much time in New York. I need to see him."

Did she actually think he would sacrifice his appointment for her whim? Graham looked at her. Yes, she did. He wasn't inclined to appease her, but neither was he too excited about the conversation he needed to have with Keith.

"We'll let Keith decide," Graham said. This woman was a handful.

Victoria raised an eyebrow. "Yes, we should. But you should know. Whatever I want, Keith wants."

As if he ever had a choice, Graham said to himself.

Keith shot into the office talking on his cell phone. Walking at a rapid pace, he threw the jacket to his expensive business suit in the chair next to his mother and kissed her cheek with a swift move. He was just an inch shorter than Graham, but something about his thinness made him seem taller.

Graham noticed again how much Keith looked like his mother. Milk-chocolate skin, light eyes, fine features. Not a stitch out of place.

"Mother." He switched off the phone and tossed it on his desk, sitting in his chair. "I see you've met Graham. I wasn't expecting you this early."

"I know, dear. The show was wonderful, but short. The fashions are too bold this year. I don't know if there's anything appropriate for a lady to wear."

"Keith," Graham said, deciding he had given enough time for catch-up. "We have our appointment."

Keith nodded. "That's right, Mother. Graham and I need some privacy. Money talks, you know."

Graham didn't appreciate him sharing the topic of their confidential conversation, and his face must have said so, because Keith shifted in his seat, showing signs of discomfort.

"Uhm, Mother. Can you just wait outside for a moment?"

Victoria pouted with a grace that Graham didn't know a pout could have.

"Dear," she said. "You know how I feel about waiting. It's just money. Can't it be postponed?"

"It really can't, Mrs. Hart." As much as Graham wanted to avoid this talk, he knew the only way to deal with an unpleasant thing was head-on. "Keith?"

"We have something very serious to talk about," she said, eyeing Graham sternly. "It's a family emergency."

"Bree?" Keith asked, seeming suddenly annoyed.

Victoria nodded. "It's urgent, Keith. Mr. Lane can understand that."

Graham didn't have time for this. "Look, Keith. If it's a family emergency, I don't want to interfere with that. I do want to deal with this today, however. So let's—"

"Graham." Keith stood up, walking toward him. "This is not an emergency. Trust me. It'll take only a few minutes, I promise. Can you wait outside? I want to deal with this today too."

Graham paused before slowly standing up, his eyes set on Keith. The man had transformed into a negotiator, almost pleading with him. Trying his best to hide his arrogance. Graham's patience was wearing thin, but he wanted to make an exception for Keith. After all he had done for him, and Sophia.

Graham was outside the office for less than five minutes before Keith opened the door and waved him back in. Something was up. It took a minimum of common sense to know this was not good. The look on Keith's face was too conciliatory.

"Can you come back in, Graham?" he asked with a high-pitched voice and a smile. "Got a great idea that can help you out a lot."

"I didn't ask for any help, Keith." Graham walked cautiously back into the office.

His eyes focused on Victoria as he sat back down. Something was different with her as well. She was upset, and looked tired. Not physically, but emotionally. How could this have anything to do with him?

"Keith," he said, heading it all off. "I don't want to get involved in your family situations. They're none of my business and I don't want them to be. Let's reschedule our meeting for—"

"Even if it meant you didn't owe me a penny?" Keith asked.

Graham sighed, willing to take the bait. For now. "What do you mean?"

"I mean," he answered, "you owe me tens of thousands of dollars for Sophia's defense. I put a lot of my time and the time of my New York and Baltimore staff into fighting Trotter Securities.

"Now, I'm not complaining. The CEO of Trotter, Davin Smith, well . . . I told you that he was a former client at the firm I used to work at before going solo. Well, I didn't tell you that he fired me. He's the only client I've ever had that fired me. It was a humiliating experience. I had never—"

"What does this have to do with my debt to you, Keith?" Graham interrupted.

"You can clear it all up. You can go to a balance due of zero. For a favor."

"I'm not in the favor business." He looked at Victoria, who sighed heavily. "Let's talk later."

"Mr. Lane." Victoria stood up, her expression weary. "You have to help us. You have to help me find my baby and bring her back to me. I'm desperate."

"Mrs. Hart." Graham was affected by her emotion. He had a soft spot for women in need. "If your daughter is missing, you should call missing persons. Surely, you can afford—"

"No," she said. "We can't do that. We—"

"Mother." Keith stood up. "Please, sit down. I'll handle this. Look, Graham. My sister is not a child, even though she acts like one. She's an adult, all of twenty-five years old. She ran away from home several months ago, and she's in New York. We just found this out a few weeks ago."

"So you've found her?" Ran away? How does a twenty-five-year-old run away? "What's the problem?"

"We haven't found her," Keith said. "It's complicated. The little brat has decided to rough it. I guess she's using another name. We had a private investigator looking for her when we tracked her here, but he let it slip out and mother had to do some maneuvering to keep it out of the Baltimore social papers."

"We can't go to the police, hire an investigator, or any of that," Victoria said. "We need someone who won't tell anyone."

"No one knows she's missing?" Graham couldn't believe he was even asking this.

"We've told everyone she's abroad. Traveling." Victoria rolled her eyes. "She's the adventurous type, so it fits. There's no way on God's green earth I'll tell people she's slumming in New York. Waitressing at some restaurant. Living with some guy that might be an ex-con.''

Graham didn't want any part of this girl, whoever she was. "Keith, Mrs. Hart. I'm sorry, but I'm just not—''

"Here." Keith handed him a folder. "This is what we found on her so far. You can just take it from there.''

"You're right here in Manhattan," Graham said. "Why don't you go find her?''

"I don't have time for this." Keith leaned against the chair next to his mother. "Besides, if she saw me, she might run again. For good this time.''

"That can't happen," Victoria said.

"She's an adult. Can't she go where she wants to? Despite an unsavory lifestyle, she's not being held against her will. And she's obviously surviving.''

"This is no life for her," Victoria said, her voice laced with anger. "Bree doesn't know what she wants. She's an adventurous thrill seeker. She thinks this stuff is cute. She's been a privileged child her whole life and she has no idea what the real world is. She jumps into things, causes a ruckus of her life and the lives of everyone else around her. I'm always cleaning up after her. I'm scared to death that I won't be there for her when she needs me this time.''

"I'm not a baby-sitter and I'm not a spoiled child chaser.'' Graham knew his words were harsh, but this was ridiculous. He tossed the folder on the chair beside him. "Either find the child yourself or let her live her life.''

"My son can play hardball, Mr. Lane." Victoria's emotion was all gone. She was done with the charade. "If you bring it to that.''

"Mother." Keith's tone was warning.

Graham traded glances from Victoria to Keith. "Are you threatening me? What is this?''

"Graham, please." Keith smiled, but the smile quickly

went away when he noticed the look on Graham's face. "No one is threatening you. We're giving you options. You can either pay me in full what you owe me for keeping your sister out of jail. Or you can find my sister and clear your bill forever."

"In full?"

Keith nodded. "Yeah, didn't I tell you? We don't have a payment plan of any kind here. It's a start-up firm, really."

Graham clenched his fist. Keith wasn't as smart as he thought he was. "Don't try to pull one over on me, Keith. You'll get a lot more than you bargained for."

Keith blinked, but showed nothing else. "Don't be so defensive, Graham. Why don't you take some time to think about it? It seems so simple to me. Are you concerned that you couldn't do it?"

Graham smiled. "It's going to take a better man than you to make me doubt myself."

Keith's face went flat. It was obvious he wasn't at all pleased. Victoria seemed to notice, and, trying to keep things from getting out of hand, took over.

"My son isn't trying to get you to doubt yourself." She floated to Graham with the grace of a well-bred woman. "Not at all. It's just that he sees a mutually beneficial situation for both of us. For us, we can find Bree and save her from herself, while being certain that the person helping us has no interest in making it public. You don't care about us or have any interest in fame or climbing a social ladder. That's what Keith said."

"Nor do I have any interest in chasing after overgrown children," Graham said.

"Not even to erase a debt of several thousand dollars?" she asked.

Graham was sighing and laughing at the same time. This was hilarious and frustrating. "You can't force someone to

. . . Look, I'm not even going to consider it. Keith, if you want to discuss money in a professional . . . confidential conversation, you know my number.''

There was complete silence as he turned and walked out. He never looked back. If he knew anything, it was to make a decision and stick with it. Looking back was a sign of regret. People like Keith and Victoria Hart pounced on regret.

Graham had learned long ago how to hold his composure with the upper crust. Growing up with working-class parents in the tough neighborhoods of Brooklyn, he never interacted with the so-called elite. His mother left them after he was five, and his father struggled through a hard life before passing away far too young. Sophia had his back, which was why he felt he owed her everything.

It was his first year at New York University on a full merit scholarship that he had come in contact with the privileged society. He had learned how to deal with them, and it hadn't been as hard as he had expected it to be. The fact that he turned out to be smarter than most of them hadn't hurt either.

Especially at Columbia. There were a lot of people like Keith and Victoria at Columbia. And people like Bree Hart. He didn't have time to be bothered with any of them. And as for the money, the tens of thousands of dollars he owed Keith—well, he would deal with that tomorrow. He had had enough headache today.

It wasn't generally his style, but all Graham could think of right now was a strong drink.

Tribeca was one of Bree's favorite areas of Manhattan. As out of the way as it was from her home in Harlem, the trip was always worth it. It was an area in lower Manhattan, below Canal Street, that ran right into China Town. Years ago it was a manufacturing and warehouse district, but it was now an active, vibrant cultural center for the city's young professionals and social elites. It was also a home for artists, an alternative to Soho, housing myriads of art galleries and some of the best restaurants on the island.

Bree loved the free-spirited atmosphere. But she couldn't really enjoy it right now. Especially not when she remembered why she was down here tonight. Detroit was the name of one of the newest bars in Tribeca. Bree had never been here, preferring the older bars that had been around since the early nineties. But this was where she was to meet Robin per her instructions.

The bar itself was a lot like the others in the area. Brick walls, with art of all kinds displayed on them in various shapes and juxtapositions. Round tables, with white cloths and wildly shaped candles lighting a dim room. The dance floor circled the dining area. To the left, just at the entrance was a bar that stretched along the wall on two sides. It was one of the largest Bree had ever seen.

At the far end of the bar, a DJ was playing some sort of Irish sound with a loud bass in it, similar to the backdrop of any rap song. Bree thought the two sounds fit well together. The dance floor was struggling for attention from the myriads of people standing around it waiting for someone else to lead the way. The tables were all filled with young people of every ethnic makeup you could think of. It was Friday night in Tribeca, and there was never an empty table.

Bree smiled at the men who stared at her as she walked by. Her petite but curvy figure played up the crimson tank top and hip-hugging black stretch pants. Her thick flops gave her a couple of inches on her five-foot-two frame.

She was a harmless flirt most times, but tonight Bree just smiled and walked on by. She wasn't trying to start any drama tonight, and after breaking up with Michael, her latest mistake, just a few weeks ago, she wasn't in a flirtatious mood anyway. She should have known better about Michael, but that was her MO. Act first, think later.

"What took you so long? I said eight." Robin Clay pressed her thin lips together as her fingers tapped at the table.

"You called me at six-thirty and wanted me to meet you on the other side of Manhattan." Bree took the seat next to her, speaking loudly enough to be heard over the music. "Now you want to nag me?"

"I'm sorry, Bree. I'm nervous."

Robin's appearance backed up her words. She didn't look good to Bree at all. Her twenty-two-year-old hazel eyes were a teary red. She usually wore her sandy brown hair kinky and natural, but it normally looked more put together than now. Her butterscotch-colored face was void of makeup, and Bree knew Robin didn't go outside without at least lipstick on. And she would never go out on a Friday night without being decked out, knowing her full figure was an attention grabber. Decked out would hardly describe her getup tonight.

"What's going on with you?" Bree noticed that one of Robin's hands was glued to her lap. "I thought you wanted to meet me way out of the way so we could hang out without Nabb gunning us down."

Robin leaned across the table, looking desperately into Bree's eyes. "You're my friend, right? When we met eight months ago in Central Park, you were looking for a place to live and I needed a roommate. I took you on your word, and we said we'd be friends."

"Yeah." Bree placed a hand over Robin's. It was shaking. "And I meant it. I've been here for you, haven't I?"

Robin nodded. "Even when you found out I had a record

for shoplifting, you didn't care. Even when I've gotten into a little mess now and then, you've still been my friend.''

"Like you haven't done the same for me. We scratch each other's backs, girlfriend.''

"You gave me the two grand to pay Nabb and get him out of my hair.'' Robin looked as if she were near tears. "You had to dig into your trust, and I know you hated that.''

Bree did, but she only smiled reassuringly at her friend. Robin was a bit of a hell-raiser like herself. But Robin had had a lot of bad breaks in life. Bree knew she herself wasn't in any position to judge her. She had been determined to make it in New York without money from her family, but this was an emergency.

"What is going on, Robin?"

She lifted a small paper bag and laid it on the table. "I owe Nabb another two grand, right?"

"And he wants it now. I told you he stopped by the restaurant last night. You're shift starts tomorrow at noon. He'll be back, I know it. If we don't show up, we'll lose our jobs and that's gonna suck. We can't avoid him much longer.''

"I plan on handling it tonight," Robin said, looking at the bag. "The money is in here."

"Where did you get it?" Bree felt a sense of relief come over her. The ambience of the room set in on her. It was a nice bar. She couldn't believe she liked this music, but she did.

"I didn't." Robin swallowed hard. "It's actually two hundred dollars that Lily let me borrow. She's a good friend, that girl. Well, I slipped two hundred on top of some counterfeit.''

"You're nuts, girl!" Bree grabbed the bag, but Robin pulled it away from her.

"No, Bree." She waved away an approaching waitress.

"Whenever I give him money, he never counts it. I've always paid him back what I told him I would. This time, it was a little more than I could pay back in time. But I've always done it. He'll look at it real quick and add it to all the other cash he collects on the weekend. Friday is collection night."

"Where did you get counterfeit? I want to see it." Bree reached again, but Robin slapped her hand away.

"Not important. I know a guy. What's important is that Nabb will leave us alone."

"It'll just make him angrier. He's going to kill you. Us. He's a thug, but he's not stupid, Robin. He'll notice counterfeit eventually."

"But not right away. He'll be back home, high on weed, countin' his money. It'll be a while before he wises up. Then, he'll never know it was me. I've always paid him tried-and-true cash."

"This has got to be the worst idea I have ever, ever heard. And I've heard some bad ideas. Most of them were my own."

"I'm doing it." Robin was resigned. "I'm meeting him here tonight. I called him. He said he's picking up money from like ten people in this area tonight. You know he lends it out to these artists down here all the time. They sell a painting or sculpture at the exhibits and pay him back. So I told him I'd meet him here."

Bree leaned back in her chair. "You're living in a fantasyland."

"I wanted you to be here to do this with me, but if you don't want to, you can leave."

Bree thought about it. Even with everything in her saying this was going to blow up in her face, a sense of intensity hit her and she didn't want to leave. She was a danger freak. "I'm not leaving you alone to do this."

Robin jumped as the music suddenly went up a few notches and people got up to start dancing.

"You're nervous as hell, girl," Bree said. "I think you know this isn't going to work. And it'll only make things worse for you. For us."

"I'm just a little anxious." Robin looked around the bar. "Where is that waitress? She ain't coming back here. I already waved her away twice. I need a drink."

"I'll get us something at the bar." Bree stood up. "What do you want?"

"Tom Collins," Robin said. She looked at the paper bag. "You know what? Make that a straight gin on the rocks."

Graham wrapped his fingers around the glass of wine. Was this his sixth or seventh? He couldn't remember anymore. He didn't care.

After he left Keith's office that afternoon, he walked around midtown. He didn't want to think about anything, so he kept walking, acting like a tourist in a city that he knew like the back of his hand. The Empire State Building, Macy's, the Chrysler Building, Grand Central Terminal, the United Nations Complex, Rockefeller Center, Trump Tower, Times Square, Carnegie Hall, Radio City Music Hall. They were all that made the city one of the most exciting places in the world.

When his feet couldn't take it anymore, he found himself in a Tribeca bar called Detroit. He never usually came this far south.

Graham was used to having everything under control. He considered himself a simple man, with very few complications. He avoided complications on purpose. But ever since everything had begun happening to Sophia, his life was getting out of control. His only real relationship in years fell apart. The person he loved most in the world, Sophia, had crawled into an emotional corner after this nightmare began. And financially, he was in debt as he hadn't been since student loans.

His only solace had been in teaching. He was able to focus, concentrate, forget the rest of the world. Now it was June and the school year was over. Something was missing in his life. Maybe it always had been, but he couldn't ignore it anymore. He needed . . .

"A gin on the rocks and an amaretto sour, please."

Like a breath of fresh air. Graham didn't know if it was the alcohol or not, but this beautiful chocolate-brown princess that stood next to him at the bar erased the rest of the world for him. For that moment at least.

She was a petite feminine woman, probably looking younger than she was. Her dark hair was set wildly around her face, ending just below her ears. Her features were angelic, but everything about her said she was a ball of fire. Her eyes were dancing even though her body stood still. Usually her type would make Graham turn and head the other way. Usually he didn't drink six glasses of wine in less than an hour. He swung his stool around to face her, wanting only to know her name.

"Two drinks at a time?" he asked, wondering if he looked as tipsy as he felt. "You must be in a rush to get your weekend started."

Bree turned to face him. He was handsome, she thought at first glance. He looked like a bit of a bookworm. One of those strong sturdy guys a gal could depend on. She didn't need to depend on any guy. She checked the hand first. Always check for the ring. She learned that lesson the hard way.

No ring. She was surprised. He looked like a ready-made husband. Still, he was entertainment while she waited.

"They're not both for me," she said with a sweet smile. "Not that it's any of your business."

"Just making conversation." Graham liked the sound of her voice. Flirtatious, but not easy. Just very sassy. "The other one for a man?"

"That's none of your business either." She felt herself relax. He was a square, but he was really cute. He'd had a few though. That much she could see. "But what if it is?"

"Then I'd say that was a very lucky man." Lucky indeed. He tried nonchalantly to lean closer. She had a sexy little outfit on too. Her skin was glowing and tempting.

"I guess I should thank you," Bree said, "but I think you're being fresh with me, so I won't."

"What's your name?" Graham asked, but she wasn't looking at him anymore. She was looking into the crowd, and that flirtatious look on her face was gone.

Bree's stomach clenched when she saw Nabb approach Robin at the table. He looked halfway decent, but in this area, looking a little different wasn't something that got you noticed.

"Fourteen bucks, ma'am."

With her eyes still on Robin and Nabb, Bree fumbled for her money in her back pocket. But the man on the stool placed his hand on her arm. It distracted her enough to tear her eyes away from Robin.

"Don't . . . think about . . . it." Graham wondered if the alcohol was making him stumble with his words, or if it was the softness of her skin. "I got it."

"Th . . . thank you." Bree watched as Nabb took the bag. He didn't even look in it. With a sigh, Bree turned to the man next to her. "Thank you. I've got to go now."

"Why so soon?" Graham didn't know anything of this woman. But he did know that he didn't want her to go anywhere. "Can't I get a name?"

Robin was upset. Her expression changed very quickly.
Bree took one step, but something stopped her. Nabb was
opening the bag! Bree felt frozen in place.

"Are you all right?" Graham tried to see where she was
looking, but there were too many people talking and dancing
in her frame of vision to narrow in.

"I'm fine." Bree turned to the man as Nabb looked around
the club. She placed a hand on the side of her face to shield
herself. She leaned into the stranger, trying to blend in. Her
mind was racing.

Graham felt a sense of excitement hit him as the girl
leaned toward him. He was fine socially, but never a suave
playboy. Women didn't make him nervous, but he wasn't
complex or complicated. Women were. He couldn't remember ever being this forward.

"What's your name?" she asked, peeking to the side at
Nabb and Robin. He was counting the money! Robin said
he never counted her money. What should she do?

"Graham." Graham could smell her now. Lavender.
"Now, your turn."

"Sasha." She hadn't used that one in a while.

She could only see Nabb from the back, but he was making
quick movements. As if he was yelling. "You're from
Brooklyn. I can . . . I can hear your accent."

"Born and bred," Graham said, taking another sip. A
long sip. "I can't call your accent. And I know dialect."

Finally Bree made eye contact with Robin as Nabb was
looking at an attractive woman dancing suggestively next
to him. Robin was petrified. She jerked her head toward the
door.

"Leave?" Bree said, not realizing it was out loud. Was
she telling her to leave?

Graham was shocked. "Leave? You want to leave?"

He had never done anything like that before. Not even in

college. It was so risky, so irresponsible. Two things he was not. She didn't look the type. What type was that? He wasn't sure. She just didn't look it, and he had never been the type either.

"Oh my God," Bree whispered, turning and leaning over the bar. Her stomach was a mess. She should never have let this happen.

"You change your mind?" he asked. "I know I've had more than a couple, but I'm a little confused here, Sasha. You want me to go home with you?"

Ignoring him, Bree turned around. She had to help Robin. She let out a gasp as she saw Robin whisk by the bar and out the front door. Bree looked back at the table. Nabb was trying to get through a group of people standing around the dance floor. He lifted his head, looking around.

He had fury in his eyes.

"What is wrong with you?" Graham knew he hadn't been drinking too much to notice this girl was acting weird. "Who are you looking for?"

"No one." Bree needed cover right now. Cover from Nabb. He was coming toward the bar. "Not anymore."

She leaned in again, and Graham's mind went blank. She faded out everything. He could be that type of guy once. He had done the right thing all his life and look where it had gotten him.

"Graham, right?" she asked, scooting in a little closer. "Tell me about yourself. I want to learn all . . ."

Nabb was coming down the bar. She could see him only a few people down from Graham. He would see her in a few seconds. And she couldn't run to her right.

"All about me," Graham said, finishing for her. "I'd rather learn about you. I'm sure you're more interesting than—"

Bree grabbed him by the back of his head and pulled his

face to hers. When she planted her lips on his, she pulled her body against him. He was a lot bigger than she, and Bree was certain he covered her completely. She wondered how long before Nabb would pass them by.

Graham felt a sensation run through him that he couldn't remember feeling before. A sense of uncertainty, desire, and confusion. Her lips were soft, but demanding. It took him a second, but the sweetness of it all hit him and he kissed her back. He raised his hand to her arm, her soft-as-silk arm, and kissed her back with intensity. He felt it in the pit of his stomach, a passionate pull that teased him. Made him want more.

The fact that he didn't know anything about this woman meant nothing. He knew that she lit a fire in his belly that made this okay. That made this right. His lips searched deeper for hers. Everything about her was soft. She made him feel . . .

Bree pushed away from Graham, keeping her head down. She quickly blocked the minor distraction of her body's trying to send her some signal or other. No time for that. She lifted her eyes to look past him. Nabb wasn't behind him anymore. Her eyes twisted to the right. He wasn't in front of her. She sighed.

"That was unexpected." Graham felt his own heavy breathing. That ended far too soon for him. His hand touched hers as it lay on the bar. "Sasha, I . . ."

Bree looked behind her. Nabb was walking down the line of the bar past her. This was her chance. She pulled her hand away from Graham and stepped away from the bar. With her eyes so set on Nabb, Bree didn't notice the waiter with a tray full of empty glasses.

She bumped into him and the tray went flying. Glass hit the floor and everyone turned. Nabb turned. His eyes connected with Bree's and they turned to slits.

"Are you all ri—" Graham reached for her, but she just looked at him with a fear in her eyes that brought him out of the daze the kiss had put him in.

Bree ran. The door seemed a mile away, but she kept running. She knew Nabb was coming after her, but she was fit and small. She could maneuver and run fast. It was all she had.

Graham stood up from his stool. What in God's name was going on? She was afraid of someone. Who?

That was answered the second a man, a large man dressed in all black leather with an afro, darted after her. When he passed, his jacket flared with the wind of his pace and Graham noticed clearly a gun stuck in his pants.

A gun. And he was after Sasha.

Against all his better judgment, Graham went after the man. He knew he was crazy while it was happening. He never did anything like this, but for some reason right now, it was all he could do. He thought of her, her smile, lavender, and those mind-erasing lips, and he went after that man.

Graham busted out of the front door, the cool evening air providing a burst of clarity. There was a crowd of people out front, but Graham could see the path that had been made by the large man knocking them out of his way. Graham followed the open hole. He reached the man, who had been slowed by the crowd.

He pushed and the man fell forward on the ground. The gun that he had at some moment grabbed, fell out and into the sewer drain. He hit the ground hard, and wasn't getting up. Standing over him, Graham felt as if he were having an out-of-body experience. Had he just done that?

The people in the crowd starting cheering, happy that revenge had been enacted upon the man who had bullied them out of his way. Graham looked up and saw Sasha, who was halfway down the street, turn around.

Bree heard the cheers and turned around. She saw Nabb on the ground. Only his head was moving back and forth as if he was trying to shake himself out of a daze. She saw the guy from the bar standing over him. Had he done this?

Their eyes connected. She could see that he was confused. All Bree could do was smile. She smiled wide enough so he could see it no matter how far away he was. He had probably just saved her life. She had to get out of there.

Graham felt a sting when she turned and ran away. Had he expected her to come back to him? To thank him? This was all too weird for him. And as he heard the man on the ground moan and start to lift himself up, Graham didn't have time to contemplate what this was all about. He went to the sidewalk and jumped into the first cab that pulled up.

The man was on his knees looking straight at Graham as the cab drove by. His eyes were slits.

Chapter Two

Graham made his way to the kitchen of his Morningside Heights apartment. His hand was against his forehead as if that were the only way of keeping his head from falling off his body. He heard himself groan as he opened the refrigerator door. The extra light made his eyes hurt. He reached for a bottle of water.

"Your friend, Professor Brenton, called for you."

Graham knew Sophia wasn't yelling, but it sure sounded as if she were. He closed the refrigerator and turned to face her. She was still in her pajamas, sitting at the tiny kitchen table with a glass of orange juice in one hand and half an English muffin in the other. Her jet-black hair was tied up in a satin wrap.

"What did he want?" Graham whispered, sitting across from her. He reached for the window next to him and pulled the shade down a few more inches.

"He said you can take his place on the panel Wednesday evening." She squinted her dark eyes as she surveyed the muffin. She turned and tossed it into the garbage behind her.

Graham forced a smile. "Great. Thanks. I'm stopping by school today. I'm sure he'll be there."

He popped two aspirins into his mouth and washed them down with the water. He looked at his sister, thirty but looking closer to forty. She had probably lost twenty-five pounds in the last six months. "You look like you're back in your funk again, Soph. Remember Thursday? We won. You're free."

Sophia sighed, looking around the dimly lit kitchen. "I realize this is a college town apartment, but you could stand to decorate this place a little. It's so . . . white."

"Sophia."

"I know," she said, shaking her head. "For a few days there, I felt like I was on cloud nine. I mean, for the last six months, I was worried about spending time in jail. With that lifted off my shoulders, I should be ecstatic. But I'm not. Because where do I go from here?"

"You find a job." Graham wished he could take some of his sister's pain. She sounded so disillusioned.

"I'm so afraid of getting out there. No one is going to hire me. I have a reputation now. I read the papers. There is no mention of my innocence, Graham. It's all about Keith's magical lawyer tactics. Everyone thinks that's the only reason why I'm free."

"Sophia, you've got to get out there," Graham said. "And don't worry about your reputation. I'm going to get to the bottom of this. We'll get that back for you."

"How can you do that, Graham?" Sophia's voice was laced with skepticism. "You've been trying to since this all started."

"But I was working then. I had too much on my plate with teaching and your trial. Now I'm off for the summer and the trial is over. This is my number-one priority. You just think about getting yourself back on your feet."

"And paying Keith's firm," she said. "Where will I get a job to do that?"

"I'm handling that, Sophia." He could see her entire body tensing up.

"You're my little brother, Graham, not my big one. You can't keep taking care of me. You already let me come live with you when I couldn't afford to pay my rent anymore. You've been supporting me like a child. I'm not letting you take on my debt too."

"We've already had this conversation."

"When we were little, I took care of you because that was my job. It wasn't a favor. You don't owe me anything for it. Especially not a decade's worth of debt. You still have student loans from Columbia."

"Sophia."

"Fine. At least, let me help you pay it back. Can you agree to that? It was my trial."

"Just get a job and get yourself up and running again. Then we'll talk about what you can help me with."

"Graham, it's just so much money. There is no way that we could pay for it. Did you talk to Keith about a payment plan?"

"Yes," he lied. There was no way he would tell her about the fiasco in Keith's office yesterday. Payment in full.

"You're not even working anymore. You have to make your money last this summer. You didn't get that summer teaching opportunity you wanted at NYU because you were caught up with me and this trial. This is a mess."

"No, it isn't." Graham signed.

It *was* a mess, and he was stupid to let his pride get in

the way of dealing with this problem. He couldn't have Sophia worrying about this. And she would until it was solved. She had too much to worry about already. Graham just had to figure out a way to make this work for him. He would.

"I know you want me out. I've messed up a lot for you."

Graham sighed. His head still hurt. When were those aspirins going to kick in? "You know that's not why I said that."

"If it wasn't for me, you and Jodie would still be together."

"You can blame yourself for that all you want, but, Sophia, I think you know that Jodie and I were on the skids before all of this."

"You loved her, didn't you?"

"Yes, I did, but . . . she changed."

"She felt neglected because you devoted everything about yourself to me."

"We broke up because Jodie woke up one day and decided that the academic life was not a fit for her. She didn't feel like it was the best path to taking advantage of this vibrant economy kick. She wanted me to leave teaching and get a real job."

"Did she say real job?"

"Her exact words. It was over between us longer than three months ago. Yes, I did neglect her and that was wrong, but it was only the final straw, not the cause of the problem. I'm fine now. I'm over her."

Suddenly he thought of last night. What he could remember of it, at least. A wicked smile came to his face without his intention.

"What?" Sophia asked, a tiny smile of her own forming.

"Nothing." He leaned back in his chair waving his hand. "Does this have something to do with why you look like hell this morning? What happened last night? You weren't even out that late.''

''It doesn't take all night to get into trouble, Soph.'' He laughed for a second, until it hurt his head.

''You never get in trouble. So what happened? And don't hold out on me.''

He told her about last night at Detroit, from beginning to end. Graham really couldn't believe it as he heard himself repeating the story. Nothing like that had ever happened to him.

''Nothing like that ever happens to you,'' Sophia said with skeptical eyes. ''If you weren't such an honest guy, I'd say you were lying.''

''So would I. But it did. I can't believe it. I mean from flirting at the bar to watching that nut stare at me while the cab drove by, it was crazy.''

''Since when do you hit on women? You never do that.''

''I've approached women before. I'm not a social hermit.''

''Yeah, but under the safest of situations. Not like that. In a bar? So do you think it was drugs?''

''I don't know. The guy had a gun. That girl sure was cute though.''

''Are you sure? You were drunk, remember?''

''Not that drunk.'' Graham tried to remember her face. There was a hint of a blur, but he remembered her. ''I'll never forget her smell.''

''Since when are you interested in the wild types?''

''I'm not, Soph.'' He stood up. ''That entire encounter was alcohol induced. I would never in my right mind have done any of that. I'm grateful the girl ran away. She's not my type at all.''

''Whatever you say.''

Graham ignored Sophia's words as he returned to his

room. No, of course he would not be interested in Sasha in "real" life. If that was even her name. He doubted it. It was a fun memory to have at a time when he needed some. He still remembered that kiss though. And the lavender.

Bree touched her lips with the tips of her fingers. She was getting that weird feeling, as though she should remember something, but she couldn't. She felt something. Something that made her want to touch her lips, but she had no idea what it was. It drove her crazy. She tried to forget it, but how can you forget something you can't remember?

Central Park. There was nothing like it. It had been her favorite part of New York well before moving to the city for good. Family vacations, getaways with friends. She loved it. It was like an island all its own. The attractions, museums, famous restaurants, and all that grass. It was a green oasis. The Upper West Side on the left, the Upper East Side on the right. The Metropolitan Opera House and Julliard.

"And some pretty hot guys," she whispered to herself as a couple of shirtless men jogged by. Bree was always one to appreciate a well-built man.

Her eyes followed them as they passed and stopped at a drinking fountain. One of them made eye contact with her. The cutest one. She smiled, her head held high. He smiled back, before turning away. The other one lifted his head from the fountain and placed a comforting, affectionate hand on the cuter one's back as he took his turn at the fountain.

"That figures." Bree turned back around. She looked down at her watch. "Where is she?"

"I'm right here."

Robin removed the sunglasses and took off the fisherman's cap as she sat on the bench next to Bree. "You're always late everywhere, so don't start with me because I am once."

Bree couldn't argue with that. Timing wasn't her strong point. "Whatever. Where did you sleep last night?"

"Is that really what's important here?" Robin tugged at her shirt. The same shirt she had on last night. She looked at Bree's obstinate stare. "Fine. You never give up. If it's so important to you, I stayed at Carly's."

"Carly Anatucco?" Bree laughed. "That girl's one notch crazier than you."

"And one notch less crazy than you, so what's your point? Why are you trying to be the reasonable one here? You're usually the one that needs some advice."

Bree bit her lower lip. "Well, maybe . . . I don't know. This is really dangerous. It's not like ever before. It's not exciting anymore."

"Tell me about it. What about you? Where did you sleep last night?"

"A hotel. And my funds are pretty depleted. Thanks for the message."

The message was code. Whenever one or the other was in trouble or needed to see the other, she would leave messages at the apartment with code names for locations where they could meet. Robin's message said to meet "at ten at our spot in wonderland." That meant meet at eleven at their bench in Central Park.

"I owed you this at least," Robin said. "You were right, needless to say. He spotted the counterfeit right away. I'm in deep trouble."

"*We're* in deep trouble." There was that desire to touch her lips again. It was so frustrating. "After you left, he came after me."

"How did you get away?"

"With the help of this guy." With a smile, Bree remembered the scene on the street.

"It was a fond memory for you?" Robin asked with sarcasm.

"No. It was scary as hell, Robin. Nabb looked like he was going to kill me. He would have. That guy saved my life. I owe him—"

"What guy is this?"

"No one." Bree didn't want to go over the story. "Just some guy from the bar."

She remembered the kiss. Was that why she kept touching her lips? Ridiculous. It meant nothing to her. It was just to keep Nabb from seeing her. It had to be something else.

"Answer me," Robin said. "How did he save your life?"

"He just knocked Nabb down or something. Gave me enough time to get away."

"What happened to him?"

Bree felt a sense of urgency. "Oh my God. I don't know. I hope he got away. I read the police blotter this morning, but it didn't say anything. It was probably too soon. I'm sure he got away. There was a crowd of people there."

"Either way, Nabb is still after us. We are out of luck, out of a job, and on the run."

Bree's mind was on the stranger. Graham. That was his name. Sure, he was okay. He had to be. This was an uncomfortable feeling for her. She had to get him out of her mind. The image was slowing her down.

"We can't go home," she said. "He knows where we live. He could be waiting for us. We can't go to work. He knows where we work. We've lost our jobs, and we have no money."

"I've been in this situation before," Robin said.

"Well, I haven't." Bree folded her arms across her chest. "This sucks."

"You miss it, don't you?"

"A warm bed? Money in my wallet? Yes, I'd have to say I do."

"Very funny. I'm talking about the life you had before you came to New York. You never would've gotten into this kind of trouble."

Bree laughed. "You'd be surprised at the kind of trouble I found a way to get into at home. Which, by the way, isn't looking too bad right now."

"I hate you being in this. If you went back home you would be free of it all. Could it be that bad in Baltimore?"

"Think of Nabb, but ten times worse. That's my mother, and what she has planned for me."

"She wants you to marry someone? I still find that unbelievable. No one does that anymore."

"The truth is, wealthy people do it all the time. Everyone thinks all these society people are falling in love and getting married. There are a lot more arranged marriages than people would think. And my mother is determined to make it happen."

"Is her will stronger than yours?"

"She has the help of the dark side, Skywalker." Bree laughed. "A little excessive, I know, but I know when I'm up against a stronger opponent. Took everything for me to get away, but I'm glad I did it."

"Even now?"

Bree looked at Robin for a long time before nodding. "Even now. Look, I'll get us some money."

"You hate going into your trust fund, girl. Don't do it. It makes you miserable."

"Well, we have to eat." Bree didn't want to get that money. It seemed as if every dollar yelled back at her "I told you so" in Victoria's voice. She felt sick to her stomach just thinking about it.

"You look like you're going to throw up." Robin leaned in closer. "I can borrow some more money from Muhammad. He still loves me."

"No, Robin." Bree didn't want him back in their lives. "He's a psycho. It took forever to get him out of your life. If you borrow money, you're just asking him right back in."

"Then what?"

Bree was wringing her hands together. "I'll see if Lily will let us stay with her for a little bit, while we figure out how to get our stuff out of the apartment. I'm going to the center Monday to volunteer anyway. We can just stay at the hotel tonight. Then we've got to get our paychecks."

"No way." Robin was shaking her head. "You know he'll go there."

"Then we'll have to look out for him." Bree saw the fear in Robin's face. "You're too scared. I'll do it."

"Bree, when he realized it was counterfeit, he said he was going to kill me." She tugged at her hat in her lap. "It's too dangerous."

"If I get that bad feeling, I'll abort the whole thing and pull from my trust. Now, how much money do you have?"

"Twenty-two bucks, probably."

"I got thirty," Bree said. She sighed, feeling uncertainty. "I never thought I would ever say this, but I think we need to get a gun."

"You, Miss Anti-handgun? Are you sure? Because if you are, I know a guy."

"You always know a guy. That's your problem. And if we get one, I want it done legally. I'll have to do it using my real identity, but I don't care. I think we need it. Nabb sure has one. He showed it to me at the restaurant Thursday night."

Robin put her hat and sunglasses back on. "Geez, Bree. I'm sorry. I'm so sorry."

The girls hugged for a long time. Bree couldn't believe she was contemplating a gun. It had really come to that. She knew Robin hated the police because of her past, but Bree would have to convince her to involve them at some point. This was getting out of hand.

"Mother, are you there?" Keith turned up the volume on the speaker of his office phone. He smiled at Graham, who was sitting in the chair across from him.

Graham did not smile back. Showing up was the most he could do on his end.

"Yes, I am, dear." Victoria's voice came over loud and clear. "I can hear you fine, but you have me on the speaker again. Why do you insist on that? I hate it."

"You don't expect Graham and me to cuddle up and share the receiver on the handset, do you?" He laughed for a moment, but not long, as he noticed Graham didn't flinch.

Graham wasn't about to engage in small talk and humor. "Hello, Mrs. Hart."

"Graham." She held an excited tone. "So glad that you came around. I think it works out well for all of us."

Keith slid the folder across the desk. "I believe you remember this."

Graham nodded, taking the folder. "Let's just get this over with. Where do I start?"

"With what we know so far," Keith said. "She lives somewhere in Manhattan. We think either Harlem or the Upper West Side."

"I hope it's the Upper West Side," Victoria said.

Graham took offense at her insinuation. "There are actually some very nice homes and neighborhoods in Harlem, Mrs. Hart. You should visit it next time you're in New York. There's a lot of history and culture."

There was an awkward silence that Graham had hoped for. Point made.

"Of course there are," she stammered back. "I was just saying—"

"I know what you were saying," he said, flipping open the folder. "So, we think she's in Harlem or the Upper West Side. Why is that?"

"She's pulled funds from her trust account from ATMs in those areas," Keith said after clearing his throat. "She seems to be having a hard time in the real world. Just a couple of weeks ago, she withdrew over two grand."

Daddy's little girl having a hard time of it? Graham knew the type. NYU and Columbia had been full of them. Kids that scream in defiance of everything their parents stand for, but have no problem spending all the money they make doing it. They fight to be on their own, but the second the bills roll in, Daddy and Mommy have to save them.

"The detective we had before spent the last two weeks snarling around both areas," Keith continued. "But you know they're too big. He did find something out, and it's all there."

"She's living with some ex-con," Victoria said with a slow, painful voice. "His name is Robin, or Robert. Or something like that. That's all we know, but that's more than enough. She's always had horrible taste in men, but an ex-con? Her life is going down the toilet."

This girl was trouble, Graham thought. He really didn't want to do this. "What else?"

"There's a list of places she frequented in New York the few times she visited here with friends and us before." Keith looked at his watch. "Stanton. The guy we just fired, started checking those places out. That's how far he got. Her picture is in there too."

Graham sifted through the information for the photograph.

He found it and had to admit it did grab his attention. She was a pretty girl, looking about twenty-one or so. Hair almost as short as his own, circling a petite face that was glowing and lively. Her eyes were big and dark, her nose as tiny as a button. She had flirtatious full lips. The look on her face said so much. *I'm a handful, and don't you ever forget it.*

But there was something else. She looked familiar to Graham. Something about her. Maybe he had seen her picture along with Victoria's and others when he was looking into Keith's background. Still, in the back of his mind, something about her familiarity was closer than a picture could be. Those eyes, those lips.

"Graham? Graham?" Keith tapped the table to get his attention. "Unless Mother has something more to say, that should be it. I have my regular Monday-morning roundup meeting to get to."

Victoria chimed in. "I have nothing more to say, Mr. Lane, but that you must find her. She's a little spitfire, so don't let the sweet face fool you. She'll run right over you if you let her. Still, she's a child and she needs me. I can't let her continue living this way. There's a future for her, one that she needs, in Baltimore."

Graham wasn't interested in any of this. He closed the folder. "I get it, Mrs. Hart. You want your daughter so you can put her back on the straight and narrow. Now, I hope you don't expect me to force her to return against her will. That would be a felony."

"We wouldn't tell anyone," Victoria said.

Graham laughed, but Keith frowned.

"Mother is joking." He looked at Graham. "But it won't hurt to try, Graham. You can't possibly be afraid of overpowering a kid?"

"I'm not afraid of anything," Graham said. "And I'm

not in the business of overpowering anyone. Especially overgrown children.''

"You know, Graham," Keith said, "principles only get you so far in this world."

Graham leaned forward, looking Keith sternly in the eyes. "I'm not much interested in getting anywhere I could without them. I'll do my best to convince her to go home."

"You're the big-time Ivy League professor," Keith said, leaning back in his chair. "I expect your best to be good enough. If you can't get her home, get her to me. I plan on being in Baltimore for a while now, but I can be at this office on any given day as well. If I have to, I'll take her home. I'm not afraid of her. Just don't give a half-assed attempt at it, Graham. I don't . . ."

Keith quit with the orders when Graham's eyes sent a warning shot. The silence was enough to make Victoria nervously speak up.

"Boys? Boys, are you still there?"

"Yes, Mrs. Hart." Graham smiled victoriously at Keith.

"I think that's it, Mother." Keith reached for the phone.

"One more thing," Graham said, holding a finger up. "I have a request."

"A request?" Keith asked.

"You know how I feel about my sister's company. Trotter Securities framed her, and I'm intent on finding out exactly who was behind this and why."

Keith stared blankly.

"Well," Graham continued, "I need your help."

"I already helped you, remember? And your end of this bargain has already been established."

"I'm adding something to it."

Keith laughed. "You're joking. No way. I'm letting you off of tens of thousands of dollars. You want more? Forget it."

"Then no deal. Good luck, Mrs. Hart."

"Keith," Victoria said. "Let him talk. What do you want, Mr. Lane?"

Graham smiled at Keith's discomfort. "I'll need to conduct a lot of research to get to the bottom of this issue, and I need your office's resources."

"So, let me get this straight."

"Keith—"

"No, Mother, hold on a second. In order for you to avoid paying fees for all the work my office has done for you and your sister, I need to give you more resources from my office for free. Sounds fair."

"May not be fair, but if you want your sister ... Or maybe you don't. It's up to you."

"I could pull this whole thing and you would be right back where you started," Keith warned.

"So would you."

The men stared each other down as Victoria called out to them.

"Keith," she said for the fourth time. "I want this over now."

Keith blinked and Graham smiled. Keith may have a few years on him, but he could call his bluff any day.

"You need to check in with me," Keith called after him as he stood up to leave. "Every couple of days, I need an update."

"I'll check in with you when I have information for you," Graham said. "What's their name?"

"Who?"

"The person in your office who's gonna help me?" Graham didn't turn around as he waited at the door. "What's their name?"

Keith sighed, frustrated with his loss here. "Damn it."

"Keith," came Victoria's reminding voice.

"Terrence Stamps," Keith acquiesced. "He can help you. He's one of the interns in this office."

"I'll call him later today." Graham opened the door, and yelled back. "Good-bye, Mrs. Hart."

"Find her, please," was her only response.

Bree strolled into the Dusty Rose Children's Center on the Upper West Side around noon. It was as busy as usual. The center was one enormous room with a dome ceiling. As soon as one entered, one came face-to-face with a long, elegantly adorned desk that held the entirely female administrative staff. No offices, no cubes, just desks set along the wall and chairs at the edge for visitors and members.

The area was elevated, and from there, one could see the open center that contained a basketball court, a nursery, a gymnastics area, three circles for classrooms set up with chalkboards and chairs, and a roller rink with a safety gate around it. The design was Gothic castle, which made it look centuries old, although it was built five years ago. A donation from the wealthy families of Manhattan and its prosperous surrounding suburbs, it was a recreation center for children five through seventeen and was entirely privately funded.

What Bree loved about the place was that it was a five-star operation for kids living far from a five-star life. It was circled by Harlem, Morningside Heights, and Washington Heights. If a low-income or poor family qualified, their children could come to the center before or after school, and on the weekends.

The center was run by professional child care technicians, former teachers, child psychologists, and volunteers. Most of them were Columbia University students who could afford to volunteer without pay. Bree did it because she loved being around kids. She loved their openness, their honesty, and the way they just wanted to have fun. At the expense of everything, they just wanted to live life. No concerns about the future, no responsibilities to keep them reserved.

"Hi, Sandy." Bree twitched her nose at the gray-haired lady who stood watch at the entrance desk. She was a stodgy old woman and she had never liked Bree. When Bree asked her why, her answer was that she made too many movements. She needed to work at being still.

Sandy Snyder rolled her eyes. "If it isn't Ebony Richardson. How long has it been? Two weeks? Not nearly long enough for me. Please say you just came to pick up one of many items you leave behind, cluttering up the whole office."

"I'm here to volunteer for the whole summer." She stuck her tongue out. "I just couldn't stand to stay away from you."

Sandy looked her up and down. "Dressing with class, as always."

Not ready to go back to the apartment, Bree had gone to a thrift store and found a bright red summer tank dress to wear. The straps were thin, the neckline showed a healthy amount of cleavage, and it stopped just above her knees. It was a little sexy for a recreation center, but it was also twelve dollars and looked new.

"I'm dressing for you, Sandy." Bree slid over the desk and came down on the other side. "I know how much you live for my next fashion statement."

"You both need to stop."

Lily McDonald stepped between the women, hands on her slender hips. She flipped her fire-engine-red hair back and traded authoritative glances between them. "Remember, there are children here."

Sandy rolled her eyes again and went back to her paperwork.

"Sandy knows I love her," Bree said, giving her friend a hug. "Can we talk?"

"Of course." Lily smiled, her honest green eyes glowing. She turned and led Bree only steps away to her desk.

Lily was a twenty-eight-year-old genius. She had the best of education, the best of social breeding. She graduated from high school at sixteen, college at nineteen. She could have gotten a job anywhere she wanted. She could have married any one of New York's elite bachelors. Instead, she spent the last eight years of her life helping others. She had been to Africa, the Philippines, and Romania. She had been with City Year and the peace corps. She had worked in Harlem; Gary, Indiana; the southeast district of Washington, D.C.; and the mean streets of Philadelphia. Now she was running Dusty Rose.

"You in trouble again?" she asked as they sat down.

"You pretty much know what's going on." Bree wasn't ready to go over it again. "I can't believe you let Robin get away with that counterfeit fiasco."

"What counterfeit?" Lily whispered in the very open environment. "I gave her two hundred dollars, because she said you guys were running from a thug she owed money to."

"She owed two thousand, not two hundred."

"I don't want to know any more," Lily said, shaking her head. "What are you here for?"

"I'm here to volunteer for the summer."

"I thought you said you needed two paying jobs this summer. Money is tight, right?"

Bree shrugged. "I know, and it is. But I hate being tied down to one job enough. I think I would choke if I had two. Dusty Rose makes me happy. I don't have a lot of that in my life right now. I need this."

"And the kids love you." Lily tilted her head affectionately to the side. "They took to you faster than any of the other volunteers. But you scare me, Bree."

"What have I done? I was doing a good job tutoring all year."

"But it's warm and beautiful out. Can I depend on you to be here with consistency? You get real antsy pretty quick, Bree. Kids need consistency."

Bree nodded. "What can I do?"

Lily paused as if considering it. She nodded. "I'll look at our summer rotation and get back to you later today."

"There's something else," Bree said as Lily stood up.

She sighed, sitting back down. "There always is with you and Robin. I'm not lending out any more money."

"What about your place?" Bree asked. "I know it's a lot to ask, but Nabb, that guy that's after us, is really, really after us. He has a gun, Lily."

"Why are you dealing with people like this, Bree? This is crazy. You can't—"

"That's her. That's the bitch!"

They both swung around to face a man trying hard to get over the counter that separated the administrative staff from the rest of the area. A security guard was pulling him back. He was in his thirties, medium height and build, with blond hair neatly cut. He was dressed in a white polo shirt and khaki pants. "How did he get in here?" Lily stood up. "Charles, get him out of here."

"I will, Mrs. McDonald." Charles, the security guard, pulled at the man. "Come on, jerk."

"I'm going to get you!" He was yelling at Bree, pointing his finger accusingly at her.

Bree thought, unfortunately, this wasn't new for her. "Who are you? I don't even know you."

"Mr. Walsh." Lily came to the counter. "You get out

of here or I'll call the police again on you. You're in enough trouble already."

The man stopped trying to climb the counter, but still tried to loosen the grip of the security guard. "That girl is trying to ruin me. None of you are going to get away with it."

Bree remembered him now. Alex Walsh. She knew him very well, but had never actually laid eyes on him. She didn't have to. "You started this. This is your fault."

"Bree, shut up." Lily looked back at her with all seriousness. "Get him out of here, Charles."

"I know the Redgraves, the Oldmans, and the Kanawas," Alex Walsh yelled back. "They're on my side and you guys are going to pay for starting this."

The man was still cursing and screaming as he was escorted out of the building.

"The nerve of that man," Bree said, shaking her head. She looked around for sympathetic nods, but only got more eye rolling. "What?"

"He does know the Redgraves, the Oldmans, and the Kanawas," Lily said as she sat back in her chair with an exhaustive sigh.

"Lily." Bree was in disbelief at her behavior. "That man is beating up his kid. I had to report him. Little Jacki had bruises everywhere."

"He denies it all, Bree."

She threw her hands in the air. "What a surprise! Did anyone actually expect him to admit to smacking his daughter around?"

"Bree." Lily waved her arms to quiet her down. "Take it down a notch. No one wants to hear this now."

"You believed me when I showed her arms to you, Lily. When I told you that he was hitting her."

"I still do, but—"

"But what? How can there be a but to that?"

"He's a very influential man. The only wealthy kids that belong to the center are kids of major donors. He's one of them. And he knows a lot more."

"Oh." Bree slapped her forehead. "I'm so sorry. What was I thinking? That means it's okay."

"Stop it, Bree. It's a difficult situation. I still believe you did what was right. It's just—"

"I'm out of here." Bree opened the barrier fence and walked through. "I'm sorry for caring."

"Bree, it's not that." Lily stood up, calling after her. "It's just that I have to think of the center for all the children."

"At the expense of one?" Bree asked. "Well, I'm sorry, Lily. He's beating her up and I had to do what I did. I'm glad I did it and I'll be proven right."

Thinking better of it, Bree decided to exit through the kitchen instead of the front door. She didn't want to run into Alex Walsh. The day was not starting off well. Could anything else go wrong? Bree asked herself.

"We're talking about me here," she said out loud. "Of course it can."

Chapter Three

"Sir! Sir, you can't go in there. Sir!"

Graham ignored the woman who trailed him into Robert Barber's office. He'd known from experience there was no chance that his sister's ex-boss would agree to see him. Not after all the threats Graham had hurled at him in the last six months. The only way to reach Robert was force. It wasn't in Graham's nature to be this forceful, but what had happened to Sophia had made him break out of all types of comfort zones.

Robert showed signs of fear with his eyes as Graham entered his office. He quickly looked around the office, in which he was obviously alone. He took a deep breath as he gripped at the edges of his desk.

"What in the hell are you doing here?" he asked, after a hard swallow.

Graham approached the edge of the desk, leaning toward the man of medium height and husky build. He had given up on the comb-over to hide his balding, because it had become too advanced. He was pale and pasty white, one man whose appearance fit perfectly with his personality. From the day she had started working with him five years before, Sophia had described him as an unapologetic jerk who knew the only way he would get to keep women and friends was if he made a boatload of money.

"Heard you got yourself a nice new job," Graham said, looking around the plush office. "This one is larger than your office at Trotter. You seem to be doing well for yourself. Especially seeing as how you kept complaining that this whole scandal ruined your life as much as my sister's."

Robert nodded to his secretary to leave them alone. "I am in the process of rebuilding my life, yes. It hasn't been eas—"

"Skip the BS, Bobby." Graham sat in the chair across from the desk. "What does CMA do, anyway? Obviously they're doing it very well to have such prime space in Midtown Manhattan. And to afford you. The best money can buy."

"I can call security on you, Graham." Robert seemed to calm down, as he leaned back in his chair. There was still a hint of caution on his face. "You have to stop harassing me. Sophia was acquitted anyway."

"No thanks to you and your perjured testimony." Graham wasn't a violent man at all, but every time he saw Robert, he wanted to strangle him.

"It wasn't perjury." Robert's brows centered. "I told the truth. I'm not proud of what I've done, and I'm sure Sophia isn't either. But at least I made peace with it. What I said was true. And I didn't place the blame on Sophia. I started it all, but I was very clear with her about what we were doing. She knew it was against SEC law, which was why we had to be so secretive about it. She helped me, Graham. She helped me and she was compensated for it. The bank shows the deposits in her checking account from mine.''

The SEC was short for Securities and Exchange Commission, the governing body and police of the trading industry. They were the ones who vigorously prosecuted Sophia. Graham hated them for it, but he treaded carefully around them. He knew he would need them again.

''Robert, you know damn well that you told her that money was an added incentive for working such late hours with you.''

''That's what she said, but I never told her that. I'm sorry, Graham, but Sophia is lying to you. *She* lied to the court. Not me.''

Graham clenched his hands into fists to control himself. This man, of all men, calling his sister a liar. ''You are going to be so sorry you did this. I know you set her up. I know you worked this into your deal with the SEC and the state of New York so you could walk away clean. Something more sinister is at play than you sharing mergers and acquisitions secrets with your AA buddies, and you knew all about it from the beginning. You were a willing participant, and my sister was always the intended fall guy.''

''A willing participant?'' Robert's eyes widened. ''My reputation in the industry was destroyed.''

''And it seems to have amazingly kicked back into gear. Was that the plan? To be willing to play the lesson-learned guy for six months and then get back in the game? And getting back in at the top, no less. Was this job a part of the deal for you putting the finger on my sister?''

''You're stretching it, Graham. Sophia is a great person, but she was a secretary. She wasn't that important to the brass at Trotter.''

"She wasn't important to anyone. That was the idea, right? She was a nobody, and it would be so easy to blame it all on her. You didn't expect her to hire a top-notch lawyer like she had. You guys thought it would be a cakewalk and the SEC would be satisfied with getting someone over this."

"You're starting to sound like your fancy lawyer. Count your blessings, Graham. Now, if you don't mind, I have a client meeting to prepare for."

Graham stood up. "It all worked out too easy for you, Bobby. And now that my schedule has cleared up, I'm going to devote everything I have to getting to the bottom of this."

The smile on Robert's face disappeared. "Look, Graham. Your sister is free. She'll get a job as soon as the media attention dies down."

"But she could have been convicted," Graham said. "She could have a criminal record or be in jail."

"That would have never happened."

Graham's eyes focused on his. Robert had slipped. "How do you know that?"

"I don't." Robert shifted nervously in his seat. "It's just that the whole case was weak against both of us."

"So why did you plea bargain?"

"I wasn't willing to take the chance. I don't want to talk about it anymore. I'm calling security now."

"I'm leaving, Bobby, but I'm not going away. I will find—"

"Don't do this, Graham."

Graham stared at him for a long time. Robert stared back. Robert blinked first, and lowered his head.

"I knew it," Graham said. "You'll be seeing me again, Bobby. You can count on it."

* * *

Bree considered going into the store to get Robin. She didn't know how long she had been in there, but it had been a while. The only thing keeping her from running in was that Bree was enjoying the moment of silence to clear her head.

With Nabb chasing after them, no job, no home, running out of money, and now the center not even wanting her, Bree had to admit she had never been this deep into it. And she had a lot to compare it to.

How was she going to get out of it? She had faced odds and obstacles in her life all the time. Trouble seemed to gravitate toward her. She wasn't to blame. Yeah, she liked excitement and drama, but she didn't want guns and homelessness. This was rough, and Robin wasn't helping at all.

But she could not, would not go home. She would not let anyone say that New York had beaten her. That she was the rich girl who couldn't hack it on her own. She couldn't ask for help from her mother. That would be worse than anything. Wouldn't it?

Bree thought of her father, something she tried not to do. He had never been there for her when he was at home. He was too busy with his White House goings-on or his mistress in Bethesda. Now that he was in jail, why should she weep over him? Just the thought of it made her feel worse.

"No," she said to herself as she stood in the middle of the busy Midtown street. "You can fix this, Bree. Everything always has a way of working out for you. It's just going to be a little harder this . . ."

It was him! Bree squinted her eyes even though she had 20/20 vision. Yes, she was right. He stepped out of the office building across the street and came to the curb to hail a cab. It was him, she was sure of it. He looked the same, like a regular guy. A regular guy who had saved her life.

"Hey!" Not waiting for the light, Bree maneuvered her way through frantic traffic to cross the street. "Hey, you!"

Graham watched the young woman run across the street, with barely any concern for her life. In New York, walking with the light was risky enough. Walking against it was sure suicide. Cars honked at her as they hit the brakes to avoid hitting her, and in effect, almost hit each other. She wasn't paying attention as the men and women yelled obscenities at her from their car windows. She moved with a carelessness that told him her guardian angel was getting serious overtime pay.

"It's you!" She approached him, reminded of how handsome he was as she got closer.

Graham tried to keep from looking at her body, which was hard to do with the tempting, very revealing sundress she wore. A smile came to him instinctively at the sight of her. He had thought of her a lot since Friday night, more than he cared to admit to himself, but he'd never assumed he'd see her again.

"I remember you," he said, not sure if he should hold out his hand to her. He had kissed her already, after all. "How could I forget?"

Bree smiled, her hands on her hips. She liked his smile. It was very genuine. "Thank you. I couldn't forget you either. You probably saved my life Friday night."

"You have some pretty dangerous acquaintances," Graham said, noticing the sparkle in her eyes. He had thought his reaction to her Friday night had been the alcohol, but that theory was fading fast. She was really a cute girl with an aura that drew people to her. "Who was that guy?"

"No one important." Bree waved her hand.

"If someone comes after you with a gun, I would think it was important." Who was this girl? Waving her hand in the air over a man with a gun.

"He pulled a gun on you?" Bree's stomach tightened.

"Not on me. He had it out when I got to him outside." He noted a hint of seriousness in her face. So she had some sense to know it was serious.

"Wow, you're kind of tall," Bree said, stepping closer to him. From far away he looked so ordinary in a pair of cotton twills and a white button-down. Close up, he looked . . . Bree wasn't sure what the word was. Interesting. That was it.

"No, you're just short." He looked down at her. "Sasha."

She blinked, biting her lower lip. "What happened to him?"

"Who?" Graham was distracted by her skipping between topics.

"Nabb. The guy you saved me from. What happened? Did he ever get up? Did he come after you?"

"No, but he would have if he could. I think I knocked the wind out of him. I got in a cab and got out of there. I'm not interested in staying around for scenes like that."

"You were pretty cool." She clenched her hands in fists, waving them in the air. "Knocking the big bad guy to the ground."

He shrugged as if he had done this hundreds of times before. "Just pushed him. I was pretty drunk."

"I noticed." She gestured as though taking a quick drink.

Graham smiled. She was quick with the comebacks. "So, are you going to tell me who this . . . Nabb was his name, right?"

"I guess you deserve to know," she said. "Saving me from him and all. He's some loan-shark jerk that wants money."

"You owe him money?" She borrowed from loan sharks? This girl was trouble. Why did he like her?

"No, well, yes. No. My friend owes him money, but . . . No, I don't. You see, I'm a waitress and she's a—"

"Where?"

"What?"

"Where do you waitress?"

She looked him up and down. He didn't look like the stalker type. What did she have to lose? "Logan's on the Upper West Side. You heard of it?"

"No, but I'll have to check it out."

Bree dropped her arms to her side. "Don't bother. I'm not there anymore."

"Got fired?"

"Quit. Had to. It's a long story."

"Does it have to do with . . . what's his name again?"

"Thanks for pushing him anyway," Bree went on. "Sorry I ruined your night."

"You kind of made my night," Graham said, remembering that kiss clearly. How it had made him feel. He looked at her lips. Very tempting. "Even though it was all fake."

"What?" Bree's eyes widened and her lip pouted a bit.

"Don't try the coy smile with me." Graham knew about women like this. "You know Friday night was fake. Whatever was going on with you and your gun-toting friend was the reason why you kissed me."

Bree saw it wasn't worth it to try to pull one over on him. He was harmless. "Well, I'll apologize if your feelings were hurt."

"Can't say that." Graham liked the way she tilted her head to one side flirtatiously. She had reckless written all over her, and that should make him walk away right now. But he didn't want to. "I enjoyed it."

"We'll always have our kiss," Bree said, sensing a pull of attraction to someone that she normally wouldn't be attracted to. He wasn't dangerous and tough enough for her. But there was something about him. "Graham."

"It took you this long to remember my name?"

"No." She rolled her eyes. "I remembered your name the second I saw you."

"Liar," he said. "You forgot all about me and our little kiss."

"Yeah, like you remember me."

"I do remember you," Graham said quickly. "You're pretty unforgettable."

Bree didn't know how to respond to that. Was he serious or was he playing the same game she was? He looked serious. She didn't pick him as one to play a lot of games.

Graham hadn't been interested in any woman since his breakup with Jodie. There had been too much to deal with during Sophia's trial. This woman was not for him, but she sure brought his senses back to life. She . . .

Something clicked in the back of his mind.

"Your name isn't Sasha," he said, morphing the picture in the folder with what he saw now. Maybe a couple of insignificant years older, hair longer, less makeup. No wonder the picture had been so familiar to him.

Bree laughed. "No, it isn't, but it doesn't matter what my name is. I mean, I'm not—"

"Bree Hart?"

Bree was frozen in place. Her entire body clenched as her mind sped into high gear. Who was this man? She felt panic set in. *Calm down. Calm down. He may just know you from pictures or society pages.*

"You're Bree Hart, aren't you?"

Bree felt the wide streets closing in on her. She looked around. She looked at the drugstore. Where was Robin? She didn't want to leave without her, but . . .

"Who are you?" she asked.

"It is you." Graham was floored by the coincidence. Were the gods smiling on him? He had done nothing to try and find this girl and she was falling into his lap.

"How do you know me? Where are you from?"

"Your mother is looking for you. She wants to—"

"No." Bree's hands clenched into fists. "Mother?"

"Bree! Bree! Let's get out of here. Run like hell, girl!"

Robin was running across the street with terror and desperation on her face. She grabbed Bree and dragged her as she ran down the street. Bree heard someone yelling after them, threatening to call the police. There were too many people and they were moving too fast for her to figure out who it was and where they were coming from.

"What is going on?" she asked, running beside Robin. "I'm not dressed for the Olympics, Robin."

"He caught me," Robin said. "He caught me stealing food."

Bree halted, her mouth wide open. "You stole from him?"

Robin reached back and grabbed her. "Run, girl. We can talk about it later."

Bree sighed and kept running. The yelling died out, but they kept running. What in the world was going on?

Graham watched with the other passersby as the store manager headed back toward the store. He was cursing and screaming in Italian and English. He looked at Graham and stopped, walking toward him.

"The one of them was talking to you. The one she grabbed! She was talking to you."

"I don't know her," Graham lied, holding his hands up in the air. "I just met her a second ago. I swear."

He looked Graham up and down and appeared to believe him. "You better check for your wallet. They stole from me. I'm going to get them. I saw both their faces. I'm sick of this city."

After a thought, Graham did as the man said and checked for his wallet. He stood on the curb for a few moments more trying to process just what had happened. He knew he could have helped the store manager, but something made him hold back on giving Bree's name. He didn't want to get her in trouble.

It had all happened so fast. He had lived a pretty structured and boring life for most of his adult years to make up for the uncertainty of his childhood. He liked it that way. He had worked hard to keep it that way. But coming in contact with this woman only introduced chaos. He didn't need any of that.

It made sense. The person that he had seen twice now, and the person that Keith and Victoria Hart had described. She was out of control. How was he going to get her to go home to her family? How was he going to find her again?

"I don't want to hear it anymore!" Robin threw a pillow in the air in frustration. "We have to eat, Bree."

Bree leaned against the window of the shady-at-best motel room they would be staying in for one more night. She was trying to control her temper. "We don't have to steal food. I thought you said you would never shoplift again."

"I never thought I would be homeless and penniless again." Robin took a big bite out of the honey bun, one of the items she had stolen. "That's why I did it before. Only because I was hungry. You can't understand that."

Bree knew she couldn't understand that. "It still doesn't excuse stealing. I can go into my trust, Robin. I'd rather swallow that pill than steal."

"I wouldn't. You act like such a baby about that. Like you think the second you take a penny out of there, your mother is going to have a SWAT team outside the door."

Bree sat on the other bed. "I wouldn't put it past her. She obviously knows I'm in New York."

" 'Cause she tracked the last withdrawal?"

"I guess. You know that guy I was talking to outside the store?"

"I wasn't really paying attention to your socializing at the time."

"He knew who I was. He told me my mother is looking for me."

Robin's eyes lit up. She leaned forward. "My God, Bree. Did you know him? Do you think he told the store guy who we were?"

Bree hadn't thought of that. "I don't . . . I don't know. I don't think so though."

"Based on what?" She tossed the bun down, looking as if she had lost her appetite.

"He didn't seem like the kind that would tell on folks, you know? Like, it would be more of a hassle for him. He's not the hassle kind of guy."

"So you do know him?"

"He's the guy from the bar. The guy that saved me from Nabb."

They stared at each other in silence, each waiting for the other to explain the coincidence.

"Maybe he's from Baltimore and he just recognizes you," Robin said finally. "Your face was in all the papers all the time, right?"

"But everyone in Baltimore thinks I'm overseas," Bree said.

"How do you know?"

"I called my sister-in-law about three months ago. She told me that's what Mother told everyone. She was too embarrassed to say I just ran off because I didn't want to be part of the clan anymore."

"You trust this sister-in-law? This is the one in D.C.?"

Bree nodded. "Yeah, Sydney. She's cool. I can trust her. She hasn't bought into the Hart thing. Matter of fact, she pretty much blew the Hart thing out of the water a couple of years ago."

"The thing with your father?"

Bree nodded. She had met Sydney Tanner in MBA school at Howard University and brought her home with her for the summer. Sydney was from the wrong side of the tracks, and needed a place to stay. From the beginning, her mother wanted Sydney out. But Bree wanted Sydney to stay, and so did her oldest brother, Marcus. Everything was made worse when Sydney found out about the family's past, how they came to be as rich as they were. Skeletons in closets as far away as Africa that Bree's father was willing to kill to keep locked away.

"That was the worst year of my life," Bree said. "But it wasn't Sydney's fault. It was Daddy's."

"Your mother never really forgave her?" Robin looked intrigued. "I mean you never talk about it, really."

"For a reason, Robin." Bree looked at the phone. "Besides, Mother forgave Sydney. If you can say she forgives anyone. She just kind of deals with it. She deals with Sydney. It's been better since she and Marcus got married and had Brandy. You know, everyone loves a baby."

"So, what are you going to do?"

Bree picked up the phone. "I'm going to find out who is after me. If that guy . . . Graham, knows that I'm missing and not traveling, then that means someone in my family told him."

"Hello?"

"Sydney?" Bree felt a sense of homesickness at the sound of her sister-in-law's voice. She missed her more than anyone in her family. Sydney and her Aunt May had been the only two people making life in the Hart family bearable. "It's Bree."

"I know who it is," she said quietly. "Where are you, Bree? You've got to tell me."

"Let's not go through that again, Sydney. I'm not telling you."

"How are you doing? Everyone is so worried about you. You haven't called in three months." There were baby sounds in the background. "Are you all right?"

"How's Brandy?" Bree missed her niece. She missed her nephew as well. Her older sister Kelly had a seven-year-old son, Jordan, whom she hardly ever saw. "She must be getting pretty big now."

"She is big and wonderful. Bree, talk to me. Don't you know how worried everyone is about you? Marcus is losing sleep over you."

Bree knew Sydney loved her brother with all her heart. What she had put up with to be with him said enough. "Tell Marcus I'm fine. Tell everyone I'm fine. I need to know something."

"Why don't you just come home for a—"

"To Mother? Are you crazy? I can't live with her anymore."

"No, not to her. To me. You can come stay with us in D.C."

"She'll find a way to get her claws into me. You know how she is."

"You have got to stand up to her, Bree."

"I have been. It doesn't work."

"You haven't been standing up to her, Bree. You've been throwing tantrums and causing all hell to break loose. That's not standing up to her."

"Is she sending someone after me?"

Sydney sighed. "No matter what Victoria is, she is your mother and in her own way she loves you. You're her baby."

"Sydney."

"Okay, yes, she has hired someone. She called Marcus and told him yesterday that she has a college professor after you. She's had one person or another looking for you in New York for over a month now. She tracked your trust withdrawal."

Bree clenched her fist in anger. "What does she think she can do? Drag me back home?"

"I wouldn't put it past her. Look, Bree. Just come here. We'll work it out. I'll help you."

"I don't want help," Bree lied. She wanted it desperately. "I can lead my own life."

"Then fine. Do it. But you don't have to live in secrecy and completely ignore your family to live on your own terms. You can handle Victoria."

"I'm not you, Sydney. I can't control her like you do."

Sydney laughed. "No one controls Victoria Hart."

"You've come closer than anyone."

"Come to D.C., Bree."

"You know she wants me to marry that idiot."

"She can't force you to marry anyone."

"She says she'll make it happen. She says the family needs it. You know there's no stopping her when she's focused on appearances."

"Bree. Is that you?"

Bree noticed Marcus's strong, deep voice over the phone.

"Marcus, get off the phone," Sydney said.

"Bree, what in the hell are you doing?" he asked.

Bree hung up, knowing nothing else to do. She knew Marcus wasn't a minion of their mother's as Keith was, but he was also a proponent of reason. He always did what was reasonable. But dealing with Victoria required more than reason. He didn't seem to get that.

"What's up?" Robin asked after a while.

Bree lay down on the bed. "He's a college professor. She sent a college professor after me?"

"Why a professor?"

"Good question, but the answer doesn't matter. Whoever that guy is, I can handle him. What's important now is us getting some money and getting back into our apartment so we can get our stuff."

"What about Lily? Can we stay with her?"

"I didn't get around to asking that. It's a long story. I'll work it out. Tomorrow, I'm going to get our paychecks."

"You're nuts. What if he's there?"

"I'll be careful." Bree felt the butterflies already. "I'll go when they open up. That way Jack won't be there either."

"I hope it works."

"It will." Bree had to be positive. She wasn't going to give in to this city yet.

Graham dipped his head into the dining room of Logan's restaurant. It was a nice, friendly-neighborhood type of place only a few miles from his home; he wondered why he'd never heard of it. He looked around. There were two young men in jeans and T-shirts taking chairs off of tables. There was a third man behind the bar, setting up. Graham chose him.

"We're closed, sir," was the first thing he said as Graham approached. "We're a dinner-only restaurant. We don't open for another three hours."

"I'm looking for someone." Graham leaned against the counter. The man looked nice enough. The way bartenders seemed to look. Someone you could talk to. "Gabrielle Hart. Or Bree Hart. She used to work here."

The man thought for a second. "No such name I can recall. I've been here for four years. What she look like?"

Graham handed him the picture of Bree.

"Ebony?" He laughed, setting the picture down. "That's Ebony Richardson."

"Really?"

"What did you call her? Gabrielle—"

"Never mind. Are you sure that's her?"

"Yeah, that's her all right. Her hair is a little longer now, but I'll never forget that face. She's a hottie. What you want with her?"

"I'm just looking for her. I'm a friend of the family."

"She said she didn't have any family." He popped a cherry in his mouth and resumed cleaning. "But she's a liar. I know enough about people to know that. The girl is trouble."

"Why do you say that?" As if Graham needed any more proof.

"She's stuck up, and she's nosy. And she's always starting drama around here. I don't know why Jack . . . I mean Mr. Ballard hasn't fired her yet. She owes him a lot, letting her stay on after being such a hell-raiser. Then what does she do? Doesn't even have the decency to quit. She just never shows up. Won't call nobody or return calls neither."

"You've been trying to call her?" If Graham hadn't been convinced before, this girl was a virtual hurricane.

"Not me. Jack is the manager of this place. He's been trying to reach her and that one she lives with."

Graham tried to recall the ex-con boyfriend's name. "Robert? Rob—"

"Robin. Yeah. He hired Robin as a favor to Ebony. Jack wouldn't usually hire ex-cons. This is a family restaurant.

The last thing we need is waiters walking around with tattoos on their arms.''

"Where is this Jack Ballard?" Graham needed to get Bree's address or phone number. Something that could help him find her.

"He won't be here for another few hours."

"I need her number or her address."

The man looked Graham up and down. Graham knew he looked harmless in his textbook college professor wardrobe. Still, the man wasn't stupid. It wouldn't be that easy. Graham pulled out a twenty-dollar bill and slid it across the table.

The bartender laughed. "Buddy, I'm gonna make close to four Benjamins in tips tonight."

"So? You'll make four hundred and twenty. It's twenty more than you had before." After getting no reaction, Graham stared straight into the man's eyes. "I really need this information."

"I don't like the wild child personally, but I'm not handing her over to some psycho dressed up like Ted Bundy."

Graham laid all his identification on the table. Driver's license, school ID, and building ID. "I'm not a psycho. Seriously, I'm a college professor at Columbia. Br . . . Ebony's mother is worried about her. You know how reckless she is. Her older sister is real sick and her mother thinks worrying about Ebony is making it worse."

The guy seemed to soften up a bit. He looked down at the identification. "I can spot a fake, you know."

"It's your living. I'm sure you can."

He grabbed the twenty still on the table and nodded for Graham to follow him. "Her contact info is in the back."

A smile from cheek to cheek covered Bree's face as she grabbed both paychecks out of the check slot in the kitty to the kitchen of the restaurant. The only two people in the back were cooks that recognized her, but didn't speak English, and apparently didn't know or care enough to question her being there.

There had been no sign of Nabb or Graham outside, and Jackson Ballard's parking space was empty. Bree headed for the kitchen. All she had to do was hit the back door, head down the alley, and the subway stop was only steps away. No Nabb, no Ballard, no . . .

"I always knew Ebony was going to just run out on us. That's her style. She just ups and leaves. Does whatever she wants. People like her don't have no concern for what they leave behind."

Bree dove behind the coatrack, which was thick with jackets that the employees always left behind, dating back to the previous winter. She probably owned a jacket or two hanging in front of her. She watched as Jerry Newman, the head bartender, led Graham into the kitchen.

Graham nodded. "Ebony Richardson, huh?"

"That's what she was calling herself."

Bree pressed her lips together in anger. Why did she have to go and tell him where she worked? He had appeared so harmless. Slowly, she stepped to the kitchen door, pushing it open just enough to listen.

"I'm not surprised it's a fake name," Jerry said. "Look at the element she runs with. That Robin is trouble." He leaned in toward the wall near an old, black telephone. "This is the call list. Where we call folks when they're late or when we need extra help. Here it is. Ebony Richardson."

Graham leaned over. Phone number only. That would have to be enough. He knew it wouldn't be hard to turn it into an address. He copied the number down.

"She lives in Harlem. I know that much. I'm from Queens, so I don't know anything about Harlem except for the Apollo

Theater, but I hear she lives in a real nice part, 'cause someone else here was saying that.''

"Striver's Row?" Graham knew that was prime New York property in Harlem. Beautiful brownstones, walk-up condos, and family-owned stores.

"That sounds right. So you say her sister is sick?"

Graham felt bad lying, but he meant Bree no harm. "Yeah. She just came down with something real bad and it's taking a turn for the worst."

Bree put her hand to her chest. Kelly! What could be wrong with Kelly? She didn't want to believe it. If something was wrong with Kelly, Sydney would have told her. But would she know? Kelly could go months without talking to anyone in the family. But if she would call anyone, she would call Sydney. Was Sydney just keeping the truth from her so she wouldn't freak out? Was that why she was so adamant that she come to D.C.? So Sydney could tell her?

The whole family was always trying to keep things from her to protect her. Bree hated being the last to know. Kelly traveled so often, no one really kept up with her.

No. Bree calmed herself down. This was a ploy by Graham. He was playing with her. But why would he say her sister and not someone even more sympathetic like a mother? Maybe he knew of Bree's relationship with her mother and didn't want to chance that Jerry did as well.

Bree jumped back behind the coatrack as she saw James head for the door. She heard Graham ask for a way out the back. Why the back?

James yelled out as he held the door open. "That door straight ahead leads you to the alley. Take a right toward Broadway. Left just goes through the alley to Broadway the long way, but it's not too pleasant back there. Pretty narrow and very cluttered."

Bree waited until the coast was clear to come out from

behind the coatrack. She knew she should just stay still until Graham was out of the way. She had her checks, and he was certainly lying about Kelly. She paced the tiny room, peeking into the crack of the door to the kitchen. She watched as he looked around a bit.

That's why he wanted a way out the back. He expected Jerry to leave, so he could look around a bit. Bree waited until he appeared satisfied that he wasn't going to find anything and left out the back door.

"Just let him go," she whispered to herself. "You got what you came for. Don't push your luck."

"Graham!"

Graham swung around to see Bree Hart standing in the doorway to the restaurant. She walked out into the alley. She was so attractive that just the sight of her evoked a reaction from him. He wasn't surprised to see her. Something in him sensed her in the restaurant. Even so, something about Bree made it only right that she pop out of the most unexpected places. Nothing about her made sense.

Bree approached him, noticing a smile on his face. "What are you smiling for?"

He shrugged. "Just nice to see you, I guess. You know they're looking for you in there. Just left them high and dry. Not very professional."

"You don't know the whole story." Bree grabbed him by the arm to pull him toward the wall. She was surprised that she felt some pretty well-defined muscles under her hand. Surprised more that she noticed. "Get out from the middle of the alley. Someone could see us."

He moved his arm away, not so sure that he liked how aware he was of her touching him. "I don't need to know the whole story, Bree. Or Ebony. Or Sasha. Whichever you're using right now. Blowing people off is unprofessional.''

"Not when a madman is . . .'' She tried to control her frustration. "What about Kelly?''

"What about who?''

Bree made a fist with her hand and socked him in the chest. He didn't really move, which only made her angrier. "I knew you were lying. How could you?''

Graham touched his chest where she had hit him. "You're the last person to pass judgment on someone.''

"Just let's get this straight. No one in my family is sick, right?''

He nodded. "Well, not physically, at least. Mentally, I can't—''

"Go to hell!'' Bree turned and headed toward Broadway. She felt Graham grab at her arm and pull her back. His grip was strong. She realized that Graham was stronger than he looked. "Let me go!''

"You might want to keep your voice down,'' he said, turning her around to him. "What if your boss hears you out here? Besides, our business is not finished.''

"Our business?'' Bree placed a haughty hand on her hip. "We have no business, loser. I know you're a lackey for my mother.''

"I'm nobody's lackey, you little brat.'' He leaned toward her. "And from the looks of my life compared to yours, you're one to be calling me a loser.''

"You're doing what my mother tells you to,'' Bree said. "That makes you a—''

"How do you know your mother . . .'' Graham didn't care. "It doesn't matter. This is a business arrangement between me and Keith.''

Bree laughed. "Of course. Wherever Mother is, Keith is

never far behind. Dealing with the devil or her son makes no difference.''

''That's how you refer to your own mother? As the devil? What kind of ungrateful daughter are you?'' Graham didn't like Victoria from what he knew of her, but this was harsh.

Bree sighed, regretting her words. ''I know. My mother is not the devil. I love her, really. I'm just tired and frustrated. And the last thing I need is a dinky college professor trying to lead me down the path of righteousness.''

''Personally, sweetheart, I don't have the time it would take to lead you so far in the other direction of where you're obviously going. What I am here for is to get you to face up to your life.''

''You don't know anything about my life.'' Bree gritted her teeth. She wanted to slap him. ''You don't even know me.''

''It looks like no one in New York knows you, Bree. How many aliases are you using, anyway?''

Bree gave him the once-over. ''You don't know who you're dealing with, Professor.''

''My name is not professor, it's Graham.'' Graham felt his temper rising and his patience growing thin. ''It's easy to remember. Unlike you, I only have one name. And what I don't know about you is irrelevant. I do know that you're twenty-five and you act like you're sixteen. What you need to do is go home, face up to your mother. Then just live your life.''

Bree laughed. ''Pearls of wisdom from nobody out of the blue. I got news for you, Grah-ham. It was unwise to go into business with my brother, because you just lost.''

Bree turned, heading for Broadway. The glare from the street lit up the alley enough to show a figure appearing at the sidewalk. She stopped, wondering if it was Jackson Ballard. No, too tall. This man was black. This man was . . .

"Bree!" Graham reached for her. "Run!"

She turned and ran the other way with him, hearing Nabb's footsteps behind them. They maneuvered down the dark alley, jumping over garbage cans and cardboard boxes. Bree had to share her attention between the ground and the area in front of her because the second she jumped to avoid a piece of garbage on the ground, she almost ran into a large garbage disposal under hanging fire escapes.

"I want my money!" The voice wasn't too far behind.

There was a tiny spot in Graham's mind that was able to think about something other than getting away from this man. That part was focused on how he could possibly be in this situation in the first place. This woman was going to get him killed.

"This way." He pointed toward the light. "Go ahead of me, Bree."

She did as she was told, only looking back when she heard a loud bang. It was Graham turning over a large garbage disposal, blocking the ever-narrowing alleyway. He turned back to her, surprised that she had stopped.

"Run!"

She kept running. She heard Nabb cursing in the background, but it sounded farther away. They finally reached the sidewalk. Bree felt relief wash over her, but she wasn't clear yet. She looked both ways for the subway entrance.

"Keep going!" Graham grabbed her by the arm and pulled her with him as he headed down Broadway. "We need to get out of his sight. He could hurt someone trying to shoot at us."

"Where is the subway?"

"Not the subway. That's a trap if he finds us. We need the streets."

Bree nodded, too scared to try to argue or fend for herself. She couldn't hear Nabb anymore, and when she looked behind her, she couldn't see anything. There were too many people and they were moving fast. He could be anywhere.

"In here," Graham said.

They slowed down and walked as naturally as possible into a hotel. Graham nodded at the doorman as if everything were okay, thinking how crazy it all was.

Bree looked up at him. "Where are we going?"

"Just go."

They walked further into the lobby of the hotel, and Graham led her past the front desk and concierge desk to the hallway. They passed telephone hotels and bathrooms and entered a side hall next to a private restaurant. They were clearly out of sight from the street, and were perfectly positioned to see anyone coming toward them.

They stood there together in silence, looking down the hallway, waiting. Their breathing was heavy, and their nerves were high. Bree felt his grip still on her arm, as her stomach loosened up. She heard him breathing behind her, she felt his chest against her upper back. Fear was subsiding, but it was being replaced by emotions that she wasn't sure she wanted. What was going on with this guy?

"What in the hell have you gotten me into?" Graham asked after finally letting her go. He stepped back from her, not liking the fact that she was so close anyway.

"You got yourself into it by coming after me. If you had minded your own business and left me alone you wouldn't be here."

"You're welcome," he said sarcastically. She had to be the most ungrateful person he had ever met.

"For what?" She lifted her arm. "You practically bruised me."

"I saved your life by slowing him down. That was the second time I saved your life from him, by the way. Not to mention that I could have turned you in to the police when you and your friend robbed that poor store owner.''

"You didn't say anything to him?" Bree sighed. "I am so relieved. I have to call Robin. Where are the phones?"

"Forget your boyfriend!"

"Who?" Bree wasn't paying attention to him, looking for a phone. "There's one over there. I have to—"

"You're going to call the police if anyone," he said.

"I can't do that."

"The man is after you with a gun. You have to call the police."

She shook her head, hands on her hips. "I'm fine now. Thank you for helping me. I can take it from here."

"Unbelievable." He had just saved her life, again, and all she was thinking about was calling her ex-con boyfriend. "Can we just sit down and talk?"

"So you can convince me to . . ." She jumped as someone came into the hallway. It was a young woman, who sent them a quick glance before walking into the restaurant. "To go back home to my saintly mother? No way."

"Of course not. Since your life is so promising here."

Bree poked at his chest with her index finger. "That was strike three for you and your insults."

"Fine." Graham found himself amused by this petite figure imposing herself so effectively. "No more insults. How about doing it just because it's the right thing to do? She's your mother."

"Why do you care so much?"

"I don't. I told you—"

"Oh yeah. The business arrangement. What are you doing in business with my brother anyway? You don't look like his type."

"If I was a smarter man, I'd say that was an insult."

She looked at her watch, symbolically. Time meant nothing to her right now. "You've got a minute to answer my question, or I'm out of here."

They were none of her business, his motives, Graham thought. Still, he needed to convince her to at least go see her brother. "I'm usually not his type, as you would say. But Keith just saved my sister from jail. My sister is Sophia Lane. You've probably read about her in the papers or seen her on the news."

Bree nodded, remembering the case she saw on television. "You were the one. The guy that had his arms around her and was leading her into the limo. You should wear a suit more often. You clean up well."

"Whatever you or I think of your brother, he's a great lawyer. And my sister was up against incredible odds. She was being framed by her company, but that's not the issue here."

"Framed?" Bree's curiosity was piqued. "What do you mean?"

He waved his hand. He didn't want to get into all that with her. "Getting to the point, he did his job and I owe him thousands of dollars. I'm a professor at Columbia, so I have no way of paying him. At least not all at once like he wants."

"What about payments?"

"Your brother is trying to . . ." Graham was getting angry just thinking about it. "Keith isn't open to that. Your mother and he suggested that I can wipe the slate clean if I find you."

"Why you?"

"Because they know that I don't give a damn about the Harts and all the drama and publicity that surrounds you. They knew I wouldn't go to the press or society pages. I could keep it quiet. No one would suspect anything of a college professor."

"So. You found me. I guess you get out of jail free. Tell them I'm fine and dandy. Congrats on your sister. I'm out."

"Wait. Bree, I have to get you to go home to pull my end of the bargain."

Bree laughed. "Just how do you expect to do that? Kidnap me? Think twice, brother. I may be little, but I know where to hit to make myself seem a lot bigger."

Graham couldn't help but smile even though she completely frustrated him. "Your mother would have been fine with me dragging you to Baltimore. But I have no intention of trying to force you to do anything. But can you understand why this is important to me?"

"I get it, but you can't expect me to go back home for you and your sister. You don't understand the situation."

"How bad could it be? Just go to her and tell her you want your own life. You're twenty-five, for Pete's sake."

"That doesn't mean anything to her." Bree sighed, leaning against the window of the restaurant. "I need to get something better going on here before I face up to her again. With what's happening right now, if I were to go home, she'd annihilate me."

"I'm not giving up on my sister," Graham said.

Bree saw in his eyes that he meant that. He was the loyal type, a lot like her oldest brother, Marcus. Family meant everything to this guy, but in the good way.

"I did save your life and keep you out of jail." Graham sensed her weakening. Through all that fight and feistiness, there was a softness there. He needed that side of her to come out now. "That has to deserve some consideration."

Bree couldn't believe she was feeling guilty. She hated this feeling. She had no obligation to Graham or his sister. Usually when faced with this situation, she would wish them the best, or give them some tips on playing dirty to put the

advantages more in their court, and be on her way. But
something in his eyes . . .

"Let's make a deal," she said, always thinking. "I know
a way that can get us both what we want."

"Don't try to con me." That look on her face sent up
red flags for Graham. It was like dealing with one of his
students. Except she was a lot smarter and a lot prettier.

Her eyes widened innocently. "I wouldn't think of it. An
honorable do-right brother such as yourself. I feel for your
situation. I really do."

Graham's brows narrowed.

"I do," she said in reaction. "But I'm not going home.
So, my plan has us convincing Victoria and Keith that I'm
on my way, but I never get there. But it won't be your fault.
You'll have done everything you can. And you can get a
guarantee of all dues paid in full before I mysteriously disappear again."

Graham was shaking his head even before she finished
the last sentence. "I don't know your mother very well, but
neither she nor Keith are stupid. I'm not . . ."

Graham's head turned only inches to the right, but that
was enough. He leaned closer against the window to the
restaurant.

"What?" Bree was intrigued by his interest in whatever
was going on in the restaurant. He was looking at a particular
table in the corner of the room. It was full of middle-aged
white men in very expensive Wall Street–type suits, all
laughing and smoking cigars.

"Who are they?" she asked.

"They work at Trotter Securities," Graham said, a flame
lighting underneath him just at the sight of them and their
celebration. But it wasn't just his hatred for them all that
kept his attention. Who were these other people? "Actually,
they run Trotter Securities."

"Which is?"

"The company that tried to frame my sister." He made a mental note of all the faces he recognized and all those that he didn't. Why were they meeting on the Upper West Side when Trotter's offices were on Wall Street in lower Manhattan? That was a long trek for the middle of the day.

"Cool," Bree said. "I mean, not cool but . . . Well, this is exciting, isn't it?"

"No." He turned to her. "It's not exciting at all. But it is curious. Come on."

She followed him without further prompting. The whole idea was worth her time, since she had all the time in the world. Specifically, it was the look on Graham's face that intrigued her. He was angry. The anger was controlled, but his eyes were lit up. Something was about to happen.

Graham addressed the hostess standing at the entrance of the private restaurant. She was a long-legged blonde, with a black minidress on. She looked like one of those waitresses at the not-so-reformed men's business clubs in the city. She was incredibly beautiful and, Bree noticed, not at all unhappy to see Graham.

"Of course I can help you," she said, showing perfect teeth with her perfect smile. She ignored Bree, focusing on Graham.

This must be important, Bree thought to herself, because Graham didn't notice or acknowledge the woman's infatuation in the least.

"That party over there," Graham said. "Those look like my old buddies from Trotter. Is that them?"

Clever, Bree thought.

"It sure is. You used to work there?"

He nodded with a fake laugh. "Before I started my own firm. Wow, it's been a while. There are so many new faces. I thought I knew everyone."

She leaned forward as if to whisper something that she shouldn't. "Well, they aren't all Trotter folks. Some of them are from Cammermeyer and Storm. That's who the reservation is under and I heard them talking while I was leading them to their table."

Graham nodded as if the name were familiar. It wasn't. "Oh yeah. That's right. I heard about this deal."

"Some type of merger or something," she added.

What a sucker, Bree thought. She had no idea she was being played. Bree could teach this girl a lot.

Graham made another mental note. "Thanks, Ms. . . . ."

"It's Holly," she added. "Would you like to say hello to them? They're in such a good mood, I'm sure they would be open to visitors."

"Yes," Bree said, wrapping her hand around Graham's arm. "Let's go say hello, honey."

He looked at her with a frown. "No, sweetheart. Not necessary. We'll be seeing them this weekend at the club."

"That's right." Bree lowered her hands to her sides. She was disappointed. She wanted to see the fireworks. "Oh well. Thanks for all your help, Holly."

Bree received a cold smile from the woman.

She followed Graham as he headed for the lobby. "Where are you going? Aren't you afraid Nabb is still out there?"

Graham had forgotten about him. His mind was focused on this lunch. He had to get to the bottom of it. Something told him it would be worth it. He looked at Bree, realizing that getting her to go home was the key to his getting the information he needed Terrence Stamps, Keith's intern, to help him with.

"I have to get something done," he said. "You're coming with me."

Bree stopped in the middle of the lobby. "I beg your pardon?"

"You want to explain your little scheme? Then come with me."

"Where?" She followed him outside, looking around but not seeing Nabb.

"To my house." He instructed the bellhop to call him a cab. "I need to get to the bottom of this, and you're the only way I can do that. So, I'll listen to what you have to say."

"What if you don't like it?" she asked, getting in the cab.

He got in, shutting the door behind him. "Then you'll listen to what I have to say. Either way, you're going home, Bree Hart."

He ignored her lips pressing tightly together as she slammed her tiny body against the back of the seat. He advised the driver to head for Morningside Heights.

Chapter Four

Bree's senses came to life as soon as she entered Graham's apartment. The smell of home cooking delighted her nose. She had gotten so used to the restaurant smell, the mixture of a hundred different foods, liquor, and smoke. Either that or her own food, which was carryout, delivery, or microwave. This smell was unique.

"Make yourself at home," Graham said as he threw his keys on the stand at the door.

Graham had never been one to care about what others thought of his home. It was neat, it was well decorated and pretty spacious considering Manhattan apartments. For some reason, that didn't seem enough right now. Maybe it was because he knew Bree was used to so much better. But why would he care? It was a college town, and this was a college town apartment. It had always been enough for him.

Bree suddenly realized, as she followed Graham toward the living room, that she wasn't just smelling home cooking, she was hearing it being cooked right now. She suddenly felt anxious. Why, she wasn't sure.

"Is your girlfriend here?" she asked, stopping in the middle of the living room.

Graham looked back at her, wishing that he didn't find her so appealing. "I don't have a girlfriend. That's my sister. I can introduce you to her."

Bree felt herself sigh. "Good. I don't want any girlfriend drama."

Graham laughed. "Of course you don't. You're the last person to want drama. Just a peace-loving soul."

Bree rolled her eyes at him. "You're so judgmental."

"I call them as I see them," he answered back.

"Graham?"

Bree smiled at his older sister standing in the doorway of the kitchen. She was an attractive woman, similar in appearance to Graham. Bree recognized her right away from the television.

"You're Sophia Lane." She approached her, holding her hand out, noticing a hesitation.

"It's so nice to be a celebrity," Sophia said, reluctantly shaking Bree's hand. "And for all the wrong reasons."

Bree saw the dark circles around the woman's eyes, and caught on to her sarcasm. "I'm sorry. I didn't . . ."

Sophia waved a hand in the air. "Don't apologize. Everyone either thinks I got away with fraud or they feel such pity for me they don't even want to look at me. You're a refreshing change."

Graham guessed the day hadn't been a good one. "Have you gotten out today, Soph?"

"No. I never got around to it." She barely shrugged, her eyes staying on Bree. "Do I know you?"

"Soph, this is Bree Hart. She's Keith's younger sister."

Sophia's lips formed a half smile. "Oh really? I pretty much owe Keith my life, so I guess any family of his is welcome in this house. Have you come for dinner?"

"Bree and I have something to discuss," Graham said. "She can stay for dinner."

"Don't hurt yourself trying to make me feel welcome," Bree said, not at all liking the reluctant way he spoke.

Graham ignored her and headed for his room. "We can talk over dinner," he yelled back. "I need a rest."

"Dinner will be ready in"—Sophia watched as Bree walked right past her—"a little bit."

Graham turned on the light in his bedroom, pulling his shirt out of his pants at the same time. He was exhausted. What this girl was putting him through! His eyes focused on his bed. It was calling him. It was . . .

Bree darted past him and flung herself on the large bed. "God, this feels good." She looked around. "This ain't so bad for a professor. I thought you guys made minimum wage. This is a pretty spacious apartment."

"What are you doing in here?" Graham stood at the edge of his bed, uncomfortable with her on it. He was a pretty old-fashioned guy, which didn't fit well in the twenty-first century sometimes. Women today just invited themselves into men's bedrooms? Oh well.

"I want to talk. You said you would hear me out." Was it Bree's imagination, or was he nervous about her being here? She found that pretty amusing. "I'm not going to attack you or anything, so calm down."

He sat down on the edge of the bed, trying to make it seem as if he couldn't have cared less that she was there. When she sat up, coming closer to him, he realized that wasn't going to be easy.

"What do you need to rest for? You're a young man."

"I'm a young man who isn't used to being chased down the streets of New York by a man with a gun. Now, this might be a daily activity for you. As a matter of fact, I'm sure it is. For me, this is weird, and I'd like to take a little rest before being forced to deal with you again."

"Forced?" She huffed. "I'm not forcing you to do anything. You said you would listen to me."

"I will." He moved a little farther back. She was really too pretty for her own good. "At dinner."

"Not with your sister around." She tugged at his sleeve. Bree wasn't stupid. She had to get him alone to convince him. Bystanders would only get in the way. "Let's talk now."

Graham ran his hand over his head with a sigh. He didn't have the energy to argue with her right now. Even if he did, he wasn't so confident he would win. "Fine. Go ahead. Let's hear your fantastic plan that's going to solve both our problems."

"Okay." Bree slid closer to him. Was he moving away from her? "What are you, scared of me? Why do you keep moving?"

"I'm not moving," he lied. "Just go on with your plan."

"Okay. So, you found me, all right? Fine." The expression on her face gave away what she thought of calling her mother. "I'll call my mother. You and I can call her and Keith. We'll tell them that you found me and that you're sending me home. I'll give this sob story about how I'm so destitute and I know the city has defeated me. Mother will love that. I'll buy the ticket and everything. They'll track my credit card, and see that I'm serious. This is where you'll get Keith to write up some document or whatever that says you did your part and you owe him nothing."

"He wouldn't do that before you're actually home." Graham wasn't buying this idea at all. "Why don't you just—"

"I'll put on a show that will do the trick for you. It's a mixture of stubbornness and conciliation that I've taken to another level. It works wonders with mother."

"I don't doubt it." Graham smiled. This woman was a piece of work.

"You shouldn't," she said with narrowed brows. "Do you need me to get Keith to write this up for you? Can you do it yourself? You look like the type that gets a little queasy in a scam."

"I wouldn't know, Bree. I've never run a scam."

"Exactly." Bree looked him over. He was cute, but needed a lot of work when it came to dealing with the Harts. "So, you want me to get it done for you?"

"I don't need you to do it. When you're home, I'll have everything taken care of with Keith."

Bree sighed impatiently. "You're not listening, Graham. I'm not going to Baltimore. But I'll have Keith and Mother believing as true as the sky is blue that I am. And you, you're so committed to holding down your end of the bargain, you're going to escort me to the airport and see me off. Maybe we can even get Keith to come. Yeah, let's get him to come. That's when he can sign that paid-in-full agreement for you."

"But you just won't get on the plane."

Bree nodded. "Finally, you're getting it. I'll go along with it all. Not too much so as to make Keith suspicious. He'll eventually let down his guard with me. Then, I'll just excuse myself to the ladies' room and you and Keith can come looking for me. But you won't find me. And that won't be your fault. You did everything you were supposed to. You get what you want and I get what I want."

Graham leaned back on his bed, wishing he could just take a quick nap. "I expected you to come up with something better than that, Bree. It's not going to work. Not for me at least. And that's the whole point. You're only thinking about yourself, and that plan works perfect for you.''

"It'll work for you too if you follow it like I tell you to." She made a fist, hitting him on his thigh. "Listen to me."

Graham sat up, rubbing his thigh. "You're pretty violent for a little thing."

Bree pouted. "Don't be such a wimp."

"Hey." He leaned closer to her. "I'm not a wimp. Your plan stinks."

Bree was distracted by his sudden closeness. She opened her mouth, but nothing came out. Her eyes looked into his, and she felt a spark of excitement in response to his angry retort. Did this guy have some life in him after all?

Graham was surprised at what he was feeling at that moment. Being this close to her, mixed with anger, frustration, and exhaustion, created a pull in his groin. In a quick second, he envisioned himself grabbing Bree by the arms and kissing her. And then some.

This time, it was Bree's turn to back away. "Well . . . what do you suggest we do?"

In his head, Graham quickly convinced himself this reaction was all a result of not having been in this bed with a woman in a long time. "How about you going home and facing up to your mother?"

"It's not about facing up to her, Graham. There's no dealing with her. She's decided to make up for all the bad things that have happened to our family in the past couple of years by throwing herself into making me perfect."

The phone ringing was a welcome diversion for Graham as he stood up to answer it.

Bree, feeling suddenly exhausted herself, leaned back on the bed. This professor wasn't going to be as easy as she thought. She would have to put a little extra work into getting him on her side. Or at least fooling him enough to get him to work for her.

"Terrence." Graham turned to the bed, seeing Bree lying there. He liked the sight of that too much for his comfort, so he turned away.

It was Terrence Stamps, the intern from Keith's office who was assigned to help him. Graham knew that if he wanted to get as much use out of this guy as he could, turning Bree over now was not in his best interest.

"Mr. Lane," the young man said. "Mr. Hart says you wanted me to do some research for you."

"Yes, and I need the information yesterday."

"I'm faster than anyone you'll ever work with."

Graham hoped that was the truth. "First, you have to check on Robert Barber. He used to work for Trotter and now he works for a financial services company called CMA. Find out what financial transactions Barber has made in the last six months. Find out if there have been any significant changes in his lifestyle. Second, find out what CMA does, who they do it for, and everyone at the top. I mean, everything. Who are the officers of the company, board of directors, and what other businesses are they tied to?"

"Got ya. Barber and CMA."

"Third."

"Third? You want a lot of information yesterday."

"And I mean it too," Graham said. "Third, find out anything you can about Cammermeyer and Storm. Everything, just like CMA. You got that?"

"Yeah, I got it. So, we've been speaking in figurative terms like saying you need it yesterday. In reality, when do you need it by?"

"Yesterday, Terrence." Graham glanced back at Bree on the bed. Something told him he would be in a lot of trouble if he didn't get her out of his life as soon as possible. "And I mean yesterday."

"Lane? Is that you, Graham?"

Graham recognized the voice immediately. Not just the sound of his voice, but the tone. He always spoke in a harsh, condescending tone. "Hello, Keith."

Bree shot up from the bed, her eyes wide and frantic. She stared at Graham, who stared back at her.

"What have you got for me on my sister?"

"Your sister?" Graham gritted his teeth. He hated lying, but he needed more time to think. More time to figure out how he could use this situation to help Sophia. "I've seen her."

Bree felt her stomach tighten as she rushed to Graham, her hands entwined in a prayer gesture. She shook her head vigorously.

"You've seen her?" Keith asked. "Where is she?"

"She works at . . . she used to work at a club on the Upper West Side, but—"

"What club?" Keith asked.

Bree threw her hands in the air. He was going to do it! He couldn't.

"Logan's. It's a nice restaurant actually." Graham had to admit he was getting a little kick out of her pleading. He wasn't usually so sadistic, but she had put him through a lot today. "I'm on my way down there now."

Bree stopped gesturing and stared at him. What was he doing?

"I'm going to show her picture around to see if anyone has seen her. I think I'll get some good leads on her."

Bree wanted to smile, but she was still too scared. He was lying to Keith. He wasn't going to turn her in. Not yet at least. Would Keith go for it?

"Fine," Keith said. "Just call me tomorrow with what you know. My mother is driving me crazy."

Graham found a little pleasure in that too. "Well, you be sure to tell Mrs. Hart that I said hello. I wish——"

Graham heard the click and knew immediately he had been hung up on. He put the phone down.

"What kind of game are you playing?" Bree asked.

"Playing yours, Bree. All you want is to work this for your benefit. Well, all I want is to work this for my sister's benefit. And when I figure out how I'm going to do that, I'll let you know how this is going to go."

"You think you're in charge?" Bree felt herself heat up at the thought of being played. No way. "You're not in charge."

"And you are?" Her fire was contagious. Graham felt his adrenaline rushing just at the sight of her getting angry.

"I could call my brother right now," she said. "I could call him and let him know the truth. If he knew you already had me and were planning on using me to get the best of him, you'd have the bill collectors at your door first thing tomorrow morning."

Graham gritted his teeth. "You're not screwing this up for me like you screw up everything else in your life, Bree Hart."

"Ooooh." Bree looked him up and down with a smirk on her face. "The professor does have a temper. Looks like we both have each other by the cohunes. It's just a matter of figuring out whose are bigger."

"I'll save you the time," Graham said, regaining his composure. "Mine are."

"We'll see." Bree turned and sauntered out of the bedroom, knowing his eyes were on her.

So, the professor wasn't going to be as easy as she thought. That was fine. The measure of difficulty only made it more interesting. There wasn't a man alive that could get the best of her, and Graham Lane wasn't going to either.

Graham sat down at the dining room table where Sophia had prepared dinner. "Where is Bree?"

"She had to make a phone call," Sophia said, motioning for him to serve himself. "What's going on with you two?"

"It's a long story, but don't worry about it." He poured gravy on his pork chop and mashed potatoes. "This looks great, Soph."

"No problem. I figure if I have to be such a burden to you, I might as well learn to cook. I need to be worth something."

"Would you stop with that?" he asked. "You know you're always cranky when you don't get any fresh air. Why did you stay in all day today?"

"Because I didn't feel like going out. Besides, it's New York City. There is no fresh air."

He poured himself a glass of wine. "Who did Bree say she had to call?"

"Someone named Robin."

Graham slammed his fork on the table, surprising not only Sophia, but himself.

"What's the matter with you?" she asked.

Graham shook his head. "Ignore me. It's just been a frustrating day, and that pretty much tops it off."

"You seem jealous," she said.

Graham refused to respond to that. He knew that couldn't be it. He was angry, though, and assumed his expression gave himself away as Bree arrived at the table.

"What did I do now?" she asked in response to the look on his face.

"I sure hope you didn't invite Robin over here. Ex-cons aren't welcome in my home."

"That's very Republican of you, Graham." Bree dug into her dinner. She was starving. "I didn't invite anyone over here. I just needed to make sure Robin was all right."

"I wouldn't worry about Robin. Ex-cons usually do pretty well taking care of themselves."

"Would you stop using that word, ex-con? People can turn their lives around, you know." Bree remembered the shoplifting incident earlier today, and figured she should probably just keep her mouth shut. He just made her so angry.

"That's all fine and good," Graham said. "I just don't want him anywhere near my home or involved in our situation."

"Him?" Bree asked.

"Who is Robin?" Sophia asked.

"Robin is—"

Graham interrupted Bree. "Robin is Bree's boyfriend. Who also happens to be an ex-con. He's behind the reason why Bree and I were chased by a man with a gun today."

"A man with a gun?" Sophia's eyes widened. "What are you talking about?"

"Robin is not my boyfriend," Bree said.

"Your lover, then. Whatever you want to call him." Graham heard his voice rising, which was rare. "He's not coming near my home."

"Who chased you with a gun?" Sophia asked.

"The same man I told you about the other night. The one I chased at the nightclub. For her."

Sophia turned to her. "You're the girl from the nightclub? The one who—"

"Robin is my roommate," Bree said. "She's a girl, you idiot. Who told you she was my boyfriend?"

Graham was silenced for a moment. "A girl?"

"Yes, you jerk. You don't even know what you're talking about."

"Your mother said . . ." Graham tried to decipher his own feelings at this news. It shouldn't have made any difference. Did it?

"I should have figured," Bree said. "You are a lackey for my mother. You just take her word for anything."

"I told you not to call me that. Your mother said you were living with a guy named Robin who was an ex-con. She got her information wrong, not me. It doesn't matter either way. Just eat."

"Don't tell me what to do. I'll—"

"Stop it." Sophia hit her hand on the table. "You're both acting ridiculous. Graham, I'm surprised at you. You always talk about giving ex-cons a second chance."

"Unless they have something to do with me, I guess." Bree shot him a spiteful glance.

"Now, maybe," Sophia continued, "some of this is none of my business. And if that's true, then tell me. But this whole thing is a little confusing. You said you didn't know the woman you met at the club. When was a guy chasing you with a gun? And what are the two of you doing together anyway?"

"You haven't told your sister what you're doing in her behalf?" Bree asked. "Don't you think she has a right to know?"

Graham let out an angry groan before turning to Sophia. "Soph, it's a long story."

Sophia leaned back. "I'm listening."

Graham noticed the smirk on Bree's face at his discomfort as he explained the situation to his sister. Sophia interrupted him several times. She wasn't at all happy with what he was doing in her behalf, but in general expressed her understanding of why he thought he should do this.

"I guess after everything," she said, "I'm just confused about the circumstances that bring you into it, Bree. How old are you?"

"Twenty-five," she answered, leaning back in her chair. She didn't know what to think. At first, she enjoyed watching Graham squirm as he explained everything. But when it came down to it, what he was doing was awesome for Sophia and she admired him for that. She wondered if either of her brothers would ever go this far for her.

"If I hadn't seen you," Sophia said, "I'd assume you were ten. How can your mother even have this happen?"

"You don't know my family."

"We know more than you think," Graham said. "Soph and I did a lot of research on Keith before deciding to take him on as her lawyer. We know that your family is like black royalty in Baltimore. We know that your father used to work for the president, until he tried to kill your sister-in-law, Sydney."

Sophia added, "All because he didn't want her finding out that the family made their fortune in Sierra Leone selling other Africans into slavery. There was a lot done to cover it up, and Sydney found out the truth and was going to let the world know."

Bree would much rather forget that time in her life. "It was only a couple of years ago, but it's still fresh. It cuts deep."

Graham felt compassion for her pain, knowing it was real. It was all so sensationalized in the media and reports, it was easy to lose sight of the fact that for those involved, the event was terribly hurtful and embarrassing. Similar to what had been happening to Sophia.

"At one time," Bree continued, "I thought things were

looking up. Sydney and Marcus got married. Keith started his own business. Mom seemed okay, even though she spent most of her time trying to hold on to some resemblance of prosperity and social propriety. But after about a year, Daddy's absence really hit her. Like never before. He was really gone.

"Marcus was gone. Keith moved out and stopped coming by as often. I think part of him sensed it was coming back. You could just feel it. Unfinished . . . grieving, I guess. I think it was too much for him. After all, it was him that Daddy almost killed, even though Sydney was his target. So I was all that was left. Still young, still a fresh plate that she could serve to society to prove the family was still there. Still a force to be reckoned with in Baltimore society."

Sophia turned to her brother. "Graham, you can't make her go back to that."

Graham tried to ignore the feeling of compassion he had for Bree based on her words. "I need you to be on my side, Soph. Bree is a big girl. She can handle herself. We need to get this bill off from around our necks."

"It's my bill, not ours," she said. "I can figure out a way."

"I made the decision to go with Keith Hart," Graham said. "So it's our bill."

"I came up with an idea," Bree said. "One that can clear your debt to Keith and let me keep my independence. But Graham doesn't even want to listen to me."

"Don't try to get her on your side, Bree. Soph is my sister. And your plan is not going to work."

"Well, figure out one that will work, Graham." Sophia pushed away from the table. "You'll have plenty of time while you two clear the table. I've lost my appetite. I'm going to bed. There's bedding for you on the sofa, Bree."

"Bedding?" Graham asked. "What would she need bedding for?"

"Sophia offered me the sofa for tonight," Bree said, sticking her tongue out.

"When?"

"Just before dinner," Sophia said. "You weren't here. She said she can't go home, and was just going to get a hotel room. But she's low on money."

"She's not low on money," he said. "She's a Hart."

"Graham!" Sophia gave him a motherly stern stare. "She's staying tonight. I don't need to argue. I'm upset already. I'm going to bed."

"Why so early?" Graham wasn't all too comfortable at the thought of being alone with Bree again.

"I need to think about this by myself." She stood up. "This is all my fault, and here you two are putting yourself in this situation to fix it. You've got her mixed up with her crazy family and she's got you mixed up with this dangerous loan shark. All because of me. I can't seem to stop causing problems."

"Soph." Graham thought to go after her, sliding back from the table.

"Leave her alone," Bree said. "She said she needed time to think."

"Don't tell me what to do with my own sister." Graham tossed his napkin onto the table. "Look at what you've done."

"Me?"

"I didn't want my sister knowing about all this. She feels bad enough. She's been so depressed since this got started that sometimes I don't want to leave her alone. She already feels like she's taken too much from me. Thanks a lot."

"Well, I'm going to bed too." Bree stood up from the table.

"You don't have anything to say to that? You just cause a ruckus everywhere you go, and walk away."

"I can't help it if you keep things from your sister."

She left for the living room. She was tired and happy to have a home to sleep in. She had checked her messages and Robin had left a code to tell her that she was spending the night with Carly Anatucco again. Bree didn't have the strength to argue with her, nor an alternative for her. So, they agreed to meet again tomorrow to figure out their next step.

Graham watched as she made herself a bed on the sofa. A tiny part of him was a little relieved that she was sleeping here tonight. Not just because he didn't want the hassle of trying to keep track of her. But at least for tonight, she wouldn't get into any more trouble. At least he hoped not.

"Are you going to help me clear the table?" he asked. "You could at least do that."

"I'm a guest, Graham." She lay down on the bed. "You don't make a guest do chores."

"You're not a guest," he said out loud, following with a whisper, "You're a pain in the ass."

"What?" She sat up. "What did you call me?"

He came over to the sofa and stood over her. "It doesn't matter what I called you. What matters is that you're not a little Hart princess in this house. You're here for one reason and one reason only. I need you to get rid of my debt to your brother and help my sister clear her name. So just keep your mouth shut, and figure out a way to fix this. Otherwise, you're going home to Baltimore."

"What do you mean by that?" Bree asked. "You need me to help clear your sister's name. Keith got your sister acquitted. She's clear."

"Just go to bed." He turned to leave, but Bree grabbed

his arm and halted him. He felt a surge of energy hit him again. The attraction returned. Had it ever left? "What?"

"Does this have something to do with what you were talking to that guy about before my brother got on the phone? Why are you asking about all these people? What about the men at the hotel restaurant today? This is all tied together, isn't it?"

Against his better judgment, Graham sat down on the sofa. He could see her eyes light up. She was a magnet to danger and mystery. The exact opposite of himself. He had to remember that. "It's complicated, Bree."

"Tell me."

He didn't want to, but those dark eyes promised to make him feel better. He believed they would despite himself. So, he told her. He told her his theory of Sophia being frame by Robert Barber and Trotter Securities, and how he was certain there was a larger plan that this setup was supposed to distract everyone from. He believed it was a big deal that had to do with Trotter, CMA, and that luncheon at the hotel today. He didn't know what it was. Everything that he had investigated so far had brought him to a dead end, but he was determined to get to the bottom of this so his sister's reputation and confidence could be restored and the people behind this could be punished.

Bree was very intrigued. She didn't know why, but these types of situations excited her to no end. She wanted to be a part of this. "So what is my brother's office doing to help you?"

"Getting to the bottom of this is what I had planned on spending my summer doing. So, while I'm trying to find you, Keith has offered to have an intern in his office do all of the legwork for me."

"That's why you didn't tell Keith the truth today, right? You want more time to get that information."

Graham nodded. With the setting sun glaring through the windows behind them, Bree's face was luminous. But it showed more than traditional beauty. It was soft and feminine, vulnerably young and honest.

"I can help you, Graham." Bree leaned forward. "Let me help you get to the bottom of this."

"How can you help me?"

"No one is better than me at getting what they want. I want to help you find out who set your sister up."

Graham warned himself not to fall for this. "I'm supposed to believe you suddenly care about my sister's good name?"

"I care about big people stepping over the little people and riding off into the sunset while the little people watch their lives fall apart. I see it happen all the time."

"Bree, if you want to help me out, just go home and deal with your family."

Bree shook her head. He could never understand. "Do you know what she wants me to do?"

"What?"

"She wants me to marry James Trapp, that assistant district attorney guy."

"Is he someone you were dating?" Graham didn't see her marrying a district attorney type. Really, he didn't care to imagine her married to anyone. He was happy that Robin was a girl.

"We went out a couple of times. It was nothing. He's a dud. All he cares about is politics and washing the right backs. When he's not talking about his Yale days ad nauseam, he's plotting and conniving to run into the right people at the right times. He has index cards he keeps in his pockets on topics to discuss with certain people."

"If your mother likes him, I assume he has connections and good breeding."

"The whole nine yards. I backed out after two dates, but she is insistent on getting me to marry him."

"That's impossible, isn't it? Last I checked, in America you can't force an arranged marriage on a kid or an adult."

Bree smiled at his innocence. He was a good-hearted person. "You're the good kind of naive, Graham. What's right is right. Only, it's not that simple when the very wealthy are involved. Go to any high-society party and I'll bet you that at least fifty percent of the marriages there were arranged. Not the same as you would find in the Middle East or someplace like that, but business agreements between parents, families, leaving people with little choices, are very common. They find a way to make it happen, and my mother is determined to do that."

"I don't see you as the type that could be forced to marry anyone," Graham said. "I think you think your mother is stronger than you because she was for a long, long time. But you're not a little girl anymore. You're a woman. Your own woman. You have to keep that in mind when you deal with her."

Bree nodded. "You're right. It's so much easier just to run away from her, but I need to stand up to her. It's just—"

"Try it with me, Bree." Graham sat up straight. "Pretend I'm your mother and I'm telling you you're going to marry this Trapp guy and that's the last of it."

Bree smiled. "Stop it."

"No, do it." He laughed a bit. "Bree, that's enough of this nonsense. I've decided you're going to marry James Trapp and that's it. You'll do it for the family."

"Never." Bree pressed her lips together to stifle her laugh. "You can't force me to do anything. I'm twenty-five years old and I want my own life."

"You don't know what you want," he said. "I know

what's good for you. It's up to you, it's all up to you, Bree. You can save this family or be the final nail in its coffin.''

Graham noticed the tender look that immediately came to Bree's face. No more giggling. ''What's wrong?''

Bree tried to control her emotions. ''She said that. She . . . said I would have to do it, or else the family would die and it would be my fault. She—''

''Damn, Bree, I'm sorry.'' Graham reached for her and wrapped an arm around her. ''I was just thinking of something to say. I didn't know.''

''It's okay.'' Bree bit her lower lip to stifle the tears. She put her head down. ''She can be kind of awful sometimes. She tells me that I'm such an embarrassment, and I don't care about anyone. That I've caused so much pain in the family that . . . that I could . . . I had to do this to make it up to all of them.''

Graham felt anger toward a woman he didn't even know. ''She didn't mean it, Bree. She's had a hard time of it, and she's desperate.''

''I've had a hard time of it too.'' Bree looked up, touched by the compassion in Graham's eyes. ''He was my daddy. He wasn't always there for me, but he was still my daddy. I wish I could help the family, but all I ever do is make things worse. And all she ever does is make me feel like the devil for it. I had to get away. No one can understand.''

''I understand, Bree.'' Graham's hand went to her face and caressed her cheek. She wasn't so tough after all. ''I understand.''

Bree suddenly felt a swell of emotion from the pit of her belly reach throughout her body. She remembered their kiss, and the moments since then when she had felt an attraction to him. She felt a little dizzy.

''Graham.'' His name came like a whisper from her mouth.

The sound of her whispering his name, the sight of the soft parting of her lips created a sense of urgency in Graham. His body reacted without warning or reason. His lips came down on hers with tender affection. All he wanted in this world was to comfort her.

Bree felt a flame light inside her at the touch of his lips. They were tender, but possessive and seductive. She heard herself let out a quiet sigh as she kissed him back. Her arms reached for his neck, pulling him closer to her as their lips explored each other. Bree was cloaked with a feeling of comfort and security.

The softness turned to a demand as Graham's body wanted more. A desire to comfort had turned simply to desire as he grabbed at her shoulders, pulling her to him. He was heating up like a volcano, as his lips parted hers. Slowly his tongue entered her mouth, and he let out a moan.

The urgent tone of his hands on her skin, and his mouth on hers, sent Bree from a flame to a fire. She ran her fingers over the back of his head, bringing her body even closer to his. Her tongue responded to his, exploring his mouth, feeling the excitement of the unexpected fueling her own.

"Bree," he whispered as his mouth left hers and went to her cheek, her chin, and settled in her neck. His tongue teased at her neck in between warm kisses. She was so soft. She smelled so good.

Bree heard her own breathing heavy and fast as his tongue felt like lava on her neck. Her hands grabbed at his shirt, wanting him to be closer. Wanting him to take more. Wanting more for herself.

Somewhere in the distance a car came to a screeching halt and horns honked out of control. The sounds jarred them both from their fantasy and Graham leaned back. Their eyes locked, as the honking got louder outside the living room window, accompanied by cursing in more than one language, none of them English.

Their eyes were connected like magnets, with all the desire, fear, and confusion they were feeling evident within them. Slowly, Bree lowered her hands to her side, and Graham did the same. Still they stared, neither wanting nor willing to let go of the least of this electricity between them.

"What in the world is that?" Sophia flicked on the living room light, closing up her robe as she headed for the window.

Graham quickly turned away and stood up from the sofa. He felt as if he had been caught doing something he shouldn't have. That was pretty much the truth.

Bree reached for her blanket, pulling it up to her chest as if she were covering up some nakedness. The light made her eyes blink. She wondered if Sophia had any idea what they were doing, but from the looks of her, she was too preoccupied with the racket that was outside.

Sophia peered out the window. "I was just getting comfortable and now this. New York. Bree, I'm so sorry for this. It probably scared you to death. College kids, you know."

Bree looked up at Graham, who was standing beside the sofa, looking down at her. He nodded apologetically to her, and in a way that hurt her feelings. Whatever it was that had made that happen between them, she wasn't sorry. Why was he?

"Come on, Soph." He turned to his sister, his voice a little hoarse. "It's dying down. Just get your earplugs."

She shook her head, walking toward him. "I'll just clear the table off and put everything away."

"Good night, Bree." Graham said before turning and heading out of the living room behind his sister, who flicked the light off.

"Good night," she called after him, but was sure he didn't

hear, seeing as how she could barely get her voice above a whisper.

What was that about? Bree still felt her stomach pulling at her, telling her she wanted his mouth on hers again. This guy wasn't her type at all. Bree had always loved the rebellious, bad boys from the wrong side of the tracks. They were so different from the boys in the social circles her mother wanted for her. They were the boys her mother hated. The type Bree liked. Dangerous and daring. They didn't care what others thought of them and answered no one.

This guy, this Graham Lane, was nothing like that. He was a college professor, for heaven's sake. He wasn't dangerous, wild, or anything that usually turned her on. So why, Bree wondered to herself, had she just wanted him as much as she'd ever wanted any man?

It had to be the emotion of the moment. The words he said that resembled her own mother's, his words of understanding, the lighting from the sunset, his closeness. The wine. Yes, that was it. Bree knew she wasn't going to get anything done if she started to have feelings for this guy. No matter what he said he understood, he was on her mother's side. That made him an obstacle. She had to remember that.

Graham sat on the edge of his bed, unbuttoning his shirt. He had no idea what had just happened to him. He was a red-blooded American man, but he had always been careful when it came to women. He thought things through before acting on them, knowing that the consequences of playing it fast and loose with romance were enormous. But with Bree, he went with what came over him.

Why? Was it because of her? She was wild and free, different from any woman he had ever been with. He couldn't plan things with her. She messed up any plans, good or bad. He had no way of getting his hands around his feelings for her, which told him that he shouldn't even try.

Whatever it was that made him want Bree Hart, he had to ignore it. He had to focus on what was important, clearing his sister's name. And getting Bree to go home was all he needed from her. Yes, he did feel bad that she had to deal with what she had. But in the long run, Graham knew she would be a better woman for it.

Besides that, he had to be done with her. She was causing too much uncertainty and bringing too many surprises into his life. Bree Hart was bad news.

Chapter Five

Wednesday morning had not gotten off to a good start for Bree. She wasn't a morning person, but the sun was at the living room window as if it was trying to break the glass. She had to wake up, and she did after getting over that second of panic when one first realizes one isn't in one's own bed.

She spent her usual ten minutes sitting at the edge of her bed, or sofa for this time, getting her head straight. Last night with Graham came back to her, speeding up her recovery. Bree wished she hadn't enjoyed it as much as she had. She wished she didn't care so much whether or not Graham had enjoyed it as much as she had.

Her plan was to act as nonchalant as possible when she saw him again. His apologetic nod last night made it clear that he regretted the incident, so she would never let him know that she didn't.

But that wasn't so simple as she entered the kitchen and saw Graham sitting at the table. He had a glass of juice in one hand and the newspaper in the other. He looked up at her, said nothing, then returned to his newspaper. Bree felt like slamming her foot to the floor. How dare he! He could at least act somewhat uncomfortable.

He continued to ignore her as she shared small talk with Sophia. Sophia explained that since she hadn't gone shopping, there was nothing for breakfast but juice. Bree was starving as usual, and could only eat breakfast for breakfast, not leftovers from dinner as Sophia was preparing for herself. Not a word, not even a gesture came from Graham's direction.

When she finally headed for the bathroom to take a shower and freshen up, Bree was fuming. She had to hide this mood because she knew there would be no justification for it. At least not one she was willing to admit to. She just wanted to get out of this place and away from Graham.

But as she showered and changed into clothes that Sophia loaned her, Bree remembered her coded message from Robin last night. At eleven this morning, Robin was planning on showing up at the apartment to get some of her stuff. She was working something out with someone and planned on skipping town. Bree needed to meet her there, and even though she was scared of Nabb showing up, she was more scared of Nabb showing up and Robin being there by herself.

It was for this that she still needed Graham Lane. Then she had to cut him loose. She had offered to help him and he had refused. She couldn't do any more for him. She only needed him to come with her to the apartment. Maybe the two of them and Robin would make Nabb a little nervous. Who knew? She was counting on a theory that three sitting ducks were better than two.

It was for this that she ignored Graham's indifference to

her and suggested they have breakfast somewhere and hash out a real agreement. He agreed. She played it polite and courteous, although inside she was fuming at this cold side to him. It wasn't until they were almost finished with breakfast that she finally lost control.

"What did you just say?" She felt her hands forming into fists under the table. The nerve of this man.

"I've thought about it and you're going home to Baltimore." Graham couldn't let the look on her face affect him. He had thought long and hard last night. Lord knows he wasn't getting any sleep after his encounter with Bree on the sofa. He couldn't think of anything but her.

"You can't force me to do anything," she said. "Besides, I still have the cards on you."

"No, you don't." He didn't even want to look at her. She was too beautiful. "I'm putting you on a plane today."

She slammed her fist on the table, garnering stares from everyone in the small diner. "I am not property. You can't hand me over."

"But you are a thief," he said. "An accessory at least. Remember, I saw you and your friend run away from that store. If you don't want me to go to the police, you'll get on the plane today. That store owner said he could identify you."

Bree felt herself explode with heat. In a fit of anger, she grabbed her glass of water and tossed its contents at his face. "How dare you! Robin has a record. She'll go to jail if she gets caught again."

Graham slowly wiped his face with a napkin. *Control yourself. Don't let this woman send you into a rage.* She was going to drive him insane if he didn't get rid of her. He really had no intention of turning her over to the police, but he had to get Bree Hart out of his life. He would never admit it to anyone but himself, but he was afraid. He was afraid of the way she made him feel. Especially after last night. In the end, he knew she would only hurt him when he no longer proved interesting to her.

"Then you understand your situation," Graham said, amazed that inside all he wanted to do was kiss her again. Despite what she'd just done. She had a way of making him feel excited, even when she was working his last nerve.

"You need me, Graham." Bree couldn't ignore the sting she felt at his betrayal. She had thought . . . She had been stupid to even attempt to make last night's kiss count for anything. "If I go home, Keith is going to pull support out from under you."

"I got a call from Terrence Stamps this morning. He called me from home. He's got the information I need."

"Impossible. You just called him at like five last night."

"He said he worked faster than anyone. Apparently, he started working the second he got off the phone with me and didn't stop until he called me this morning. Likes a challenge."

Bree fought the panic that was setting in. She needed more time. It was okay. She could handle this. She wasn't beaten yet. No way. "But it's not everything you need. You'll need him for more."

"No, I won't." Graham couldn't believe he had to actually tell himself to stay strong. Why would he need to? "I can do the rest by myself. I just needed him to get me started. We're going to the office to get the information. Keith isn't there today, but we'll call him and let him know you're coming home. Then I'll drive you to the airport."

Bree pushed her plate away and folded her arms across her chest. "You're an ass."

"Bree." Graham squeezed his fork. "Just go home and deal with your problem. You want to make things right for my sister. This is how you do it."

"You would really turn me and Robin in?" she asked.

Graham took a deep breath. "I'll do what I have to for my sister."

"I was wrong," she said. "You're more than an ass. You're downright cold-blooded."

"Stop it." He looked down at his plate.

"Last night," she continued, "you said you understood me. You said—"

"Don't bring up last night," he snapped, looking back at her with restrained anger in his eyes. "Don't you do that."

"I don't get it. Do you hate me because of last night? Why? I didn't force you to do anything."

"I know that," Graham explained. "I wanted to kiss you. I wanted to do more than kiss you last night. But there is no way that's good for either of us."

Bree paused at his words. She wanted to feel some victory in affecting him, but she didn't. He seemed tortured by it, and that made her feel bad. "I'm sorry. I didn't mean to—"

"You didn't do anything," he said. "Don't apologize, Bree. I already feel bad enough."

"So you make yourself feel better by ruining my life?" She wasn't giving up, even though her softer side told her to take it easy on him.

"I'm not ruining your life. You're just going home."

There was a thick pause that stretched between them as Graham ate and Bree thought. Bree couldn't get his words about their kiss out of her mind, but she had to. She was fighting for her sanity here. For lack of a better word, she was desperate. She couldn't let Graham do this.

"What are you afraid of?" she asked finally.

Graham wasn't falling for this reverse psychology. "Just face it, Bree. You lost this battle. Go home and face the music."

"Your life is so orderly," she continued. She may have lost the battle, but she was winning this war. "You dress orderly. You eat orderly. You talk orderly. You plan everything through and through. But this thing with Sophia, me . . . it's all got you reeling and you can't handle it."

"Be quiet, Bree. Eat your breakfast."

"Chicken." She brought her plate back toward her and started eating again.

Graham put his fork down, looking at her. Part of him wanted to wring her neck, the other part wanted to laugh at her ridiculous accusations. "I am not chicken."

"Oh yeah. You are." She never looked up, just continued eating. She knew he was looking at her.

"This isn't going to work," Graham said, feeling his frustration grow just as she had intended. He was aware of her doing this to him and didn't stop it. "I'm not going to give in to your ridiculous plan just to prove that I'm adventurous. You've been nothing but trouble since the first moment I met you and I want to be rid of you."

"You loved it." She leaned back in the booth, knowing she had won. It was just a matter of reeling him in.

"Now it's my turn to laugh. I didn't love it. I didn't love any of it. Particularly the gun part. I want to forget it all."

"You ran home to tell your sister first thing." Bree saw him blink. She had caught him off guard. She wasn't going to Baltimore. No way. "Sophia knew all about that night in Tribeca when we first met."

"When you deceived and used me, you mean."

Bree waved her hand, dismissing his comments. "That's a matter of opinion. What's important is that you couldn't wait to tell her. She said your eyes gave you away."

"She didn't—"

"While I was in her room she did. While she was looking

for something for me to wear, we bonded. That night excited you."

Graham remembered that kiss and knew she was right. Their first kiss. "I had the hangover from hell because of that night."

"Your being a booze hound didn't have anything to do with me."

"My sister didn't notice anything. Nothing is exciting about violence. At least not for me."

"You think a man chasing after me with a gun is exciting for me?" Bree asked. "I don't like violence and I don't like drama. I don't like drawing unnecessary attention to myself."

"Ha!" Graham laughed out loud, throwing his head back. "That's a bunch of bull if I ever heard it. You're an open book. This is your lifestyle."

The fact that he was pretty much telling the truth only made Bree more determined to prove him wrong. "No, it isn't. This thing with Nabb is an isolated incident. Nothing like that ever happens to me."

"It *is* you!"

Both Graham and Bree looked up to see a man walking toward them in anger. Bree braced herself, grabbing the edges of the table. It was Alex Walsh from the Dusty Rose.

"Of all the places," she said with a sigh.

Graham realized the man was about to dart at Bree, so he quickly got up and intercepted him. "What's your problem, man?"

He tried to push Graham out of the way, but Graham grabbed the man's arms and threw them back.

"I'm going to get you, you bitch!" He tried to walk around Graham and get at Bree.

Graham grabbed the man and pushed him back again. He

smelled liquor. This early? "Stay away from her. What are you, crazy?"

"This isn't helping your case, Mr. Walsh!" Bree yelled at him. "All you're doing is proving you're violent."

Graham turned halfway around to face her. "You know this guy? I should have guessed."

"To hell with you!" the man said. "Get out of my way. This is between me and the little liar."

Graham grabbed the man, who was a little smaller and not as fit as he. He turned the man around and pushed him hard enough so that he hit the ground face first. The man rolled over, grabbing his bleeding nose and moaning.

"Get him something," Graham said to the waitress standing near him. "He's bleeding."

"Wow." Bree slid to the edge of the booth, looking down at Alex Walsh.

Graham threw a twenty-dollar bill on the table and reached for Bree.

When he grabbed her, Bree was shocked. The look on his face was angry and dangerous, but she knew he wouldn't hurt her. He was running on adrenaline, a testosterone high after winning this quick battle with Alex, and Bree found it tantalizing. This was why she didn't protest as he pulled her out of the booth and out of the diner.

"Not what I would expect from a professor." Bree took quick steps to keep up with him as he continued pulling her along. "Hey, slow down."

Graham stopped, swinging Bree around to face him. He took a deep breath. "This is exactly what I'm talking about."

"What?" It hadn't passed by Bree that she wasn't too happy when he finally let go of her arm.

"That guy in there." He pointed back at the diner. "You knew him, right?"

"That's a long story, and it's not my—"

"It's not your fault. It's not your fault that people want to kill you. It's not your fault that there is an unusual amount of activity going on around you wherever you are. I'm not buying it."

Bree was angry now. "That man beats his child. I reported him, and that's why—"

"I don't want to hear it, Bree." Graham looked at his watch. "We're going to the university so I can prepare for a panel I'm sitting on tomorrow night. Then we'll go the office where you can call—"

"Graham, please." Bree pulled at his shirt. "Just give me another chance."

He shook his head as if he wasn't listening. "You can call Keith and we'll buy the plane tickets. I'll drive you to the airport."

"I will *not!*" She stomped her foot on the ground.

"Don't forget your little shoplifting incident."

Bree leaned in closer, her eyes squinting as she looked up at him. He was really tall to her. "You wouldn't dare."

"Try me." He leaned in even closer, his frustration getting to him before he realized he didn't think so clearly when he was this close to her.

The silence was deafening between them, as they both stared each other down. Bree leaned back. She had to keep her wits about her. Whatever this guy was doing to confuse her, take her off her guard, he was good at it. But no one knew determination like her. *Concentrate,* she told herself.

"One thing," she said. She needed time.

"What?" Graham heard himself say it, but he couldn't believe it. He was giving her an inch, what he promised himself he wouldn't do. She would take a mile, and he would be in trouble all over again.

"I need you to come with me to my apartment. I want to get some stuff."

"What stuff?"

"Clothes, personal belongings. Things that mean something to me. I'm not homeless. I don't want to leave them behind."

"Behind?" There was no way she was giving in, Graham knew that much.

"If I'm going to Baltimore, idiot." She turned and started walking toward the subway stop. "Come on."

"What do you have up your sleeve?" he asked, following her. "And I haven't agreed to do this."

"I'm going with or without you." She kept going with her head up, hoping to God he was following her. Of course he would follow her.

"This is it," Bree said as they approached the brownstone. "This is . . . my apartment."

Graham watched as she nervously looked around. "You think he's going to show?"

"Let's go inside," she said, ignoring his question. "Hurry."

"Bree, why don't you just call the police? You're scared to death." He looked around as they entered the building. He was a little concerned himself, but that wouldn't help the situation. Bree didn't need to see that.

"Quit asking me to do that," she said, using her keys to check her mailbox. There was nothing there. There usually wasn't. "The police make things more complicated sometimes, Graham. Especially when an ex-con is involved."

Graham shook his head. "You're thinking like an ex-con. Do you realize that? Is this what you wanted when you came to New York?"

"Graham," she warned. "I don't need to hear this right now. This day has gotten off to a bad start. I just want to get some stuff and get out of here without any more surprises."

"There you are."

Bree's heart jumped and she reached for Graham's sleeve. When she saw it was not Nabb, but Frida Jenkins, her landlady, she let go and let out a sigh. "Frida. You scared me half to death."

"A new one, I see," said Frida, a woman in her forties with a housedress that looked as if it could have been ordered from one of those ads in the *TV Guide*. "Not your usual type."

Graham frowned, looking at Bree, who rolled her eyes.

"It's not like that," she said. "Frida thinks having more than one date every six months makes you easy. I wouldn't . . ."

Bree was stopped in her tracks as they reached the front door to her apartment. An eviction notice as bright and clear as day met her at face level.

"What!" She turned to Frida. "You are not kicking us out. Our rent is paid."

"For once, yes, it is up to date." Frida placed haughty hands on her frail hips. "But I'm kicking you out anyways. You and your girlfriend brought trouble to this building for the last time."

"What happened this time?" Graham asked, ignoring the angry glare from Bree.

"Two days ago, that guy shows up. The one that comes by here looking for Robin all the time." Frida made a smacking noise with her lips. "The one that's always so rude to me."

"Oh man!" Bree rushed with her key in the door but the door opened automatically.

"He broke the lock!" Frida yelled. "He was in there

raising all kinds of hell. I had Jason from downstairs tell him to get out. He pulled a gun on him.''

''I'm sorry, Frida.'' Bree's hands fell to her sides. ''Is Jason okay?''

''Scared out of his wits, but yeah. I called the cops. Before they could get here that guy went up and down this building kicking on the walls and doors and yelling how he was gonna kill everyone if he didn't get his money.''

''Was anyone hurt?'' Graham asked. He had to get the police involved, whether Bree wanted them or not. She didn't grasp the urgency here.

''Just a little rattled.'' Frida smiled at him for a moment before turning to Bree with a look of disdain. ''He was gone by the time the cops got here. They would like to speak to you, by the way. And I've had it. So has everyone else here. You and your friend are out.''

''Frida, I—''

''Your little sob story won't work this time. That's it. You're out of here. I don't care if you're on the street. Why don't you move in with your boyfriend here? As long as you're out of this building.''

Frida leaned to the side, her hands still on her hips. She rolled her eyes and neck before turning and walking away.

''Oh my God.'' Bree looked around the apartment. It looked like a tornado had hit it. Not only were all her things thrown about, but they had been ripped to pieces first. ''We barely had anything to begin with. Now there's nothing.''

Graham had never seen such a mess. ''This guy is no joke, Bree. You have to call the police.''

She didn't reply. She felt as if her stomach had dropped ten feet. She leaned over, picking up this and that and placing them back on the floor. In her bedroom, she couldn't even muster a sigh at the sight of it. She shouldn't have expected anything better than what she'd already seen, but it almost looked worse.

Suddenly she remembered the most important thing she had come back here for and quickly panicked. Quickly she rushed to the bed, reaching under the mattress that was torn with springs stretched out everywhere. She reached for her jewelry box. She didn't feel anything.

"Oh no!"

"What are you looking for?" Graham asked as he watched her frantically toss the mattress to the side and kick all of the clothes and broken pieces of dresser around her.

"My ... My." Bree felt the tears coming as she got on the floor looking underneath what was left of the dresser. Nothing. "I can't—"

"Calm down, Bree." Graham could see she was getting hysterical. He reached down for her. She was crying as he carried her to the beanbag chair that was ripped and almost completely flat. He sat on the floor on his knees next to her.

Graham placed his arms around her and rubbed her arms gently. She leaned forward, placing her face in her hands, and sobbed. His heart was tugging at him. It was affecting him more than he could have imagined to see her like this. This tough girl, this hell-raiser was so fragile. She was in pain and he couldn't stand it.

"Bree." He spoke calmly and affectionately. "Everything is going to be okay."

Bree raised her head, speaking between sobs. "My ... jewelry box. It was the only thing I really wanted. It had the ring that my Great Aunt May gave me. It was a family heirloom. My daddy got me this necklace when he went to Italy when I was a baby. That was ... I can't believe it's gone. All the other stuff is just jewelry, but those two ..."

"I'm sorry." He gently caressed her hair with his hand.

She was calming down. "What's important is that you weren't here when he came."

Bree wiped her tears with the back of her hands. "This is not what I wanted. You think this is, but—"

"I don't think that, Bree."

"I had such high hopes. I thought I could do it. I was certain I had it in me. I knew that getting away from Mother would be a great new beginning. . . ." She took a deep breath. "But she was right. I'm no match for the real world. I've made such a mess of my life. I have nothing now. No job, no home, no money, nothing that matters."

"You have me, Bree." Graham meant every word he said. And as she looked at him, her eyes wet with tears of regret, it only confirmed what he thought. He was developing feelings for Bree Hart. He had to be to feel her pain so deeply. What he had thought was a mere physical attraction was more. "I'm here for you, Bree. You aren't alone. I can make everything okay."

Bree was speechless. As his finger gently wiped away a tear from her left cheek, she was overcome with a sense of warmth and comfort. Her sadness disappeared. Her fear was a distant memory. She looked into Graham's eyes and saw an honesty and purity that she had never known a man to have.

She didn't move as his face came closer, his mouth came closer. It seemed as if it were happening in slow motion. Bree closed her eyes in sweet anticipation as she felt his lips come to hers. A smooth tingle waved its way through her body as her own lips responded to his. Everything was wiped away. There was nothing but this kiss and this man right now.

Graham felt a hunger that was stronger than any common

sense or emotion he had felt before. His hands at her shoulders pulled her to him as he opened her lips with his tongue. He wanted nothing more in the world than to wipe every tear from her eyes away, to make her forget about everything but him. Everything but the two of them.

She was feeling dizzy, storms building inside her body. Bree grabbed at Graham's shirt as her tongue played with his mouth. She wanted him. She wanted him not just because she felt desperate, but because she really wanted him. Her body told her that only this man would quench so many of her thirsts. She pulled at his shirt, lifting it out of his slacks. Her hands reached under and caressed his stomach. She felt the muscles under her fingers contract just as Graham let out a moan. She kissed him harder, wanting more. Her hands wrapped around his waist, feeling him warm to her.

She could never be close enough to satisfy him. Graham's mouth sent a trail of kisses from her chin, across her cheek.

"Bree, I want you." He pressed his lips softly around the edges of her ear.

His hands traveled under the loose T-shirt that was a barrier between them. Her body was so warm.

"Graham." Bree could barely say his name as her body was on fire. Her hands went to his, covering them, guiding them over her body. She let out a hungry groan as his strong hands cupped her small breasts, the tips of his thumbs teasing the nipples.

Their mouths returned to each other, this time in a more fervent, more desperate attempt to be closer. Bree loved the pain of his lips crushing hers. Their bodies moved to the floor, with Graham on top of Bree. Her head went back as his mouth went to her neck. As his tongue led a path of fire down her neck, Bree's body arched. She felt out of control.

Graham wanted every part of her. He positioned himself

between her legs to ease his weight. She was a tiny woman, but all woman, and he knew she could feel that he was all man now. There was no hiding that.

He leaned up, lifting her shirt above her breasts. She wasn't wearing a bra. His mouth came down on her right breast, circling the nipple with his tongue. Her wriggling body beneath him only made him more crazy.

When he took her breast in his mouth, Bree called out his name. Her hands grabbed at his shoulders, her nails digging into his skin. What was happening to her? She didn't know, but she knew she wanted it, needed it. Had to have it now.

"Oh my . . ."

Bree's eyes shot open, able to decipher Robin standing in the doorway to her bedroom before her mind could. Her body was even later catching up as she tried to push Graham off of her. Robin quickly left the room.

"Graham." She called to him with a deep, husky voice still caught up in the passion of their lovemaking.

Graham looked up, his entire soul taken over by the passion. Somewhere in the back of his mind was a voice telling him something was wrong. "Bree?"

"Robin is here." As he lifted a bit, she took the opportunity to slide out from under him. It was confusing. Her body didn't want to move, so it wasn't a simple action. She had to concentrate to get away. Her body was acting as if it had a mind all its own.

Graham tried to pull himself together. "Robin?"

"She saw us." Bree swallowed, trying to soothe her dry throat. She pulled her shirt down, but it didn't hide the movement of her chest as her breath kept pace.

Graham wanted to know what had just happened to him. He looked around. He was on the floor in a disaster area, rolling around in mad passion with a woman he had only met a week ago. And he wanted every bit of it. He still did.

"I . . ." He stood up, reaching his hand out to Bree to help her out. "I'm sorry."

Bree helped herself up. She didn't trust his hand. This guy had an effect on her that went against every bit of better judgment she had. Which she knew wasn't too bountiful to begin with. "Don't apologize again, Graham. You have no idea how degrading that is."

"That's not what I meant to do." Graham didn't know why he was apologizing, and as he followed her out of the room, he realized that he wasn't at all sorry for what had just happened between them.

"I knew this would happen!" Robin kicked at the debris on what used to be the living room floor. "That bastard. He destroyed everything but the phone and the answering machine, so he could check our messages. Good thing we were using code."

She turned to them, looking Graham up and down. "Done with the show? Sorry to interrupt you. I didn't know you guys were coming."

"I wasn't going to let you do this on your own." Bree was still tucking her shirt back in. She wanted to fan herself, but that would be too obvious. She looked at Graham, who didn't appear happy.

"You knew she was coming?" he asked.

"I knew you wouldn't," Robin said, as if she hadn't heard Graham. She began searching for salvageable items.

"Of course you did," Graham said, not sure where his anger was coming from. Maybe he was mad at being interrupted from one of the most passionate episodes of his life. Maybe he was mad that Bree lied to him about the basis for coming here.

"I beg your pardon?" Robin looked at him, placing a hand on her hip.

"You knew Bree would show up. She's got your back and you take advantage of that."

"Graham." Bree shook her head. "It's okay."

"No, it isn't," he said. "You get yourself into these situations and drag Bree down with you. This whole thing with Nabb is your fault, but Bree is the one running for her life from a gun. It's just like that shoplifting incident."

Robin's eyes widened and her hands fell to her sides.

"Don't worry," Graham said, "I'm not calling the cops."

It was Bree's turn to be surprised now.

"It's just an example," he continued, "of you getting yourself into trouble and dragging her along with you. Now look around. And Bree's jewelry box was stolen, filled with items that have significant meaning to her. All to pay off your debt."

"You don't know a thing about me," Robin started. "You want to pass judgment on me because of my past."

"I don't give a damn about your past!" Graham's brows narrowed. "I'm talking about right now!"

Bree reached over and gently touched Graham's arms. He immediately calmed, turning to her. Their eyes met and he understood that she wanted this to stop. He nodded, and then stretched his neck, which seemed unusually tight at the moment.

Bree smiled at him, still reeling from the fact that she had come so close to making love to him. She wondered how far they would have gone.

"It doesn't matter anyway," Robin said. "I'm getting out of her life, so you should be happy."

"What are you thinking about doing?" Bree turned over what was left of the coffee table and sat down.

Robin smiled. "I got this second cousin out in Washington

County. She says she'll let me come stay with her. She runs a beauty shop and she needs a shampoo girl. So, I'll do that for room and board until I can get back on my feet."

"That sounds good." Bree was thinking about her grand-mother's ring again.

It saddened her and made her want to be in Graham's arms again. This was too confusing. She didn't even know him a week ago. Suddenly, he was her first-choice source of comfort?

"You can come too, Bree." Robin looked from Bree to Graham. "Unless you think I'd be dragging you down."

Graham looked down at Bree. It was an unusual feeling hitting him. His whole purpose for being with her was to get her to leave. Now . . . Well, everything seemed different now.

"We both need to lie low for a while," Robin said. "I know how much you love Manhattan, but the block is hot right now. Just come out there for a couple of seasons. Come back at New Year's. I might."

Bree didn't know what she should do. "I don't know, Robin. I—"

"No," Graham said, knowing at the same time he had no right to butt in here. "Bree doesn't want to go to the country with you, just so you can get her into trouble there."

Robin laughed. "Bree knows how to get in trouble pretty well by herself. She doesn't need my help."

Bree smiled. "Thanks a lot." She wondered why Graham was protesting, but tried not to. Putting too much thought and analysis into words or even actions softened her reflexes. "I don't think I'll go."

Robin shrugged. "I'm going into my room to see if I can get anything that hasn't been ripped apart. I'll be as fast as I can. Let me know if you change your mind."

"Wait, Robin!" Bree called after her.

Was she changing her mind? Graham wondered. No.

"What?"

"How are you getting to your cousin's?"

"She can't come get me. She doesn't have a car and she thinks the city is the den of Satan. She's scared to death of it. I guess I'll have to take a train and a couple of buses. I don't know. I'll figure it out."

"Let's go, Bree." Graham reached his hand down to pull her up, but she didn't take it.

"Where are you going to get the money to get there?" Bree asked.

Robin cursed under her breath. "I'll figure something out. I was expecting to find something here."

"Among your things or Bree's?" Graham asked. "I wonder."

Robin rolled her eyes. "I'm assuming there's nothing of value left. Nabb sure saw to that."

"Bree." Graham shook his hand a bit, but she still didn't take it.

Bree looked up at him and bit her lower lip. She turned to Robin. "We'll take you. Graham has a car."

"No way," he said.

"I don't need handouts from anal, judgmental Republicans," Robin said.

"What? I'm not—"

"Stop it, both of you." Bree finally stood up on her own. "Robin, you and I have gone too long relying on our ability to figure something out. It's time we have a plan. We'll just give you a ride. Hurry up and get your stuff together. I don't want to be here too long. You never know when Nabb might try again."

With Robin in her bedroom, Graham made no whispers about his displeasure at Bree's offer.

"Bree, I don't appreciate you offering my services." He looked at his watch. "We've already taken too long."

Bree didn't speak. She only stared at him. He was really an attractive man. She wondered if he was calming her. She was never the voice of reason, the problem solver, the peacemaker. What effect was this professor having on her? Or was it this place? Her Great Aunt's ring was gone. It meant so much.

"Do you want me to go back to Baltimore?" she asked.

Graham just looked at her. He didn't know what to say. Part of him wanted to tell her that she had to go back. He needed her to. The other part . . . this new part of him wanted her to stay and be with him. He needed her to.

"Tell me," Bree said. "Because I'm out of answers. I'm admitting defeat here. I lost this one, so it's up to you. If you want me to go home, I'll go. I won't give you a hard time anymore. Sophia's debt will disappear."

"What if I don't?" he asked, never imagining that this dilemma would come to him.

"If you don't, tell me that." Bree ran her fingers through her hair. "I'll stay and I'll help you with Sophia."

"Things are different now, Bree." He wanted to touch her again. Part of this felt unreal to him, because it was happening too fast to make sense.

She nodded. "I know."

"I usually have all the answers," he said. "I'm usually the one that answers all the questions, qualms all the fears, has all the explanations and fail-safe plans."

"Well, I never do," she said. "So this feeling is pretty normal for me."

"Not for me." He was looking affectionately into her eyes, giving away his uncertainty. "You said it yourself. My life is all about order."

"My life has never had order," Bree said. "I think I prefer it that way."

"So, what does that mean?" Graham wondered if he was trying to make more of this than he could ever reasonably expect there to be.

"Do we have to know?" she asked, unable to answer. "Can't we just feel it and let it happen? Besides, we have other things that require our immediate attention."

"And?" Graham asked, wondering if he had ever let himself "just feel it." He couldn't remember. Could he give it a try?

"And I've got a plan. Let's just try it."

"We'll see," Graham said. "I have the idea that all your plans involve a degree of danger, and I'm not letting you start that up again."

She smiled. "I'll keep you in mind and take it easy. Why don't you go on to Columbia to prep for your speech, and Keith's office to do your other thing?"

"Keith." Graham suddenly remembered how he had had this day planned from the beginning.

This was supposed to be about Sophia, but now Graham wasn't even thinking of her. That made him feel guilty on top of everything else. What he was feeling for Bree he couldn't decipher, but he knew it was stronger than a simple physical attraction. But was it worth putting himself back into this situation? It seemed so simple in the beginning.

"Hear me out, Graham." Bree knew he was thinking about his sister right now. He really loved her.

"Go ahead."

"Just don't call him yet," she said. "Go talk to that Terrence guy and get your information. When you get back with it, we'll work through it together. After we drive Robin out to Washington County, of course."

He sighed.

"Graham," she admonished. "With Robin safe and away, I won't be so worried. I can concentrate. I know I can help you if I can concentrate on what's going on with your sister."

"Fine." He nodded, then reflected on her words. "Wait a second. You were talking about me. Only me. But you're coming with me."

"No. I'll meet you back at your place. Robin and I will be waiting for you."

Graham thought it over. Did he trust her? A week ago, that was an easy question. No. He wouldn't have trusted her as far as he could throw her. But now . . . yes. Yes. It didn't make any sense, but yes. It was weird how things had so suddenly changed between them. He knew if she chose to ditch him, with or without Robin, he would be back at square one. But she wasn't going to. The unreliable Bree Hart was trying to be reliable.

"I'm trusting you, Bree." He looked at her with all seriousness. "I need to know that that's okay."

"You wouldn't have gone to the police about the shoplifting thing, right?" Bree asked.

Graham shook his head. "I guess I gave myself away."

"I knew you wouldn't. I felt that about you even when you said you would. What do you feel about me?"

"That's a loaded question," he said. "So, I'll just trust you. Because you know if you try to ditch me, I'll hunt you down like a dog, and there won't be any mercy then."

"Compared to what?"

"I'll ignore that." He looked toward Robin's room. "Tell her to hurry. I'm not leaving until I know you're safely out of here."

"I'll get her."

"And, Bree." Graham waited for her to turn around and look at him. "We need to at least talk about this. Us. At some point."

She nodded with a wink. "Sure thing."

Graham watched her leave, wondering what in the world he was letting himself get into. Whatever it was, he couldn't ignore that he liked it. Bree was something new and refreshing for him. But was she good for him? That was the question he had to answer for himself before he let this go too far.

"You're a lifesaver!" Robin ripped open the envelope holding her last paycheck from Logan's restaurant. "I can't believe you got them."

"I almost forgot I had them." Bree looked down at her own check. Almost nothing, but almost nothing was better than nothing. "With everything that happened since the restaurant yesterday, I forgot that I had picked them up. It wasn't until you asked me how I hooked back up with Graham that I remembered."

"A good thing too," Robin said. "I can't believe Nabb chased you down Broadway with a gun. He generally likes to keep his stuff on the down low."

"I think he's pretty much had it with us." As an older woman got up, Bree took her seat on the subway. "I don't think there are any check-cashing shops in Graham's neighborhood. We should get off here and find one before heading back to Morningside Heights."

"There's one at the next stop," Robin said, looking at the map on the wall. "I've been there before. It's right next to that famous popcorn shop."

"We can get our cash and hop right back on. We'll be at Graham's by—"

"What is this, the twilight zone? You sound like a wife, Bree. What happened to you?"

Bree placed her hand on her chest. "Me, a wife? Please, girl."

She had no idea how she sounded. She was still trying to get her head together, and it wasn't until they parted ways with Graham before getting on the subway that she was able to start.

Robin leaned over, her eyes narrowed as if she were studying a piece of art. "You sound like you're reading the daily schedule he left for you on the refrigerator before heading off to earn the bacon. Get everything done in time to look fresh and ready for loving when the hubby gets home."

Bree shook her head. "It's nothing like that. I'm just trying to stick to some type of schedule."

"That's a joke in itself. Besides, it sounds like his schedule. When was the last time you let a man determine how you run your day?"

"He doesn't determine anything for me," Bree said, stubbornly trying to look unaffected by Robin's observations.

"You're trying to make it sound like he's nothing to you, but I walked in on you two a little while ago, remember? Which was really confusing since I thought you said that the professor was your enemy."

Bree remembered what she had said and thought about Graham. It wasn't so clear anymore. "I'm revising my opinion."

"That's a pretty vague way of stating it. What do you mean?"

"I mean he's not a lackey for my mother like I thought."

"Or so he would have you think."

"What are you trying to start?" Bree asked, seeing the skepticism in Robin's face.

"He's an Ivy League professor with a big debt on his shoulders, according to you. Don't you think he'd be willing to convince you of anything to get you to go back to Balti-more? He can't force you, so he's got to make you think it's what you want.''

''Stop, Robin.'' Bree didn't want to mistrust Graham, but she had to remember why they were together in the first place. ''He could do that, yeah. But that's not Graham. He doesn't play tricks with your mind. He's a straightforward guy. What you see is what you get. What he says is what he means.''

''Which,'' Robin said, ''if true, then what are you doing with him? You hate those boring types. You always want a challenge, a project. He's a professor, for Pete's sake. He has conservative written all over him.''

''He wears it well, though.'' Bree smiled, remembering their last encounter. ''I can't believe it either. I would never have thought I would—''

''Would fall for him?''

''No,'' she answered, shaking her head. ''Yes. I don't know. There's just something about him. I can't put my finger on it, but I like it. I can't believe it, but I like it.''

''I think I can put my finger on it,'' Robin said. ''It's called sex. You haven't had it in a long time and you're letting it confuse you.''

Bree laughed. ''I can't argue it's been a while, and I can't argue that the physical thing is kicking with an unlikely man. But that's not all that intrigues me about him.''

''Just be careful.''

''You're telling me to be careful? You don't see the irony in that?''

''Ha, ha, ha. I'm just saying that you're being pulled in all directions right now. Partly my fault, I admit.''

''How observant of you.''

''But your life is crazier than usual. So, don't let this guy take advantage of that.''

"He wouldn't do that," Bree said. "I don't think he would. He's really committed to his sister, which is what I really like about him. But I think he wants to work with me on this. Besides, I don't really have a lot of choices right now, so maybe he's the choice I need to make."

"Is that why you want him?" Robin asked. "Because you've run out of choices and he's looking pretty good right now? Don't do that. Because once you get back in your groove, he won't be looking as good as he does now."

"That's not what I meant." Bree didn't want to believe anything Robin was saying. "I'd never be with a man because he was a last choice. Don't worry about me. I can handle myself, Robin."

Robin shrugged. "None of it will matter anyway if you let him trick you into going back to Baltimore."

"No man is going to trick me into anything," Bree said with a defiant frown. "And I'm not going back to Baltimore anyway."

"You didn't seem so sure of that earlier at the apartment."

"My mind was on other things then," Bree said. "But that's not going to happen again. I'll figure something else out, but I'm not going to Baltimore. Not for Graham. Not for anyone."

Graham knew what was coming when he stepped onto the floor of Keith Hart's office. Seta was standing next to the receptionist talking into the headphone she was wearing. She waved for him to come over.

"Yes, I know." She was looking at him, but talking on the phone. "I know that, Keith. Please."

Graham turned to the now familiar receptionist. "Where do the interns work?"

She blinked flirtatiously. "In the library, Mr. Lane."

"No." Seta reached for him, tugging at his corduroy shirt. "Mr. Lane, please stay. Keith, I know. I told you I would . . . Yes, that's what I'm trying to do."

Graham didn't really want to talk to Keith. Not that he cared about lying to Keith Hart, but he just didn't care for the act altogether. When Seta motioned for him to reach over the receptionist's desk for the phone, he did so.

"Here he is, Keith." She sighed with relief as she flipped a switch on her headset. "What a pain in the ass. He wants to talk to you."

"Keith—" Graham began.

"What do you have for me, Graham?" Keith interrupted. "It's been a week. I want some results."

"I was just—" Graham tried again.

"Mr. Lane." It was Victoria Hart's voice coming over now, with all the sweet venom mixture of a practiced society woman. "It's my fault. I need to know what is going on with my daughter. I am barely holding things together here. Everything will fall apart if she doesn't get back here soon."

"What's wrong?" Graham asked. "The assistant district attorney doesn't feel like waiting anymore?"

"How do you . . ." Victoria gasped. "You've talked to her! You found her. Oh, thank goodness. It's about time."

"Good," Keith said. "When will she be in Baltimore?"

"How is she?"

Graham was surprised by the tone of genuine concern in Victoria's voice. He shouldn't have been, considering she was Bree's mother, but he was. "Mrs. Hart, Bree is doing fine." He knew that wasn't exactly the truth. "She's healthy."

"She's in trouble, isn't she?" Keith asked.

"Is she in danger?" Victoria followed.

Here it goes. "Bree is fine, like I said. She's got a lot of activity around her right now, but I'm sure that's nothing new for her. She's unharmed. That's all that matters."

"We don't need you to tell us what matters with our own family," Keith said. "I can tell you're keeping something from us, but I don't care. Just tell me when she is going to be in Baltimore."

Graham was definitely keeping something from them. He was falling for Bree. That wasn't at all what Keith had intended, and he was certain Victoria wouldn't approve of it.

"Where did you find her?" Victoria asked. "Was she with that . . . ex-con?"

"Robin is a girl, Mrs. Hart." Graham could hear from Victoria's sigh that she was as relieved as he had been when he first heard that fact. "She is . . . she was Bree's roommate."

"Was?" Keith asked. "Is she dead?"

"Keith," Victoria said. "Who cares about her roommate? Bree is healthy, happy, and found. Now she can come home. I can keep things together for a few more days, but—"

"I need a little bit more time with that." Graham had expected yelling, but there was a silence.

"Time? No," Keith said. "No more time. You put her on a plane today."

"That's not likely, Keith. Mrs. Hart, just hold off on telling folks she'll be back from overseas tomorrow."

"What is going on?" Victoria asked, that hint of sweetness all but disappeared. "You've found her, haven't you? Is she in jail or something? Why can't she come home today?"

"She doesn't want to," Graham said, amazed that Victoria was acting as if that weren't even a possibility.

"Bree doesn't know what she wants," Keith said. "Graham, if you want your debt cleared with me, you get her on a plane ASAP.''

Graham took a second to compose himself. Usually when a man talked to him with Keith's tone, Graham pulled out the intellectual guns and figuratively annihilated him. But that couldn't happen now. Instead, he took a deep breath as he watched the receptionist investigate a bouquet of flowers delivered to the desk.

"These need to go to the hospital," she told the delivery man after reading the card. "He's in the hospital. Can you take this to General?"

The guy nodded, grabbing the bouquet, and headed out.

Graham returned to the phone. "I will get her to you. I need some time to convince her that it's the best thing for her. I don't think that will be too hard, so don't have a fit. I'll let you know what I—"

"Don't try to play me," Keith said.

"I'll call you when I've made progress." Graham hung up the phone without waiting for a response.

"Are you okay?" He placed a hand on the shoulder of the receptionist. She had been so courteous, remembering his name, but he hadn't remembered hers. She looked as if she was about to cry.

She nodded, trying to compose herself. "I'm okay. It's just that the flowers upset me. Poor Terrence."

"Terrence Stamps? Has something happened to him?"

"You know him?" She looked at Graham a little confused. "He's new, so hardly anyone knew—"

"What happened to him?" Graham asked. "I spoke to him this morning. He called me from his apartment."

She swallowed. "He was attacked on his way into work. Some guy mugged him and beat the living tar out of him. He's at General right now."

Graham charged out of the office. People were mugged every day in the city of New York. But for some reason, he had the weirdest feeling that this was no senseless act of violence. This was about Sophia. And if it was, the danger was only beginning.

Chapter Six

"What juicy info did you get?" Bree asked Graham the second he entered the apartment.

Entering the living room, he looked at her. Lying back on his sofa in a tank top and a pair of blue jeans, a bowl of popcorn on one thigh, remote control on the other. The sight was calming to him. He could see himself getting used to coming home to Bree Hart. The question was, was she the type of woman that would be home waiting for him?

"Change of plans, Bree."

"What's up?" Bree sat up as he joined her on the sofa. The look in his eyes excited her.

Graham Lane was a deceptive man, she realized. He seemed boring on the outside, but there was a fire inside this man. Maybe that was why she liked him. She had been spending the day trying to think of reasons not to like him, letting Robin's warnings get to her. It hadn't worked. It was all demolished by the lift in her spirits when he walked into the living room.

"We have to go to General," he said.

"Oh my God! The hospital? What happened?"

"Terrence Stamps was attacked this morning."

"I don't understand. You talked to him this morning. He was fine."

"Yeah, I talked to him after he had spent the day before tracking down the information I requested. He was attacked on his way into work this morning. They're calling it a mugging, but I don't think it was."

"You think it has to do with Sophia?"

He put his finger to his mouth and hushed her. "She'll hear."

"She's not here," Bree said, checking her watch. "She should be at Sak's right now, getting her pores exfoliated."

"What are you talking about?"

"It's a long story, but your sister is very depressed. You should be aware of that."

"I am aware, Bree. I know my sister very well and she would never be interested in any of that spa stuff."

"Is that so?" Bree asked. "Well, then why is she at Sak's day spa getting a manicure, pedicure, and facial treatment? Thanks for leaving your credit card on your dresser. I talked her into going there. She's been under a lot of stress lately, and she hasn't had anyone to talk to."

Graham found that unbelievable. "What? I've been here the whole time."

"But you're a guy, Graham. She needed a woman to talk to. Most of her so-called friends backed out on her when the scandal hit. I know what that's like. We connected."

Graham remembered Bree's life had been rocked by a scandal not too long ago. Although she wasn't the main subject, her family had been, and it was a painful situation that was still manifesting itself in her today.

"You do have a lot in common with Sophia," he said. "I'm glad you were here for her. You were able to get her out of the house at least. Thanks a lot."

"That's not all," Bree said. She felt proud of his approval. She hadn't felt that way in a long time. It had been a while since anyone that mattered to Bree had been proud of her. "I got her a ticket to *The Lion King* on Broadway tomorrow night."

"You've had a busy day," Graham said, leaning back on the sofa. He kept his eyes on her. She was delightful to look at. Her cute little nose, her sexy full lips. Her eyes were so soothing.

Bree had been trying all day to make sense of her feelings for Graham. Now, with him looking at her the way he was, she realized there was no making sense of it. She was beaming in his admiration. The pleased look on his face as he listened to her was so satisfying. Such a little thing, but so satisfying.

"I checked the machine at my old place for a message from Robin, and my friend Lily from the Dusty Rose where I volunteer left me—"

"You volunteer?"

"Yes," she said, with a smile. "I'm not the selfish little spoiled brat you think I am. Well, not mostly."

"I don't think that anymore, Bree." And he didn't. He didn't think most of the things he thought about Bree before he got to know her.

Bree never cared what other people thought of her. Not that much at least. In general, when she did care it was because she wanted them to be angry with her. To show some emotion. But she did care about Graham's opinion of her. How had he become that important to her?

"So," she continued after a while. "Lily and I had a little mix-up the other day. And don't look at me like that. I didn't start it. It was about that guy in the diner. Don't look at me like that. That wasn't my fault either. Well, it was, but . . . that's not the point. Anyway, Lily knew she was wrong, so there."

"I'm not arguing with you, Bree." Graham was holding back his laughter.

"Well, quit it with the looks. Can I continue?"

He nodded. She was so stubborn and proud. Could he ever get a handle on this woman? He didn't think so.

"She wanted to apologize, so she told me she was leaving a ticket for me at the booth for tomorrow night's show. I told Sophia she could take it. She loved the movie, so she's very excited."

"Wow." Graham didn't even know that. How close had the two of them gotten? It didn't matter. He was grateful to Bree for bringing out some light in Sophia. "Bree, this is great."

"You're welcome," she said. "And you're probably thinking about Nabb. Because he was listening to my messages."

"What if he listened to that message?"

"He'd have to get back into the apartment, and I don't think Frida would let that happen again. Remember, before we left she said she was changing the locks to the outside building and getting a new door for our place so she could rent it again?"

"Why did you even leave the machine there?"

"For Robin and me to keep communicating until we're both somewhere permanent. Anyway, there's no danger. Even if he came by and checked the messages, he doesn't know Sophia. When he doesn't see me, he'll leave."

Graham thought about it for a moment. "Everything you

say makes sense, but I still don't like it. I don't like him anywhere near my sister.''

"Nothing is going to happen, Graham." She placed a hand on his lap. "Don't be so responsible."

He looked down at her hand, feeling the effect of her touch. He watched as it slowly slid away, clearly knowing he didn't like that. They needed to talk about this. Not that he had had time to think about what he was feeling, or whether or not she was feeling the same. There was no time for that now, which reminded him of why he was here.

"We have to go to General, Bree." He stood up. "I tried to stop by there earlier, but they weren't allowing nonfamily visitors yet. The head nurse on the floor said if I came back around two, she could let me in."

"Let's go." Bree clicked off the television, and placed the popcorn on the coffee table. "Oh, wait. What about Robin? How long will we be there?"

"I don't know." He realized Robin wasn't around. "Why isn't she here? Weren't we going to give her a ride to . . ."

Bree nodded. "Change of plans. Like you said."

Graham threw his hands in the air. "What happened?"

"We were cashing checks at the currency exchange and Robin ran into an old friend. They were gabbing and jawing. Then her friend mentioned a gig she had for the two of them that could get her some cold, hard cash today. Robin wanted as much ammo as possible before she starts a new life."

Graham didn't like the sound of this at all. "What did you call it? A gig? Unless she's a musician, that can't be a good thing. More like a score perhaps? Bree, you have got to cut this girl loose."

"I know, but until then I can't control her. I don't believe in controlling people. She is who she is. Either way, she's not getting back until early evening."

"What checks were you cashing? I thought you didn't have any money."

"Our paychecks that I picked up from work. You know, before Nabb saw us in the alley and chased—"

"Don't remind me." Graham went over time in his head. "I have the panel discussion tonight at Columbia, so I can't drive her tonight. She'll have to catch another ride."

"Graham, I promised."

"Do you want to find a way to get her out of town or help me get these guys who framed my sister and now possibly attacked Terrence?"

There was no contest there. After getting close to Sophia today, Bree was more interested than ever in helping her. She genuinely liked the woman, and hated how she had been harmed by all this.

"I'll figure something out," she said. "I always do. Let's go."

In all the rushing and change of plans, it hadn't passed by Bree that Graham didn't bring up the issue of the two of them again. Was it still a huge issue for Graham as it was for her? Had this thing with Terrence pushed them to the back burner, or was Graham just not interested in talking about it right now?

Bree believed in going with her feelings, not talking about them, analyzing them to death. But she knew Graham was probably the opposite. And as they grabbed a cab for the hospital, Bree wondered if that fact was all the discussion that was necessary.

Terrence Stamps was a twenty-year-old that looked more like a thirteen-year-old. Maybe it was the trauma of being attacked, but to Bree he looked like a wet puppy just brought in from the rain. He couldn't have been over five feet seven, barely 130 pounds or more. His caramel skin had assorted acne, mostly on his chin. He had a bandage around his head, stitches on his left cheek, his broken left arm was in a cast, and two broken fingers on his right hand were taped together. He reached with considerable pain to shake Bree's hand when they were introduced.

"You look awful," Bree said, looking down at him in the hospital bed. "They really messed you up. How many were there? Three? Four?"

"One," Terrence said with a tone that made it obvious he was embarrassed by that fact. "It was only one, but he was big."

Graham was standing on the other side of the bed. "You think it was about me or a mugging?"

"I think it was definitely about you," he answered. Terrence squinted as if the nodding gesture he'd made was painful. "That guy was looking for something."

"How do you mean?" Bree asked.

"He was grabbing at my briefcase, right? But I'm not trying to give up my briefcase, man. All my work and everything. I reached in my jacket pocket and handed the guy my wallet. I told him, 'Here's my wallet, take it.' I figured that was what he wanted and he just assumed it was in my briefcase."

"But he didn't take your wallet?" Bree asked.

"Yeah, he took it. But it was like . . . I can't really explain it in words. He was like, 'Oh yeah, whatever' and took it. It wasn't what he was after. It was like midway through it, he realized that this was supposed to look like a mugging, so he took it."

"So when did he beat you up?"

"Bree." Graham sent her a quieting stare. "Go ahead, Terrence."

"When I wouldn't give up my briefcase was when he

started in on me. I guess I made him mad, 'cause even after he got it he stomped on my arm a couple of times.''

"He was ticked because you gave him a fight," Graham said. "He probably thought you'd be easy, but you showed him."

Bree noticed a smile form at Terrence's lips. Graham had made him feel better about getting the snot beat out of him. Graham was one of the nice guys that Bree thought always finished last. She wasn't so sure of that anymore.

"Did he say anything to you?" Graham asked.

Terrence paused as if trying to remember. "He was calling me names a lot. He kept telling me to hand it over, hand it over. I think that was it. Nothing about you or what I've found out."

"What did you find out?"

Terrence shook his head. "I can't remember everything right now, but you called me around five, and I got right on the phone afterward. I called the offices of the places you gave me. CMA, Trotter, and Cammermeyer and Storm. I asked a lot of nosy questions, using the usual tactics that we learn in law school. I got a lot out of them considering they were all shutting down for the day. I got this guy that the firm uses in public records for the government to help me out too. Then, I got on the Internet and did some searching all night long. I made a few other calls and came up with some good stuff.

"I found out about that guy you asked about, Barber. He didn't make any big purchases in the last six months, but he did buy an insurance policy for a boat."

"Without buying a boat?" Graham asked. "Maybe he already had one."

"Don't think so. The insurance policy covers a model owned by Robert Barber. It's a Quest Ray 250. That's a pretty top-line model. It's one of those cutting-edge mini-yachts. Cost about sixty grand. He's keeping it at the North Cove Yacht Club, which is right off Battery Park in the financial district. I don't even want to know how much it's costing to dock it there.''

"Graham," Bree said. "Sophia told me today that Barber had to pay a six-figure fine as part of his plea bargain with the SEC. He was out of a job for six months and he has an Upper East Side mortgage, alimony, and child support to pay. Where does a new boat come from?''

"That's just it,'' Graham said. "There's no record of him buying a new boat, but he bought the insurance. So, the boat must have been a gift.''

"Bingo," Terrence said. "A gift from whom is the next question. Not sure exactly. But when I did all the other stuff you asked, you know, trying to find out where those three companies are connected, I found something interesting.''

Bree leaned closer, getting more excited by the moment. Terrence looked at her and smiled shyly. He kept looking at her until Graham loudly cleared his throat.

"So," Terrence went on. "CMA stands for Crist, Monroe and Anson. It's just the names of the partners, nothing interesting there. It's one of those new-wave financial services companies that are supposed to be more focused on individuals. Fewer clients, more care. Every investor has to invest in nonprofit to belong, etcetera. Anyway, one of the senior officers of the board is Cheryl Ripley. She's pretty active in the philanthropy world. Among others, she's on the board of this grant committee run by Westchester blue bloods called the Buckley Organization.

"Now, that org came back on the screen when I looked up the background of another executive. Cameron Moore doesn't work for Cammermeyer and Storm, but he is on the board of directors. Come to find out Cameron Moore is married to a woman named Lucy Ripley. Possibly an aunt or something. There's about a twenty-year age difference in the women. Not Cheryl's mom. She died a year ago. It was in the society papers.''

"How did you find all this out in twelve hours?" Bree was impressed.

Terrence shrugged, then winced as he realized that was not the wisest choice for a man in his situation. "I'm the bomb when it comes to research. What else can I tell you?"

"Go on, Terrence." Graham was trying to hold off a million thoughts in his head until he heard everything.

"Well, turns out that Cameron Moore is the son of the former Alicia Moore, who is now Alicia Farnsworth, wife of Charles Farnsworth, owner of a long-held family company called Nautical Luxuries."

"Which just might happen to be where that brand of boat that Robert Barber has recently come to possess comes from." Bree slapped her knee. "He got that boat from Cameron Moore."

"Can't be sure," Terrence said. "I tried calling and couldn't get anything out of them. But the Quest Ray 250 is one of their top sellers. Because of the styling and detail, the price is pretty high and only a few companies in the country carry that particular line of boats."

Graham was shaking his head. "So, how did this get started and why was my sister pulled in? What else did you get?"

"Nothing that made much sense to me, but I gathered everything I could. I was planning on getting some more today. I've left messages with about everyone in the world."

"I think that was your problem," Bree said. "Either you left a message with, or in your phone-call frenzy yesterday spoke to, the wrong person."

"I should have been more careful."

"You did great, Terrence." Graham went to give him an

encouraging tap, but thought better of it since he wasn't sure where it hurt. He looked as if it hurt everywhere. "I'm sorry you got hurt. I'm sorry you lost your briefcase. All of your hard work."

"I'm used to getting no sleep. I guess the work can be replaced. Besides, those were the copies. I was going to hand those papers to you, and keep the originals for myself. I expected you were going to ask me to do more, and I wanted to keep original copies of everything I'd done already."

"Where are those copies?" Graham asked.

"My apartment. They're in the refrigerator. Don't ask. When you've been up all night, you leave things in weird places. It always makes sense at the time. There's a spare key behind the painting of a dog at the end of the hallway. I'll give you my address."

"You shouldn't be here." Graham located the hidden key just where Terrence said it would be.

Bree was hurt by his words even though she knew he meant no harm. "You barely speak to me all the way over here, and the first thing you have to say is that I shouldn't be here?"

"I didn't mean to ignore you," he said, standing at the door. "I've had a little on my mind."

"I know. I just wonder how much the police could have found out if they looked into this. Some of these relationships had to be going on before Sophia was framed."

Graham turned the lock with the key. "Barber was probably more careful about hiding it in the beginning. Nothing that could tie him in until after both trials were over. Besides, why would the cops do the work when they didn't have to? Barber gave a full confession. All the fabricated evidence gave them everything they needed. The SEC took it from there. Trust me, I'm going to be sure to point their mistakes out to them.''

Bree followed him inside. ''Barber timed it right. But how did he know? How did he know how this would all turn out? He would have to be taking a big chance. Maybe he didn't know what was—''

''Well,'' Graham said, looking around. ''This is starting to be a familiar sight.''

They both entered the apartment that was ransacked. Not as bad as Bree's, but undeniably a crime had been committed here. It said, nothing personal, but what must be done, must be done.

''Are you sure you've never been here?'' Graham asked, stepping over a pile of books that were once neatly on the bookcase. ''This has you written all over it.''

''Shut up.'' Bree pushed him out of her way and headed for the kitchen. ''Those guys who framed Sophia are serious. They must have assumed there were copies too.''

''No good lawyer would be without them.'' Graham opened the refrigerator. ''Whoever they sent didn't cover all of his tracks. The papers are right here.''

He pulled the manila folder out from under a jar of olives on the second shelf.

''Can we go?'' Bree said, looking around. ''I don't want to be here anymore.''

''He's gone, Bree. I don't think those guys wait around too long. Besides, he knows Terrence isn't coming back anytime soon.'' Graham leaned over the counter and opened the folder. ''I just want to take a quick look. Call the cops.''

''Cops?'' Bree thought she heard something. She looked down the hallway and saw a tree branch hitting against the window. She calmed down a little. ''Why don't we just tell Terrence and have him call the cops?''

Graham turned around. "Bree, come on. The guy is in the hospital. His place has been torn apart. Call the cops."

With a huff, she reached for the phone on the kitchen wall. The cord had been ripped out of the socket. "That wasn't necessary. I think I saw a phone in the foyer. I'll try that one."

She headed for the front of the apartment. If they called the cops, would they have to wait for them? She had a bad feeling about this place.

Graham flipped through the random pieces of paper. Based on what Terrence told him, he thought he would get the furthest with Cheryl Ripley. Based on her philanthropy and background, which Terrence had in great detail, she seemed like a pretty nice person. Hopefully she wasn't all smoke and mirrors. As he'd hoped, Terrence had gotten her address. Montgomery County. A good three hours from Manhattan.

Engrossed in what he was reading, Graham didn't hear the steps coming from behind until they were right up on him. Quickly, he swung around, coming face-to-face with a sea of red. Then a ski-masked face let out a growl as large arms raised in the air. It was an instinctual move to duck. Graham felt the wind whiz by him as the man's strike missed.

Graham didn't lift back up. He grabbed the larger man by his waist and darted forward, knocking them both to the ground. He was only on top of the man for a moment before his awesome strength rolled Graham over.

"I'm gonna kill you!" he growled as his hands went to Graham's neck and squeezed.

Graham used the butt of his palms with all the force he had, and slammed them against the man's head. He heard him let out a howl and fall back. Graham kicked his way out from under the man, but wasn't fast enough. Cursing a myriad of obscenities, the man grabbed Graham's leg and pulled him back. With his other hand, he made a fist and aimed for Graham's face.

Thud.

Bree screamed as the man's huge body fell with a thump on top of Graham. She threw the heavy pot to the side.

"Graham. Are you okay?"

"I'm going to suffocate to death," he said, trying to push the man off of him. "Couldn't you have hit him with a swing to the left or right?"

"You're welcome." She placed her hands on his hips. "I pretty much just saved your life."

"I would have taken care of him." Graham finally got him off and lifted himself up. "It was just a matter of—"

"Yada, yada, yada." Bree looked at the massive figure in a bloodred jacket and black jeans. He had a ski mask on and black gloves. There was no identifying him.

"I can only assume this is Terrence's attacker. He mentioned a red jacket, didn't he?"

Graham reached for his ski mask, but just as he got there, the man flipped himself over and grabbed his hand, pulling him to the ground.

Bree jumped back, screaming. The man got up quicker than she had seen anyone of that size move. He turned to Bree, his eyes searing at her. She let out a gasp. He lifted his hands as if he was going to come after her, but was distracted by Graham getting back up. He kicked Graham in the stomach, turned, and ran out of the apartment.

Bree rushed to Graham on the floor, wrapping her arms around him. "He's gone, Graham. Are you okay? Do we need to get to a hospital?"

"No." He shook his head. "It's not that bad. Just knocked the wind out of me. I need a second to catch my breath."

Bree was trying to calm herself, but it was hard. She sat

on the ground next to him, all of her emotions building up within her.

"I was so scared," she said, feeling as if she could hardly breathe. "I thought he was going to kill me. And you ... the way he was kicking you, just a few more inches and it would have been your face. What if he had a gun? He would have ... oh, Graham."

Without thinking, Graham grabbed her and pulled her to him. His mouth came over hers in one fell swoop and pressed. The kiss was hard and aggressive. It was what he felt right now. Maybe it was the excitement of what had just happened to him, but right now Graham wanted nothing more than to kiss this woman with all the energy running through his body.

Bree was breathlessly shocked as his lips devoured hers. She was even more shocked by her own reaction. She wrapped her arms around him and pressed her lips harder against his. She reached her body over, her right leg swinging over his lap. Her body seemed to explode as desire hit her like a sharp whip. She was melting into him, hearing herself moan in pleasurable unison with his.

Graham's hands grabbed at her hair, pulling her head back. His mouth went to her neck, his tongue leaving lava-hot marks everywhere. He had never gotten so out of control so fast. He wanted to take her right here. Right now.

"Neither of you are Terrence."

Both Graham and Bree jumped so high, they were able to stand straight up. They were both thinking, had he returned? Fortunately, they came face-to-face with an elderly Asian man standing in the door to the kitchen.

"Who in the hell are you two?" he asked. "And what kind of pornographic activity are you engaging in on my floor?"

Graham cleared his throat. "This is Terrence Stamps's apartment."

He shook his head, taking an extra second to look Bree over. "No, this is my apartment. I rent it to Terrence. I hear screams. A hooded thug almost knocked me down running out of here. The door is wide open, this place is a mess, and I find you two making babies on the kitchen floor."

"Terrence gave us the key," Graham said. "He's in the hospital. He was mugged this morning."

"And this place was messed up before we got here." Bree didn't care what it looked like. She used her right hand to wave some air on her face. "By that guy that ran into you."

"Don't worry," Graham said. "We called the cops."

"No, we didn't."

Graham turned to Bree. "Yes, we did. You did."

"No, we didn't," she replied. "I didn't. The phone in the foyer was ripped out of the socket."

"So," the little man said, looking from one to the other. "What do we do now?"

Graham looked at his watch. "We have to go. You should call the cops."

"You're leaving?" he asked.

Graham grabbed the folder from the counter and nodded to Bree. "Let's go. I have my panel discussion."

"Bye!" Bree waved to the man as she passed him, smiling compassionately at his bewildered expression. "Terrence is going to be okay. In case you were concerned. But you should go visit him. He's at General."

As soon as they reached outside, Bree let the wind hit her face. It was a warm night, but there was a nice breeze on the busy street. She took a deep breath as they stood at the sidewalk for Graham to hail a cab. She could still feel her heart beating wildly, but she wasn't sure if it was from a near-death experience, or the carnal desire that had taken her over on the kitchen floor.

A cab pulled up and Graham turned to Bree. She looked frazzled, her eyes were wide, her hair dishelved. Was she shaking? "Bree, are you all right?"

Bree nodded, as she stepped inside. "I'm fine. I . . . I just . . . I'm fine. You. You're the one he tried to kill."

Graham shut the cab door behind him. "I'm fine, Bree. I shouldn't have brought you with me."

"At least this time it wasn't my fault."

"Where?" The driver spoke in a monotone voice without looking back.

Graham gave him the address and turned back to Bree with a smile. He appreciated the humor. When she smiled back, her eyes sparkled like usual. Graham knew that whatever trouble he had gotten himself into over Sophia's situation, it was nothing compared to the trouble he was getting himself into with Bree Hart.

Sophia sat on the sofa with her mouth wide open. Robin was hitting a soft fist on the coffee table with excitement.

"That is so awesome," Robin said. "It's like a Wesley Snipes movie. God, I wish I had been there."

"You're nuts, girl." Bree leaned back on the sofa, happy to be safe at Graham's apartment. She looked down the hallway. Where was he, anyway?

"He's getting dressed for his panel discussion," Sophia said as if reading Bree's mind. She raised her voice, inflecting it toward the back of the apartment. "It's starting in less than an hour, by the way."

"I know!" His voice yelled back from somewhere no one could see.

"This is unbelievable," Sophia said, shaking her head. "That man could have killed both of you."

Bree waved her hand, finding confidence in hindsight. "No way. He couldn't have gotten both of us."

Bree hadn't told them everything. She had carefully left out the passionate scene between her and Graham, which was not so surprisingly what she remembered the most.

"What if he had a gun?" Robin asked. "That would have been awesome."

Sophia hit her on the arm. "You are crazy!"

Robin laughed, Sophia joining in.

"So what is this?" Bree asked. "You two bonded in the one hour you've known each other."

Sophia shrugged, getting up from the sofa. "I just felt like laughing. That day at the spa saved my life."

"Cool." Bree reached for the remote, wondering when Graham was going to come back out. "What's on TV?"

"I'm going to find something for dinner," Sophia said as she left the room.

Robin was sitting on the floor between the sofa and the coffee table. "You've had a pretty incredible day. I bet the professor is just ready to enter an asylum. He's probably not used to any type of excitement."

Bree flicked the channels. "You'd be surprised. Graham handled himself well. He may not be used to any of this, but he just might be a natural."

"Thanks." Graham entered. "But I don't think I ever want to get enough experience with this kind of thing to be considered a natural."

Bree felt herself light up inside at the sight of him. He looked so clean-cut and handsome in his casual business suit. Graham winked at her, feeling that her presence seemed to make the room brighter.

He noticed Robin on the floor, staring up at him with defensive eyes. "Hello, Robin."

"Before you start," Bree said, "Robin knows you can't give her a ride tonight. But I just told her when we got back. So she's going to use her cash to get a train ticket first thing tomorrow morning. Tonight she's sleeping here."

"Your sister said I could," Robin added. "On account of you reneging on your offer."

"It wasn't my offer," he said. "It was Bree's. But don't worry. Go ahead and spend the night here. And I can give you a ride to Washington County tomorrow afternoon."

"Why this change of heart?" Bree asked. He was acting peculiarly calm after what had happened less than an hour ago.

"I'll tell you about it when I get back," he said. Looking down at her, he wanted to kiss her good-bye before heading off, but thought against it. He nodded to Robin. "I trust you'll behave tonight."

Robin shrugged, returning her attention to the television. "Basic cable. Please."

"When will you be back?" Bree asked, wishing that he wasn't leaving. In such a short time, she had found herself getting used to his presence and liking it.

"Late," he said. "The panel is two hours and then the usual meet and greet. Don't wait up. I'll see you in the morning."

"Okay." Bree watched as he turned and headed for the hallway.

Graham said good-bye to Sophia, who was standing in the archway with a towel in her hands. She turned to Bree with a very serious look on her face and Bree wondered how long she had been standing there. The look on her face concerned Bree enough to follow her into the kitchen.

"Do you need any help?" Bree asked, standing in the doorway.

Sophia didn't look behind her. It was as if she had expected Bree to be there. "You can keep me company. I'd like to talk to you, Bree."

"I was hoping to ask you some questions too." Bree sat at the table. "Terrence found out some interesting information."

"I suppose he did. He's certainly paid a price for it. I wish Graham had told me about this before. I think it's too dangerous what you two are doing."

"He feels so bad about what happened to Terrence, but there's no stopping Graham. Nothing means more to him than getting to the truth."

Sophia nodded, washing off a head of lettuce. "Graham is a pretty laid-back guy, but when he's after what's right, he turns into a panther."

"When you were working at Trotter, did Robert Barber ever mention CMA?"

"No. Never."

"What about Cammermeyer and Storm?"

She turned around, her brow creased in concentration. "Who is that?"

"It's the company that's merging with Trotter Securities. New news."

"The only merger I knew anything about was the merger that Trotter was supposed to have with McLaughlin Silverman before everything went down. I can't think . . ."

Bree could tell she had rung a bell. "You remember something?"

"I can't be sure," she answered. "But Cammermeyer sounds familiar. It's not a very usual name. Robert used to get a hundred calls a day. Clients, other brokers, headhunters, girlfriends. I think I remember that name, but I can't be sure. If it was a name I remember, it would have been after we had already started the merger with McLaughlin, so Robert wasn't a part of it."

Bree bit her lower lip. *Who knows?* she thought. There was something there.

Sophia turned around, leaning against the counter. "I'm sorry, Bree. I'm a little out of sorts over this. The fact that what Graham and I have always believed is coming to form scares me. I can't really concentrate. I keep thinking that it doesn't make sense Robert would talk to Cammermeyer. He was all excited about the merger with McLaughlin. Why would he take calls from another company that wanted to merge?"

"Is that even legal?"

She shook her head. "It's a gray line in that business. Almost every conversation can be seen as illegal."

Bree was trying to think it through. "I wish I knew more about the industry. What I think is maybe they wanted to merge with Trotter, but obviously Barber said they were already having that discussion. So, after it all fell through, they called again. But by then Barber was gone, so they just worked with someone else."

"So why is Cammermeyer giving gifts to Barber?" Sophia asked. "He was there during this merger. As a matter of fact, he was staking his career on McLaughlin. I'm sure he would have done anything to discourage the Cammermeyer merger if he had still been at Trotter."

"There's an explanation for that somewhere. And in it is how to clear your name. I'm going to read those notes Terrence took. I'll figure it out."

Sophia smiled. "I bet you will. You seem like the kind of sister who always gets answers. One way or another. Can I ask some questions, now?"

Here it comes, Bree thought. With Graham as loyal as he

was to his sister, there was no doubt it was mutual. Most mothers, or sisters in place of mothers, didn't care for Bree. She was reckless, wild, and only out to break hearts. That's what they would say.

"I know what this is about," Bree said.

"I don't like to interfere with my brother's life," Sophia said. "With Graham, there's hardly any reason to. He doesn't screw up, he doesn't get caught up with a bad crowd. He almost always makes the right choices. In reality, it's been more like he's the older one, not me."

"I have a brother like that," Bree said. "Marcus. Just as close to perfect as perfect gets. Kind of gets on my nerves."

Sophia smiled. "I know what you mean. For example, when it comes to women, Graham has always gone after the same type. He's had very few relationships. They tend to last a long time."

Bree wasn't stupid. She could read between the lines. "Sophia, Graham and I haven't really—"

"I know," she said. "But something is going on between you. I've noticed it from the beginning, which wasn't long ago at all. And especially just now. There's an obvious electricity between you two."

"I don't know what to tell you, Sophia." Bree leaned back. "If you want to know what's going on between us, I can't tell you. I'm trying to figure it out myself. Everything has been so crazy and confusing."

"I'm sure it has." Sophia's voice was compassionate and understanding. "I'm still reeling from what happened to you two today. Now, I know that wasn't about you, but what you're bringing into his life is only adding more of the same. You have to understand that I'm concerned about my brother. Maybe this kind of lifestyle is fine for you, but this is not Graham."

"It's not me, Sophia. I swear. I know I live a kind of

crazy life, but this thing with Robin and Nabb is not what I'm used to either. And that whole scene with Alex Walsh. Well, that's just—''

"Who is Alex Walsh and what does he have to do with anything?"

Bree realized that Sophia knew nothing about this, and that was for the better. "Nothing. Never mind."

"Graham just ended a long-term relationship a few months ago."

"So did I." It occurred to Bree that she had not thought of her ex, Michael, once since meeting Graham. He wasn't that memorable in the end. "Well, it wasn't a long-term relationship."

"That's just it, Bree. All of Graham's relationships are long term. They're long term, very adult, and very calm and orderly. Like everything else in his life. That may seem boring to you, but it's how he likes it."

"I know what you're trying to say," Bree said. "I'm not his type. I never thought that I was. Not from the moment I saw him. He's not my type either. But there is something between us that seems to be very strong."

"You're a very attractive young woman."

"It's not just physical," Bree said. "I was thinking that at first, but it's more than that. We just haven't had a chance to deal with it."

"Because I think you both know what concerns you might be what keeps you from being together."

"That I'll never be good enough for him?" Bree asked, realizing as she said it that that was what she was afraid of.

Sophia shook her head. "No. Graham doesn't think like that. He doesn't look down on other people. He doesn't think he's better than anyone else."

"Not in that way," Bree said. "But Graham associates with the intellectual types. Women whose lives are in order, have accomplished careers, and are focused on something. Women without a lot of, to use his words, activity around them. Nothing like me.''

"For Graham, I think he's afraid that he'll fall for you, you'll have fun together, and when you get bored, you'll leave him behind. Can you promise that's not true?''

Bree wondered if Graham really thought that. She wouldn't know unless she asked him. They had to stop dancing around this. "How could I promise that if I don't even know what we are?''

"You're right. I don't mean to put pressure on you. I'm sure you're under enough right now already. I just want you to think about this stuff, because I know Graham is. He always thinks relationships through before going forward.''

"I never do.'' Bree shook her head. Was this even worth trying? Seemed like more work than she had ever put into a relationship and she hadn't even started this one yet. Not formally, at least.

"Go on and join your friend.'' Sophia got back up and returned to the counter. "I'll cook something up for us in about a half hour.''

Bree stood up, feeling somewhat like a child that had just gotten a good talking-to in detention, and was being sent back to class.

Graham saw the light from the television as soon as he entered the apartment. He was glad to be back home. Tonight, he had been a major participant on a panel for American and African economic trade. At Columbia, these televised panels were a privilege usually left for the more tenured professors. Experts on the topic from the best schools and think tanks in the country had been there. But did he care?

All he could think of was Bree and getting back to her. He thought he hid it well, and all the compliments he received after the discussion was over confirmed that. Still, his heart had not been there, even if his mind was. He entered the living room, tugging at his tie. When he'd seen the light, Graham had been hopeful that Bree was still up even though he told her not to be.

He sighed as he looked down at her. She was sound asleep on the sofa, wrapped in a blanket. She looked so young, so innocent. He leaned over the back of the sofa, holding his hand out. His index finger gently trailed her cheek, a feeling of warmth and home coming to him at the touch of her soft skin.

It was no surprise to Graham that he was attracted to her. She was beautiful, sexy, exciting, and vibrant. There was a physical chemistry between them that he had never had with another woman. What was surprising to him was that he believed there could be something real between them.

They were polar opposites in every way. She was a Hart, and he knew it wasn't wise to have anything to do with that family on a personal level. Most importantly, Bree thrived on excitement. Wouldn't she tire of him soon? And what about Baltimore? He needed to get her there to free himself and Sophia of their debt to Keith. But solving one problem brought on another. He didn't want Bree going anywhere. Especially if marrying someone else was the ultimate destination.

As he noticed the folder they had retrieved from Terrence's apartment lying open on her chest, Graham remembered he was losing focus. He was at the cusp of the truth about the who, how, and why of Trotter framing Sophia. This is where he had to focus his efforts.

Carefully he closed the folder and slipped it from under her hand. With a tender smile, he took a few more moments to look at her before retrieving it. Her nose squinted a bit and she twisted around a little, but never woke up. No one could tell from looking at her that she was such a little hellion.

He glanced at Robin, who was fast asleep on the love seat. The television was on, but it was low enough not to disturb him, so he left it alone. He headed for his bedroom, folder under his arm. He had some reading to do.

Chapter Seven

From his eight-year-old Chevy, Graham watched as Bree and Robin said their good-byes on the porch of what could best be described as a modern farmhouse. It was all to his relief to finally have this moment come, considering what they had been through to get there.

Morning drama had been taken to another level today. Initially, no one would get up besides Graham, who had a habit of getting up the same time every day whether or not he had work to go to. Then, like clockwork, all three women in the house got up at the same time. The morning ritual of women was one still foreign to Graham, especially en mass. There were times when he thought he'd be better off leaving, times when he thought he was going to get knocked to the ground. In general, he kept to himself as much as possible.

Graham, Bree, and Robin headed out of New York a little

before noon, but Robin wanted to eat lunch at her favorite Harlem restaurant for the last time. Bree was all for it, despite Graham's urging that it would slow them down, not to mention the danger. He lost that argument and they weren't back on the road until 1:30.

Graham successfully put his foot down to squelch a minor revolt caused by an exit for an outlet mall. However, he did not walk away unscarred. At the peak of his frustration, as he yelled a reminder that they were flat broke, his voice cracked. Both of the women laughed at him, only serving to make him angrier.

It didn't make it any easier that the address of Robin's cousin was misleading. She lived at the edges of Washington County, which was about a half hour to the far left of where he wanted to go. Her cousin's home was on the outskirts of town, and was what most New Yorkers would consider a farm. Robin made no secret of her disgust, vowing that she would have to return to civilization soon or she would shrivel up and die here. Graham just wanted her out of the car.

During it all, Graham had engaged in small talk with Bree. Although almost every conversation they had led to an argument, as they seemed to disagree on practically everything, he didn't mind. He liked the sound of her voice, the inflection of her vowels when she was making a point. The way she would try to bait him with an almost southern twang at the end of her questions.

Her glances confused him. He wasn't a ladies' man. He wasn't an expert in the art of male-female communication or the rules of flirting. Her looks had meaning, but of what he wasn't sure.

Now, as she headed back for the car, he wondered if he would find out. He remembered looking down at her sleeping on the sofa last night and the feelings that stirred within him. It was nothing like the feelings he had felt when they were on the kitchen floor in Terrence Stamps's apartment. They were feelings his experience told him only came with time. It was time to talk.

Bree slid into the seat, closing the door behind her. "She won't last twenty-four hours."

"Watch," he said. "You'll come back in five years and she'll be a housewife with a kid and a half, living on a farm of her own."

"Oh yeah, right!" Bree laughed at the idea. She turned to him, admiring his profile as she had all day. "Hey, Graham? Thanks."

He kept his eyes on the road. "For what?"

"You know," she said. "You didn't have to help her out, but you did. You made something that could've been very complicated very simple."

Bree never thought reliability was a quality that would attract her to a man. She figured she could only count on herself. She always went for the unpredictable ones. The ones that didn't always let you down, but screwed up enough to keep a sufficient amount of drama in the relationship. But Graham wasn't like that. He would be there for her whenever. He would always follow through on his promises. Why would he want her?

Graham pulled back onto the highway. "I have to admit that I had ulterior motives. Cheryl Ripley lives in Montgomery County."

"I remember reading that in the folder. That's near here."

"Not as near as I thought." With his right hand, Graham reached for the map he had used to get as far as they had. "Check that out. I'm gonna need your help. I've gone a lot farther than I expected."

Bree looked over the map. She didn't understand it and grew immediately impatient with it. "I can't read anything on this. You want to confront her?"

"Yes, I do. She's the key to this."

"Why do you think it's her and not anyone else from Terrence's info?"

"I think she's a good person," Graham said. "I think she knows something and she's not sharing, to protect her family and her company. But if she's pushed a little she'll give. Terrence must have thought the same thing. He collected more information on her than anyone else he studied. Even Barber. He even recorded her unusual work schedule."

"Why would that matter?"

"Cheryl Ripley works Monday, Tuesday, and Wednesday. She works half days on Thursday and works from home on Friday. She has a young daughter in some flexible-hours-type private high school up here."

Bree decided to give the map another try. *Stick with it for Graham,* she told herself. "I think I found it. Look, you have to take this next exit on the left. It looks like we're only a little more than a half hour away. Not bad."

"Thanks."

She put the map down, still looking at him. "I can't believe we're going to just confront her. Just show up on her porch. This is so . . . spontaneous of you. So risky."

A smile formed at the edges of his lips, but he kept a serious tone. "You don't have to go inside, Bree. As a matter of fact, I want you to wait in the car."

"Please. I live for this stuff. It's old hat for me. But you . . . This is flooring me. I didn't know you had it in you."

"I've done some pretty risky things in my life."

Bree leaned back against the passenger-side window, placing her feet on the dash. "Take some aspirin after the expiration date on the bottle?"

"Very funny." He winked at her. "Sophia didn't tell you? You two seem to be the best of friends now. I'm surprised she hasn't told you our life story."

"Give," she said, gesturing with her hands for more information.

"I got caught stealing once."

"You're kidding?"

He shrugged. "I was only six at the time, but those candy corns at the local grocery store were screaming my name."

"You're wasting my time, Professor."

"I used to jump the gate at the local high school in my neighborhood with a couple of buddies and play hoops on the court."

"Better, but I need much more than that."

Graham thought hard. He really hadn't been risky during his youth. Not that he had anything to be ashamed of. He had never gotten into trouble. Seemed kind of boring in reflection. "I mooned the Deltas during my junior year in college. Almost got charged with indecent exposure."

Bree bit her lower lip, pretending to consider this. "That has potential to impress. But not unique enough."

"Fine. Your turn. Or should I even risk asking?"

"There's nothing really to tell. I'm a kitten."

Graham laughed out loud.

"Okay," she admitted. "There were the occasional public disturbances, inciting of riots, running away, class disruptions, school expulsions. I still don't understand how one can get kicked out of Sunday school."

"You got kicked out of Sunday school? You've got to be kidding me."

"Look, honey. If that floors you, then I can't tell you anymore. You wouldn't be able to take it."

"If the last week is any indication, I think I'd rather be spared."

"This has been a little too crazy. Even for me. I know it's more than you could ever have expected."

"To say the least." Graham had to laugh at the way he

had thought this would go when he agreed to "find" Bree. "Your mother and Keith said you were a handful. I brushed it off. Big mistake. I guess taking you on is the biggest risk I've ever taken."

"Do you have any regrets?" The mention of her family took the humor out of the situation for Bree.

Graham looked at her for a long time before returning his attention to the road. So this was when they would talk. "Should I?"

"I am who I am, Graham. I'll never be anything else."

There was a short silence as Graham reflected on not what she said, but what she meant by it. "I know that. I have to say I'm the same way, Bree. I'll always be Graham Lane, the college professor."

Bree felt her stomach tighten, nerves setting in. "So I ask the question again. Regrets? And be honest."

"Honestly, yes." He turned to her briefly, unable to decipher the look on her face. He felt tense and uncertain, but knew it had to be said. "I had a plan in place, an objective of extreme importance in sight. I have serious issues that need my attention. I never expected this."

"What is this?" Bree asked.

"Whatever is happening between us," he answered. "Do either of us know exactly what that is? I don't. I just know I didn't expect my personal feelings to get involved in what I thought was a business transaction."

"I'm a person, Graham. Not a business transaction."

He nodded. "I know. I just . . . I've been careful all my life to have a minimum of surprises."

"I've been careful all my life to ensure a maximum of surprises."

"I think first, act later."

"I act first, think later. Or not at all."

"I make decisions based on sound reasoning and rationalization. With my mind."

"I make decisions based on my heart, my whim. The way I'm feeling at the time."

"I need to know what's going to happen."

"I just need to know something's going to happen. I don't care what it is."

"I believe the greatest gift you can offer someone is structure and stability."

"I believe the greatest gift you can offer someone is a wild ride and killer memories."

Here it goes, Graham thought as he took a deep breath. "I want to find someone who is completely devoted to me. Who loves me as much as I love her, and will stick by me through thick and thin."

"So do I," Bree said, feeling almost breathless at his words. "I want that more than anything."

He looked at her, noting the intensity in her eyes, the seriousness on her face. "Did I mention forever? I want that forever. Not just for a few months or until something more exciting comes along."

Bree turned, looking out the window. "You don't think I could do forever, do you?"

"I think you could do whatever you wanted to, Bree."

"Then you don't think I want to."

"Bree . . . I think you're the most beautiful, exciting, and interesting woman I have ever met. I don't think I've ever felt such a sexual attraction to anyone. I have never been pulled so emotionally to a woman. That's what I think."

"But," Bree said, her heart aching at the turn this conversation was taking. "But I'm also a spoiled little rich brat who doesn't know the meaning of reasonable, moderation, and order. I'm not reliable. I don't have feelings."

"Bree, stop that. I never—"

"No, better yet. I do have feelings and those are the only feelings I care about. No one else's matter."

"Stop it!" Graham could tell she was repeating words she had heard before, probably from her own mother, and probably more than a few times. So much for the perfect childhood of the rich. "That's not what I'm saying. Don't put words in my mouth."

"I wouldn't have to if you would say what you meant." Bree wasn't really sure where these defensive walls were coming from. It was just that this scene was familiar to her. "Stop trying to be so nice about it."

"About what, Bree? Look, I'm not judging you."

"You've been judging me from the moment you met me," she answered. "Scratch that. Since before you met me. You soaked in everything Mother and Keith said and I could tell it from the first look you gave me after you knew who I was."

"I'll admit, I had an idea of who you were, but you can't blame me for thinking that way."

"I never blamed you for thinking anything, Graham. I just would appreciate it if you would be honest about it."

"I can't be honest if you're going to jump all over me the second I am." This wasn't going as Graham had planned. He was usually so good at steering conversations, keeping a handle on them.

"It's just that I've heard it all before." Bree couldn't bear to reflect on the memories of past disappointments. "I just can't . . ."

"Can't what?"

"Nothing." Bree reached for the radio, turning up the volume. She turned toward the window, tugging at her seat belt. "Just forget it."

What she couldn't tell him was that she had heard it all

before and had lived through it. But something deep inside her told her this time would be different. This time, when Graham realized one day that she needed some fine tuning to fit into his world, she wouldn't live through it.

"Forget it?" Graham felt a dull pain hit him inside as she physically rejected him. "Is that what you want, Bree? To forget it? Everything that has been happening between us?"

She didn't respond. This was what she had been afraid of. Getting attached to a guy. She could cause enough trouble for herself on her own.

"Fine," he said, even though a voice in the back of his head told him not to let this go. "If you want to leave it all behind, we'll do that. All I want to focus on is the truth behind what happened to my sister. I just want it stated for the record that I was *not* judging you."

They drove in silence the rest of the way, both disappointed in the outcome of a talk that they both thought would make things clearer. In fact, they were more confused.

Graham studied Bree as she looked around Cheryl Ripley's mansion. They were allowed in by a maid and directed to wait in a sitting room. The room was opulent, an intentional, yet not insulting message to all visitors of the resident's social status. They were waiting in silence for Cheryl Ripley to arrive. Graham noticed Bree was looking with familiarity at the furniture, the art, the lifestyle.

"Do you miss it?" he asked.

Bree turned to him. Could he read her mind? "I don't know if I'd say I miss it. But our house is beautiful. It's very large and very well decorated. Mother spent years making it into a dream house. Whenever I wanted to change my room, she would hire decorators to be at my beck and call. I can't even imagine how much my whims cost the family. I had to have changed my style at least six times in high school and college."

"Am I actually on the verge of hearing some positive memories of the Hart household?"

Bree smiled. "I never said there weren't any. I have a lot of good memories, although not recent ones. You should meet my Aunt May. She's the best. I really miss her."

Graham couldn't stop the feelings that swelled within him when she let her guard down. It was a vulnerable, soft side that contrasted with her tough armor. "I'm sure she misses you too."

"Is this all part of you still trying to get to me to go home?" Bree tried hard not to think of her aunt, which always made her consider going home.

"No. I'm just certain she misses you." He leaned toward her on the sofa. "I know I would."

There it was again, fast becoming a familiar emotion for Bree. She felt her temperature rise at his closeness, her body awaken as she looked into his eyes. He *would*.

"Am I interrupting something?"

They both turned to see Cheryl Ripley, standing a few feet away from them. She was an attractive woman in her late thirties. She had Nordic features with almost white blond hair to her shoulders and dark blue eyes. She was wearing a rose-red moleskin tank dress that flattered her very thin figure.

"Sorry." Graham slid away from Bree, figuring from the effect she had on him in that short moment, he needed to increase the distance between them. "Thank you for agreeing to see us, Mrs. Ripley. You probably didn't recognize our names but—"

"I know who you are," she said, slowly taking a seat in the oversize chair across from them. "You're Sophia Lane's brother and you're Keith Hart's sister."

"We've never met," Bree said, finding her knowledge immediately suspicious. She went on her gut when meeting people, and something told her this woman was about to lie her teeth off.

"Based on CMA's relationship with Robert Barber, which started a few months before we hired him, we had been following the trial. Keith Hart is the new man about town. You're too young to be his daughter, and he's not married. That's how I know you. What I don't know is why you are here."

Graham wasn't interested in the niceties of introduction. "I want to get to the point. What do you know about Trotter Securities framing my sister?"

Bree noticed that the woman didn't blink.

"I don't know anything about that. And I find it offensive that you would suggest such a thing."

"We've done our research," Graham said.

"I'm aware of that," she responded. "Someone called our offices requesting information on us."

"And that someone is in the hospital now." Graham's tone was very obviously accusatory.

She blinked once, twice, before a nonchalant sigh. "First of all, there is no reason for me to believe that. Secondly, even if that were true, which I certainly would not take on your word, I can say without hesitation that CMA had nothing to do with it."

"But you do have something to do with Robert Barber,"

he said, with no need to go further about Terrence. He had planted that seed and that was enough. For now. "And that goes back to Trotter and this case."

"You're wasting your time trying to tie CMA to Trotter. We found Robert Barber through a search firm. The old-fashioned way. Whatever happened at Trotter, and I am not even aware that anything illegal happened there, has nothing to do with CMA or me."

"What about the boat?" Bree asked.

She blinked again. Bree watched with satisfaction as she gave herself away. She must have thought this was nothing she couldn't handle, because she was certain she knew everything. But she didn't. She didn't know about Terrence in the hospital, and she didn't know about the boat. She wasn't certain if she should say that or if she should pretend as if she did. Bree figured she was pretty much wishing she had never let the two of them in.

"I allowed you in my home out of kindness and consideration. I'm certain your trip was long and you seem to be nice people. I don't—"

"Robert Barber just bought insurance for a boat that was given to him as a gift. The boat was sold to him by Nautical Luxuries. That . . ."

She let out a laugh attempting to seem amused, but no one was buying it. Not even she. "Your imagination is very . . . Mr. Lane, no one wants to believe their loved ones have done something wrong."

"Including you," Bree added. "Your uncle is Cameron Moore. The stepson of Charles Farnsworth. Who happens to own Nautical Luxuries."

"What do you care?" She turned to Graham. "Your sister was acquitted. She's eligible for a healthy severance package now. She can move on with—"

"How do you know that?" Graham asked. "How do you know about the severance agreement?"

Cheryl blinked rapidly, sharing her attention between Bree and Graham. "I'm just assuming that . . . The policy with most companies is to—"

"Don't BS me, Mrs. Ripley." Graham leaned forward on the sofa. "My sister's severance package was held at Trotter contingent on the outcome of her trial. If she was convicted, she would get nothing under the grounds that she was terminated due to illegal activity. If acquitted, she would get a full package because Trotter didn't want to have to combat her claim in court if she chose to do so. They just wanted to be rid of her. But that deal was not at all common knowledge."

"Okay." Cheryl's hands were entwined tightly. "I asked. I was concerned about her. She seemed overwhelmed during the trial. So I asked Robert what would happen to her financially, because I knew she would have a hard time getting another job after she was acquitted. My concern for your sister does not make me a conspirator in a conspiracy that doesn't even exist."

"I'm going to give you a last chance, Cheryl." Graham wasn't buying anything she was saying. "A last chance to be honest with me."

"Are you threatening me?" She looked alarmed.

"No," Bree interjected. "Not at all. We just want you to help us get to the truth. No matter how painful that might be. Sophia deserves this."

"My sister's reputation has been destroyed," Graham said. "She's been depressed almost to the point of a medical condition since this got started. It's drastically altered her life, my life forever. Financially, we are up to our necks in debt and—"

"Is it about money?" Cheryl asked, a hint of desperation in her voice. "Because if it's money, I—"

"Don't you dare," he said, not even wanting to hear what she was about to propose. "The only thing I want from you is the truth."

"You know something, Mrs. Ripley," Bree said. "Why else would you offer to give him money? That's what you were about to do, wasn't it?"

"I give money to people in need," she answered. "It doesn't mean that I agree with what either of you are saying. Even if there was some truth to it, I don't know—"

"You know something," Graham said. "I know you do. And that was your last chance to offer your help. I will bring down everyone involved in this deal, including you. You can count on it."

"I want you to leave now." Cheryl stood up from her chair. "I'll have Linda show you out. I tried to be hospitable to you, but I can see that you only came here to threaten and frighten me. You should be happy I don't call the police on you."

"So you can start another frame-up? This one on me?" Graham stood up.

"Get out." She turned toward the hallway. "Linda!"

"Wait a second." Bree stood up. "Mrs. Ripley, wait."

"I've had enough of this." She turned to Bree. "I'm sorry for your situation, but I can't help you."

"Yes, you can," Bree said, placing a hand on Graham's shoulder to calm him. She could tell he wanted to go off. That would only make a tense situation worse. "You said that you asked Robert about Sophia's financial situation during the trial."

"I said I was concerned."

"You said you were concerned because you knew she would have a hard time getting another job after she was acquitted.'' Bree stepped in front of Graham, closer to Cheryl. She tendered her tone. ''How could you know she was going to be acquitted? Barber always said she was guilty.''

Cheryl had no response. She just stared at Bree.

''How did you know?'' she asked again.

''I . . . I was just considering an alternative. It's a simple question.''

''You said when . . . not if.'' Bree knew she had trapped her. She closed in for the kill. ''You knew she was innocent.''

''I want you both to leave.'' But Cheryl didn't move. She continued to stare at Bree.

''Neither of us think you planned this,'' Bree said. ''We know you just became a part of it by default. But you are a part of it, and it's up to you to fix it. You know right and wrong. I know you do. Don't wait until it's too late for you. You have a daughter.''

Graham could tell she was about to give in. Thank God for Bree. He had come so close to losing his temper, as unusual as that was for him. He would never have gotten this far. He would never have expected Bree to be the one cooling hot heads.

''She is free and clear.'' Cheryl whispered as Linda entered. She turned to her. ''Thank you, Linda. I'll show them out myself. You can leave now.''

After she was gone, Cheryl moved closer to Bree and Graham, still speaking in almost a whisper. ''Nothing will ever happen to Sophia. You should let this go.''

''Let what go?'' Bree asked, studying Cheryl's face. She suddenly realized an amazing conclusion. She'd had it all wrong. ''You didn't know she was innocent. You knew she would be acquitted whether she was innocent or not.''

Cheryl looked at Graham, shame written all over her face. She took a deep breath. "Look at the testimony. Look at the witnesses called by the prosecution. Look at that ridiculous evidence. There was no way she would ever have been convicted. I'm sorry she was put under so much stress, but—"

"It was fixed?" Graham asked. "The trial was set up to acquit her. That was part of it. Why?"

Bree put a hand up to Graham. "Let her speak. Mrs. Ripley, go on. Tell us how it happened?"

"I can't do that." She ran her fingers through her hair. "You don't understand how business and the law are so tied together. Sometimes to do something right, you have to do something wrong. When that right is a right that can change the lives of thousands for the better, you have to do it."

"What are you talking about?" Graham asked.

"And then there's the money," she continued as if she hadn't heard Graham. "That has never meant anything to me, but to others it's everything in the world. You have to deal with people like that to get things done. There's just so much of it, and there was no way Sophia was going to be convicted. Not even a misdemeanor. Not even a fine. If you let me pay her legal bills, you have to let this go."

"What are you talking about?" Graham asked again, trying to concentrate. She wasn't making any sense. "What does this have to do with law and business?"

"Are you familiar with the Century Forward bill?" she asked, waiting for a response. "No, of course you aren't. It hasn't even been introduced yet. I can't do this. For the same reasons you think I should. I believe in the end that what is right is what is being done. I won't say more than that."

"Don't you walk away from me." Graham started after her as she turned and walked away, but Bree grabbed at his arm. "Let me go, Bree."

"No." She pulled at him. "Stop it. You'll only get yourself in trouble and make this harder. You know that."

"I know what I'm doing," he said, even though he didn't. He was just so angry. He couldn't ever remember being so angry.

"Now you know you're doing something wrong if I have to be the voice of reason, Graham." She noticed him calming a bit at her attempt at humor. "Let's just go. We won't get anything more out of her. I think we may have gotten everything we need anyway."

"I only have more questions."

"That's a good thing." She led him out the front door of the house. "We were stumped before, but not anymore. She's given us a lot. We have to jump on it now. Let's get back to Manhattan."

In the car, they went over everything that Cheryl had told them. There was so much information that repeating it all only served to frustrate them more. Between Bree jumping to conclusions and Graham trying to make sense of it, not much progress was being made.

"Let's focus on one thing at a time," Graham said. "The trial. She was trying to say it was fixed."

"This is incredible," Bree said. "So the SEC was in on this too."

"Maybe not the SEC. But they were basing their prosecution of Sophia on what Trotter was providing them."

"Why would Trotter want Sophia acquitted?" Bree wasn't getting it. "They were trying to prove that she was a partner in this. She and Robert Barber single-handedly ruined their chances of merging with McLaughlin Silverman, which would have made them all rich. They had to hate her.''

Graham had to get more information. ''Do you have a cell phone?''

''Had to sell it. Robin and I needed the money.''

''I have to get to a phone. I need Terrence to find . . .'' He suddenly remembered where Terrence was. He couldn't help him. ''I've got to do this myself.''

''*We've* got to do this, remember?'' Bree asked. ''I know Sophia isn't my sister, but I feel almost as close to this as you do now. We're on the verge of blowing this out of the water. With Terrence in the hospital, you need my help.''

He glanced at her for a moment and somehow found a smile for her. ''We have to get the names of all the witnesses. What was behind their testimony?''

''I was watching the television coverage and they said that it was the weak testimony of the witnesses that made it impossible to convict.''

''Looking back on it, they were awful. But I was just so caught up in the situation that I didn't think it could be staged. I knew she was innocent, so I didn't expect the testimony to be strong in the first place.''

''What about Barber? Was his testimony harmful or helpful to Sophia?''

Graham shook his head. ''He was the most puzzling. The words out of his mouth were damaging, but he had no credibility with the jury. Keith pointed that out very well. He made Robert look like a fool. I thought it was good lawyering.''

''Keith is a good lawyer,'' Bree said. ''But Barber made it easier on him. Maybe Cheryl Ripley and the folks at CMA asked him to. But why? What's at stake for them? Just for Robert?''

"Don't forget CMA's ties to Cammermeyer and Storm. Brings it full circle to Trotter. I have to—"

Bree grabbed at the edge of her seat as she heard the first popping sound. Then the car seemed to jerk and another sound came out. "What was that?"

"Damn!" Graham didn't want to believe it, but the smoke that started coming from under the hood told him it was true. "This car."

Bree looked around. Nothing but trees. They weren't even to the highway yet. "We can't stop. Cheryl Ripley's house has got to be the only one near here. She's not going to let us back in."

"We'll keep going." He turned off the air-conditioning, the radio. He wasn't a wiz with cars. He barely drove this one, but he knew it was old. "The less we ask of this car the better. It's been driven more today than it has in the past two years."

"It's not going to last long."

"It only has to last until the nearest phone." Graham didn't need this right now. He had to get to a phone and get some answers. Cheryl Ripley had thrown a few new wrenches in this mess and he had to jump on them.

"We're closed."

Bree and Graham stared at the man as he repeated himself for the third time. He just sat there, on his old wooden stool. He was leaning against the front of the door to the gas station. His gas station. It was called Jim's Gas and the label on his jumpsuit said JIM. Jim looked more like a good ole southern boy than a resident of New York. He was a prime example of how many different cultures existed within an hour from the most powerful and modern city in the country.

Graham took a deep breath before speaking again. "I am

aware that you are closed, sir. However, as you can see from my car right here, I have no way of getting home.''

The man looked from Graham to the smoky car that had just made it to the gas station, then back to Graham. He made a smacking sound with his tongue. "What in the heck are you doing all the way out here anyway? Aren't those city plates?"

"What does that have to do with anything?" Bree asked, losing patience. "It's late, it's getting dark, and we have no ride. We need our car fixed."

"We're closed," he said again. "Doug and Alex have gone home. They work on cars. I just pump gas and run the shop. They'll be back tomorrow morning at eight."

"Fine," Graham said, eyeing the pay phone inside the store. "Can I get into the store? I need to use your phone."

"Don't work." Jim shook his head, folding his arms across his chest. He looked at Bree, exaggerated his glance at her, adding a smile with a wink.

"Yeah, right," she said, rolling her eyes.

"The phone doesn't work?" Graham asked. "How are we supposed to call for someone to come pick us up?"

Jim pressed his lips together, looking around the deserted gas station. "I can pump you some gas if you want it. That's all I can do for you."

"Why don't you just look at it?" Bree asked. "It might be something simple that any gas station guy could fix."

"We're closed. We don't do work after six."

Graham looked at his watch. "It's only five-thirty."

"Except Thursdays. Thursdays we close at five. On account of dollar everything night at Carrey's. As a matter of fact, you're making me late."

Bree pointed to the old truck next to the garage. "That car work?"

Jim beamed. "For ten years and one hundred fifteen thousand miles. That's my Gail. But you can't have her. I need her to get home.''

"Then give us a ride," she said.

"You city folk never heard of asking nicely?"

Graham leaned toward the man. "Please."

"Where?" he asked, seeming a little unnerved by Graham's sudden assertiveness. "I'm not driving into the city. I don't want nothing to do with that Sodom and Gomorrah."

"Where is the nearest phone?" Graham asked.

"Hmmm." Jim looked as if he were in pain, as if thinking brought on a migraine.

"I would say University Lodge. It's about ten miles that way."

"Fine. Can you drive us there?" Graham noticed hesitation. "We're not serial killers. We're perfectly civilized people who need to get to a phone."

He looked Graham up and down and shrugged. "What about your car? You just leaving it here?"

"Well, yeah. You said Doug or Alex can work on it tomorrow, right?"

"Depends on what's wrong with it," Jim said. "Now, if it's the transmission, the carburetor, or the ignition, Alex is your man. If it's—"

"That doesn't matter," Bree said. "Can we get going?"

"On one condition."

"If you want money, I can give you twenty bucks." Graham reached into his back pocket.

"No, I don't need your money," Jim said. He looked at Bree, again with a smile and a wink. "I want her to sit in the front."

"I'm going to throw up." Bree turned and headed for the truck.

* * *

Bree sat on the bed in the only available hotel room at University Lodge. She watched as Graham paced the room. It hadn't been going well at all. They had arrived at the lodge, which was ten miles north, taking them even farther away from the city.

Graham immediately called home, but Sophia never answered. He tried her three times before Bree realized that she must be on her way to *The Lion King* show. Frustrated, he tried to call a few other people, but couldn't remember their numbers, they weren't home, or refused to come out this far for someone who hadn't even bothered to say hello to them in the last six months.

His frustration only grew as the local cab company refused to drive him to the nearest train station, since tonight's being dollar night at Carrey's, they had plenty of business driving drunken locals to and fro.

Bree suggested they get some rooms. She was hungry. They could eat and would have time to think about what to do next, get some sleep after a hectic day, find out about the car in the morning, and get back into the city tomorrow. Realizing nothing else could be done tonight, Graham agreed.

Then came the next problem. There was only one room.

"On account of this being dollar night at Carrey's," the young desk clerk told them.

Turns out, Carrey's was a restaurant and bar connected to the hotel. On dollar everything night, beer, mixed drinks, and shots were a buck. It was the event of the week for the locals. Instead of braving the dark, woody roads after getting wasted out of their minds, many of them got rooms at University Lodge. The designated driver was not a popular role with this crowd, so they did the next best thing.

So, there they were. In the one and only room left at the lodge. It was the only one left because the television did not work and the flashing UNIVERSITY LODGE sign was right outside the window, beaming neon green and blue into the room all night long.

"Don't!" Bree yelled out as Graham reached for the phone.

He pulled his hand back, looking at her. She was sending him a threatening stare as she popped a cocktail shrimp into her mouth. "Bree, you don't even know who I was about to call."

"It doesn't matter, Graham. No one can help you right now. And what's with your friends? Why are they all mad at you?"

He sat in the chair at the work desk in the corner of the room, looking at the burger and fries he had ordered. He didn't want them. "I haven't been the best friend in the last six months. I've pretty much blown off everyone I know for the sake of Sophia's case."

"No wonder they don't want to come out here and get you. It's a lot to ask. I feel like I'm in another part of the country."

"We are pretty far out." He picked up a french fry and put it back down.

"Why did you order that if you didn't want it?"

"You were nagging me to order something."

"You need to eat something. You're getting crazy." She waved him over. "Why don't you try my jumbo shrimp? It's good."

He joined her on the bed and reached for a shrimp. It was good. "I'm still not hungry. My stomach is crazy thinking about this."

"We know what we have to do. We have to get into Keith's office and get a list of the witnesses. We'll do the same research on them as Terrence did on Barber. Any recent purchases to show they suddenly have some money."

"I want to talk to them."

"We will, but that's second. We need some ammunition to get them to talk. Look how it helped us with Cheryl Ripley."

"Next, we have to find out what she was talking about when she mentioned all that right and wrong stuff. It has something to do with CMA and its philosophy of philanthropy."

"Something about how they want to do good for others with their company," Bree said. "But then she talks about all that money. What does that mean?"

"Third," Graham continued, "we have to figure out what this Century Forward bill is."

"We'll get on the Internet and find that out. If it's in Congress, my brother Marcus can tell me about it."

"I can't wait to tell Sophia about all of this. She'll be so happy to hear we're making progress."

Bree could feel her heart tug as she saw the affection in his eyes for his sister. "You love her so much."

He turned to Bree, realizing for the first time how close he was to her. He had let all the new news block his feelings for her and make him forget how horribly their last talk had gone. Now, here she was only a foot away from him on the bed, looking at him with those breathtaking eyes.

"Yes," he answered softly. "Sophia is my whole family. She's all I have left in this world. She's been there for me through thick and thin when we were growing up. I wanted so badly to make this go away. For a while there, I didn't think I could. I just couldn't make any progress."

"But you never gave up." Bree couldn't help the way she felt about this man. He was different from any other man she had known. He was 100 percent genuine. "Even when it cost you."

"Money doesn't mean anything to me," Graham said.

"That's not what I meant." Bree placed her meal on the nightstand, leaving nothing between them. "I'm talking about the friends that won't come and get you tonight. I'm talking about Jodie."

"Sophia told you about her?" Graham wasn't sure how he felt about that.

Bree nodded. "Did you love her?"

"I did." He nodded. "I . . . guess just not enough. I mean, if I really, really loved her, I would have done whatever I had to do to keep her or get her back. But I let her go."

"Sorry." Bree said, placing a hand on his thigh. She felt that jolt, and thought better of it, pulling her hand back.

Her hand on his thigh for that brief moment snapped Graham out of the past. He looked at Bree, feeling a connection to her that he could never deny again. Jodie was the past. Bree was the present. But would she be the future?

"Bree." He slid toward her. "When you thought I was judging you earlier, I wasn't. I would never judge you. What I meant was that you've disrupted my life. Whether it had been as a boring little mouse or the exciting psychotic that you are, you messed up my plans. All I cared about was saving Sophia, and getting you home was a means to that end. I had no intention of falling for you."

"Falling for me?" Bree almost didn't recognize herself, feeling so affected by his words.

"Yes." Graham nodded. "Somehow in all of this, I've fallen for you and I don't know if that's a good or bad thing."

"Why does it have to be good or bad?" she asked, her own emotions bubbling over. "Why can't it just be?"

"I don't think that way," Graham said. "I'm not used to it at least. But I'll do it for you. I'll throw caution and all common sense to the wind because I want you, Bree. I want you more than I've ever wanted any woman in my life."

Carried away by his own emotions, Graham reached for Bree. When his lips came to hers, he let out an almost tortured moan. His body's reaction was immediate. His mind was gone.

Bree's stomach swirled sensations as she kissed him eagerly. She wrapped her arms around him, pulling him closer. Electricity surged through her entire body. As his lips pressed harder, she met him with every turn. She had never felt this way before.

He couldn't be close enough to her now. Graham's hands went to her waist, his fingers digging into her flesh over the clothes.

As if reading his mind, Bree tugged at his shirt. She wanted him so badly.

"Bree," he whispered as their lips separated for only a moment. "I want you more than I've ever wanted anyone."

She lifted his top off and pushed him backward on the bed.

"Graham," she said, biting her lower lip in naughty anticipation as she looked down at him. "I want you too, Graham. God, I do."

Graham's breathing picked up as a floodtide of ecstasy came over him. His hands caressed her head as she laid enticing kisses all over his chest. He heard himself making sounds of delight, his body arching as if lighting up like a firecracker.

Bree desperately needed the taste of his lips again, and

she returned her face to his, the sheer passion in his eyes further igniting the flame growing inside her.

"My turn," Graham said. Gently he flipped her over and straddled himself on top of her. He lifted her shirt, exposing her small, perfect breasts. As he tossed the shirt to the side, his mouth returned to her, kissing her deeply before traveling downward.

A burning sensation pierced through to Bree's soul at every spot he kissed her. Her neck, her chest, her left breast, then her right.

"Oh, Graham." Her body arched in reaction to his mouth taking possession of her left breast. She dug her fingers into the top of his back. His other hand caressed her other breast softly. Bree felt intoxicated, but at the same time more sexually aware than ever before in her life.

Her blood was boiling as waves of passion crashed within her. His lips were at her belly button, his hands tugging at her shorts. Her body made it easy for him to slide the pants down. She didn't wait for him to get to her panties, taking those off herself.

"Slow down," he said, his voice cracking a bit. He was so full of desire, he felt as if the room were in a haze.

Graham looked down at her perfect little figure. Tiny, but curvy. He reached for his pants. Suddenly, his eyes widened and he looked at Bree.

Bree smiled at him, thinking the same thing. "Try the bathroom. I think I saw them next to the tampons and first aid kit."

Graham was reluctant to leave her for even one second, but he knew he needed protection.

"Hurry back, Graham," Bree said as he got up.

When he returned to the bed, he could see her nakedness in all its perfection. Her body glistened, her skin radiating youthful beauty. She held her hands out to welcome him back to her. Graham didn't hesitate.

Both of them naked now, Bree could feel his hardness against her thigh. She opened her legs to let him position himself comfortably on top of her. It didn't hurt. It felt good. It felt right. Her whole body flooded with desire as his lips returned to hers.

He said her name again and again between kisses. The magnitude of his desire had not tempered at all. He felt close to hysteria, but would not move before she was . . .

"Now, Graham." Bree's tone was affectionate, but direct. "I can't wait any longer. The strength of his male body, the clean smell of him, and the softness of his skin surrendered her patience.

A hot tide of passion possessed her as he entered her. She let out a groan, her lips quivering at the sweet pain of him inside her.

"Oh, Bree." Graham's desire mounted to insanity as he moved inside her. She was so warm, so welcoming. He buried his face in her neck, kissing her in uncontrollable joy.

A volcano scorched through their bodies as they were bound together by a soul-melting tempo. Together, they moved as one, both losing their minds in this exquisite harmony of man and woman. Their passion soared higher and higher, Graham's thrusting deeper and more forceful.

They made no silence of it, the ecstasy spiraling through them preventing any sense of control. Bree moaned as Graham groaned. She called out his name as he called hers. There bodies were sweating from their vigor and urgency.

The power of erotic pleasures built to such a crescendo within Bree that her body began to vibrate. The core of her soul heard music as she burst free from reality. She felt a tremor run through her like nothing before.

Graham had waited to hear her yell. The sound was all he needed to reach his point of ecstasy. He felt his body shudder, and heard himself call out her name one last time before heaven came.

Chapter Eight

Bree stretched as she rolled over in the bed. The smile on her face was cheek to cheek. She was so pleasantly rested after a long, passionate night of lovemaking. Again and again. She had experienced quite a few amazing moments in her life, but she was certain that last night was a life-altering one. She had really fallen in love for the first and last time last night.

She expected to roll into Graham, but didn't. Sensing his absence, she slowly opened her eyes. Where was he? She lifted herself up, bringing the sheets with her. The room was empty.

"Graham," she called out.

"Right here." He strolled out of the bathroom, buttoning his shirt. He winked at her. She looked beautiful with her hair a mess and her eyes half open. "I thought you'd never get up."

Bree took in a good look of him. She smiled as he tucked his shirt in. He was so deceptive, with that all-American nice-guy look. "What time is it?"

"It's nine in the morning," he answered, sitting on the edge of the bed next to her. He leaned forward and kissed her.

Bree felt her toes tingle at the touch of his lips on hers. She felt warmth flow though her. A warmth she knew she would feel every time he kissed her for the rest of her life. "Now, what did you get dressed for? You know I'm just going to make you take those annoying clothes off."

He growled and kissed her again. The sweetness of her lips was like a drug to him. "Don't think I wanted to get dressed. But remember, as perfect as last night was, we have work to do."

Perfect. Yes, Bree thought to herself. Last night had been perfect. "I know. How long have you been up?"

"About a half hour." He went to the desk, looking at the phone. Where was Sophia? "I didn't want to wake you. I called Jim."

"My boyfriend from the gas station." Bree reached over the side of the bed and grabbed her T-shirt, pulling it on. She loved the feeling of contentment she had right now. It was a rarity in her life. Graham had reintroduced her to it.

Graham laughed. "Yeah, him. The car isn't going to be ready for a few days. They have to order a part. So, he was nice enough to get in touch with his cousin Cal who works at the train station. He's going to drive by and give us a ride. He would have been here earlier, but he couldn't."

"Don't tell me," Bree said. "On account of dollar everything night at Carrey's?"

"You got it, missy."

"How good the hearts are of these small-town folk." Bree studied Graham, noticing his uneasiness. "What's wrong?"

"I've been trying Sophia since I got up, but she isn't answering the phone. I'm starting to get worried."

"She's probably sleeping in." Bree propped the pillows up behind her and leaned back. "She had a big night last night."

"The show was over early."

"I told her she'd be sitting next to Lily. Lily's a great girl. They probably made friends and went out. Besides, we have a ride to the train station. We'll get into town."

"I know, but I'm still worried." Graham reached for the phone and dialed the number again.

Bree reached for the laminated menu on the bed stand. She wondered if they could get some breakfast before ten. She glanced at the bathroom. Maybe she should get ready. She tossed the menu aside, wanting only to make love to Graham again.

"Hello?"

"Soph?" Graham didn't recognize this voice. "Is that you?"

"This is Alice Gibson," the voice said. "Who is this?"

"Alice, it's Graham." Alice was one of Sophia's old friends. What was she doing there? Sophia hadn't spoken to her in a long time. Maybe his sister was reaching out again. "You visiting Sophia?"

"Graham?" Alarm laced her voice as she spoke in almost a gasp. "Thank God I found you. Where are you?"

"What's wrong?" Graham's antennae went up. He looked at Bree, who was quickly at the edge of the bed. "Where is Sophia?"

"Okay." Alice took a very audible deep breath. "Sophia is fine. Understand that first."

Graham gripped the phone so tightly, his hand hurt.

"She was attacked last night, Graham. She wasn't raped. Don't think that. Some guy was waiting outside for her at the show last night. She saw him outside when she went in and saw him when she came out. She didn't think anything about it, but he followed her to the train and roughed her up a bit.''

"Oh my God! Where is she?'' Graham felt sick to his stomach and filled with rage. Nabb!

"She's at General right now. She called me last night. I came over to get some of her stuff. She wanted me to find you. How soon can you . . .''

"What is it?'' Bree felt a shiver down her spine at the look on Graham's face as he turned to her.

Graham was so filled with anger, he could barely speak. "Sophia was attacked last night.''

"Oh my God!'' Bree jumped up from the bed. "Attacked? Is she okay? What happened?''

Graham's fists were clenched so tight, his nails were digging into the skin of his palms. "Nabb was at the show last night. I knew he would expect to find you there. He listened to your message and went looking for you.''

Bree was shaking her head, trying to understand. "That's not . . . No. He doesn't know her.''

"He knew something. He knows your friend Lily, doesn't he?''

Bree thought back. "He doesn't know her either. He's seen her before. He's seen her at the club with Robin and me before, but he didn't remember her. He couldn't—''

"Yes, he could!'' Graham grabbed his keys. "He didn't see you, but he saw Lily and remembered you. He probably tried to get Lily too. He's just trying to get anyone attached to you and Robin.''

"Graham!'' Bree didn't want to believe it, but it was believable. Nabb didn't care who he hurt. If he thought for a second he could get his message through, he'd go after anyone. He'd chosen her because of Robin. Now he had chosen Sophia because of her.

"I knew this would happen!" Graham stood at the door. "You've been nothing but trouble since the first day I met you, Bree. I already had enough problems, but you've made everything worse. Worse than I could ever have imagined. You and Robin and your ridiculous lifestyle could have cost my sister her life!"

"Wait, Graham." Bree reached for him, but he backed away. The look on his face was so painful. He hated her. "I'm sorry. It's not my fault."

"Nothing is ever your fault, Bree Hart." Graham wasn't thinking. He was only feeling. Fear, rage, helplessness, regret. Anger. "I'll take the blame for one thing. I let my guard down with you. When you told me about Sophia taking that ticket for you, I didn't like it, but I let you convince me. I'll never make that mistake again. You can stay in New York. You can go back to Baltimore. You can go to hell for all I care! Just stay away from me and my family."

"Graham!" Bree felt as if a bullet pierced her gut as he slammed the door behind him.

She was frozen in place. She couldn't move. What had just happened? Sophia was hurt. She had to be okay. Where was Graham going? He hated her! That hurt so much, she couldn't stop the tears that suddenly came. She felt selfish, knowing Sophia should be all that was on her mind right now. But she wasn't. Her heart had just made her aware she was in love with a man at the same time it was broken in two by him.

And it was all her fault. She had been warned by so many people. Her impetuous behavior, careless lifestyle, nonchalant approach to everything were going to get her hurt one day. Or worse, they were going to get someone else hurt. Someone least deserving. And that was Sophia.

Bree paced the hotel room. "Okay, think, Bree! You can't fall apart right now. You can fix this. You can make everything okay. You have to keep your head together."

No use. The tears were flowing now. She could only see that look on Graham's face before he turned and left the room. She could only hear him say, "Sophia has been attacked."

She wiped her tears. What did she have to do now? She had to get back to New York. She had to make sure Sophia was going to be okay.

"I don't even know where she is." Bree went to the phone. Whom could she call?

She hoped Cal was still coming at ten. She wondered if Graham would wait for them or if he would leave without them. She doubted he would wait for another second. He was probably running to the train station on foot right now.

To keep herself from going crazy, Bree had to find out about Sophia. She couldn't do anything until that.

Bree picked up the phone and pressed the redial button.

Bree approached the receptionist desk at the New York law offices of Keith Hart. She knew she would be spared uncomfortable introductions as the look on the receptionist's face told her everyone in this office knew who she was.

"Your brother is looking for you," she said, smacking her gum. "Do you know your brother is looking for you?"

Bree nodded, not in the mood even to fake a smile. "I know. Is he here?"

She shook her head. "He had big stuff going on in Baltimore today. He won't be in the office until Tuesday. Are you all right?"

"I'm fine," she said. Fine aside from a broken heart and a guilty conscience that threatened her sanity. "I need your help."

She flipped her braids back, leaning forward. "Sure."

"I need to see where Terrence Stamps works."

"Oh, Terrence. He's not here today."

"I know. He was doing some research for ... for me when he got hurt. I need to get it."

She hesitated, appearing not at all certain she should even be talking about this. "If he's not here, I don't know if—"

"It's fine." Bree leaned back to look at the nameplate. "It's fine, Alicia. I'm Keith's sister. Look, if you show me where he sits, it doesn't mean you gave me anything. Besides, you get to be the person that tells Keith I've been found. He'll love you for that."

"Love me?"

So, she knew Keith pretty well. "He'll appreciate it at least. That's the best he can do. Alicia, I really need your help. This could be a matter of life and death."

My own, Bree thought. After finding out that Sophia's physical damage was limited to cuts and bruises, and she was being held over for observation only because she fell on her head, Bree was able to concentrate on her next steps. She had to make up for what had happened.

Maybe it would make no difference with Graham. Remembering the hate laced in his tone and piercing his eyes, Bree didn't think anything she could do would make a difference. She had been the breaker of hearts plenty of times and had been the heartbroken one a few herself. But this was different. Before, she would cry her eyes out over a pint of chocolate ice cream and move on. That wasn't going to happen this time. She couldn't feel sorry for herself. It was what she deserved, for all she had caused.

But she could help in some way. Graham was going to

be at the hospital. He wouldn't leave Sophia's side. So it was up to her to follow up on what Cheryl Ripley had told them. Bree wanted to blow this secret wide open. The only place she could think of to go was to Keith's offices.

She didn't care that it meant Keith would find her. None of that mattered anymore. She would probably end up in Baltimore again. But at this point, she didn't care. The attack on Sophia was all the proof she needed to know her life had gotten out of control. As much as she hated to admit it, her mother was right.

Bree only wished she had learned that lesson before losing Graham.

"Stop thinking about him," she whispered to herself as she sat down at Terrence's desk. "You have to concentrate."

As she sat at the small desk placed in the middle of a growing library, Bree was at least grateful to be alone. She couldn't possibly speak to anyone. She was barely keeping it together. She had never before felt so full of regret. It was like a physical pain in her belly.

Bree had Terrence's file for Graham, which he had left in the hotel room, in front of her. She turned on his computer. She was certain Keith wouldn't approve of that sticky note with the username and password placed right on the keyboard, but to her it was a godsend.

It would be hard, trying to think of anything other than Graham, but she had to. She would find the truth behind Trotter framing Sophia and present it to him. He had to at least stop hating her, even if he still wouldn't want anything to do with her.

He had to.

* * *

Bree watched the activity coming in and out of General. The ambulance lights were glaring, the automatic doors whipping open and closed. Sophia. It could have been worse.

She leaned against the glass wall of the telephone booth across the street. It was seven now and getting dark. She had so much to share with Graham, but she was scared. She was scared that the second he saw her, he would have her kicked out of the place, refusing to see her or even listen to her for one second. Bree wasn't sure she could take that right now. She was already so tired and frustrated. She was hungry too.

Most of all, she wanted to be in Graham's arms. She closed her eyes, taking herself back to last night. It had been so perfect. She remembered the unexplainable kiss on Terrence's kitchen floor, in the bedroom of her old apartment, even their first kiss at Detroit's in Tribeca. Bree felt sensation run through her body and . . .

"Hello?" The voice was yelling on the other end of the receiver. "Hello?"

"Lily." Bree snapped back to attention. "Is that you, Lily?"

"Yeah," she answered. "Who is this?"

"It's Bree. How are you?"

"Hey, Bree. I'm fine. Met your friend Sophia last night. She was pretty cool. She seemed . . . normal. Not like most of your friends. Let me shut up. I'm one of your friends."

"I'm glad to hear that," Bree said. She really was. She felt as if she didn't have any friends right now. "About last night. Did anything happen to you?"

"What do you mean? Where are you calling from?"

"A pay phone outside General."

"General? What happened?"

"Nothing. Did anything happen to you last night? After you left the show, did you get home okay?"

"I appreciate the concern, but I'm fine. I met Steve at the Starbucks a couple of blocks from the show for coffee right after."

Bree wondered if that's what stopped Nabb from bothering her. Steve was Lily's fiancé. He played football for Harvard and was well over six feet and 250 pounds. "I have a favor to ask you."

"What trouble are you and Robin in now?"

Bree groaned at that familiar question. "It's just me, and it's not really trouble. I just need a place to stay tonight."

"What is going on with you?"

"Lily. I feel bad enough already. I'm about to do something that I know is going to be more painful than I can take. Emotionally, I mean. And I would really like not to sleep in a hotel room by myself tonight. It's just tonight. I'm leaving for D.C. tomorrow."

"Who's in D.C.?"

"Family."

"I thought you didn't have any family."

"Lily."

"Okay, okay. You can't blame me for asking questions. You and Robin. It's always something with you two. Yes, you can come over. But if this thing you have to do is so painful for you, maybe you shouldn't do it. You already sound like you've given all you can today."

"I have to. It's really important to someone. To Sophia. I owe her."

"The free ticket wasn't enough?"

"The free ticket was the problem."

"You sound like you need some good news, girl. And I got it."

Nothing but news that Graham would forgive her and

give her another chance would make Bree feel better. Everything else was just information. "Take a shot."

"You were right about Alex Walsh. Some guy from children and family services made him crack today. It was just a preliminary thing where he asks some simple questions. He just let go."

"Really?" That was good news to Bree. She had believed so strongly that he was abusing his daughter.

"Well," Lily said with a cautious voice, "he didn't confess to beating her. He admitted that he may have gotten physical with her. He claims that she bruises easily, but he did admit that the bruises were caused by him."

"What's happening to Jackie?"

"She's living with some rich aunt of her mother's in Chappaqua. Poor thing. Her mother passed away. Her dad abuses her. You were right, Bree. I'm sorry I ever doubted you."

"Thanks, Lily. I really needed to hear that. I feel like I'm screwing up so much these days, I can't remember the last time I was right about anything."

"Come on over and we'll talk about it."

"You don't have to listen to me whine, Lily. Letting me stay there is more than enough."

"I'm getting used to it," she said. "When Robin was here, we were up all night. She's got more problems than you, if you can believe it. She couldn't stop talking about that Nabb guy. Where is she?"

"She's out of town long term. She needed to get away from Nabb."

"That's funny. She didn't even have to leave."

"What do you mean?"

"Didn't you read the *West Side Story* yesterday?"

"No." *West Side Story* was a local newspaper that covered

nightlife, dining, and, of all things, crime on the West Side of Manhattan.

"That Nabb guy was in it. He got arrested a couple of days ago for trying to break into a Harlem apartment. The residents called the cops. They caught him inside. He resisted arrest. Even pulled a gun on them."

Bree felt herself hyperventilating. "Are you sure?"

"The police blotter gave word for word. His real name is David French, but they mentioned his street name, Nabb. That's how I knew it was him. I already remember seeing him at Spinning Wheel, that crappy bar you and Robin try to drag me to all the time."

"What happened to him?" Bree could hear her own breathing, it was so quick and heavy.

"Uhm, let me think. He had a couple of stolen guns on him, a lot of counterfeit money, and some weed. He couldn't cop bail because the resisting arrest and pulling the gun on the cops thing put it so high. So he's in jail for a long time. He'll probably cop out. The blotter says his arrest record is as thick as a trashy novel. Either way, he won't be roaming the streets of New York for a long, long time. So Robin can—"

"Lily. You said this was in yesterday's paper?"

"Yeah."

"So it happened Wednesday?"

"Wednesday night, it said."

"Oh my God!" Bree realized he could never have attacked Sophia. "Lily, I have to go."

"When are you coming over?" she asked.

"I might not need to. I'll call you back."

Bree hung up before she could get a response. She almost caused a multicar pileup as she ran across the street toward the hospital. What was for one moment great news would quickly become even worse news than before if what Bree thought was true.

Graham stood at his sister's hospital bed looking down at her. She was sound asleep. He wondered what she was dreaming about. The attack? He had been struggling all day to control his anger. Knowing that Sophia was going to be all right made it easier. Physically all right, at least. She was very shaken up, but she had been given medication to calm her. And after a few good naps she was able to explain last night's incident to him.

After that, Graham was only angry with himself. Based on her description, he knew who Sophia's attacker was. The red jacket, the size of the man. It was the same man who had attacked him and Bree Wednesday afternoon and Terrence earlier that morning. Not only had he wrongly blamed Bree for everything, but he himself, and his investigation, was to blame.

He had wanted to find Bree to try and salvage some of what he had destroyed earlier that morning. It had been hard enough before he'd known the truth. He wanted to hate her, but still he cared for her. He knew he was falling in love with her, and that fact only made him angrier when he thought that she and her mischief had caused his sister's attack. But when he found out that she had nothing to do with it, he wanted desperately to take back everything he had said, begging her to forgive him. He had been so cruel, fueled by the stress of the situation and the fear of not knowing how Sophia really was.

But he had no idea where Bree was. There was no way of reaching her. He tried a long shot by calling the lodge, but she had left shortly after he. His stomach tightened at the idea that he could very likely never see her again. She would probably go somewhere her mother and Keith couldn't find her. When he realized he couldn't bear that thought, he knew he wasn't falling in love with her: He was already in love with her.

But he couldn't obsess over that right now. If what he suspected to be true really was, then whatever he and Bree were uncovering about Sophia's frame-up had reached a level of severity that forced his hand. He couldn't have his sister in danger like this. He had tried several times to call Cheryl Ripley, certain that she had spurred this on, but he never got through. He met with the police officer in charge of his sister's attack, but the response he got was less than understanding. He was a beat cop who would much rather chock this all up to a street mugging than a corporate conspiracy.

Now, as he watched his sister sleep peacefully, Graham was faced with decisions that he had to make. He wanted to strangle everyone he thought was behind this. He wanted to destroy them all. He would. Nothing would stop him.

But he had to make sure Sophia was safe.

And yet, despite all of this, he had to find Bree. He didn't know how, but he had to find her and at least try to earn her forgiveness.

"Graham."

Her voice. Graham felt the wind blow against his face as he heard her call his name. He thought he was imagining it because he wanted it so badly.

"Graham."

When he turned to her, Bree's heart jumped. He looked so terribly sad and exhausted standing at his sister's bed. She wanted to take him in her arms and take away all his pain. He blinked, as if he didn't think she was really there. She slowly walked toward him.

"Bree?" Graham felt overwhelmed with relief at the sight of her. "I thought . . . I can't believe you're here."

She looked at Sophia, sleeping in the bed next to her. "How is she?"

"She's okay," he whispered, wanting only to hold Bree. He needed her so much. "She's sleeping."

"Graham." Bree could barely talk. "I have so much to tell you."

"It wasn't your fault," he said. "Bree, I'm so damn sorry. I can't even begin to tell you. The things I said—"

"Forget it, Graham. You were so upset. Sophia is your sister. Your only family, like you said. You thought I had almost gotten her killed."

He felt rejuvenated by her reaction. He had been prepared to get on his knees and beg for forgiveness. And beg over and over again if necessary, all pride set aside. "I shouldn't have just left you like that, no matter what I thought."

"Cousin Cal gave me a ride to the station." She smiled, reaching out to him. She gently touched his arm.

He smiled back, pulling her to him and hugging her tight. "Bree, I thought I would never see you again."

Bree felt redemption in his arms. This was where she belonged. It felt so right, so good. "You'd never get rid of me that easily."

He held her away for a moment. "You look so tired, baby."

"I am. And so are you." She caressed his cheek. "How did you get here?"

"I practically commandeered a young couple's car in the parking lot. Actually, I just told them the truth and they gave me a ride to the train."

"You know?" she asked, looking into his eyes. "About Sophia?"

"Yes." He nodded, looking back at his sister. "It was

the same guy who attacked us and Terrence. She described him just as well as we could have."

"I've found out a lot. A lot about what Cheryl Ripley told us. I've been researching. This is huge."

"I know." He took her by the arm, leading her out of the room. "Let's go outside and talk. I need some air."

After convincing the head nurse that the floor security guard needed to stay outside Sophia's room, Graham and Bree headed outside. They settled on a bench in a private courtyard type area set up on the corner out front. It was surrounded by shrubbery and dimly lit.

"You are such a beautiful sight for my tired eyes." Graham gently removed straying strands of hair from her face.

Bree let her cheek rest in his hands, loving the warmth of his touch. "I felt the same. When I thought my foolishness had caused all of this, I was sure you would never want to lay eyes on me."

"Even if I had thought that was Nabb, you meant Sophia no harm. Besides, Robin really started this. You didn't—"

"I could have stopped him. I should have gotten the cops involved earlier like you said."

Graham shook his head. "They can't help. They won't help me now. You saw how hard I had to fight just to get that security guard to stay near Sophia's room. The cops think I'm crazy. They don't want to hear any conspiracy theories."

"I don't think they'll come back," Bree said. "I think that was a message they wanted to send. Like with Terrence. They don't intend on killing anyone. Not yet at least."

"Thinking it through, I can only think that Cheryl Ripley called someone after we left her home. This is really my fault."

"This is ridiculous," Bree said. "We're sitting here trading blame. This is not our fault. This is all their fault. Who-ever 'their' is.''

"That's the key," Graham said. "The more we get into it, the bigger it gets."

"Which gets me back to the point." Bree pulled the rolled-up folder out of her back pocket and handed it to Graham. "I've been talking to the witnesses all day and doing some research."

"How?"

"Not important. Most of them hung up on me the second I got to the point. One guy yelled at me, telling me he was a Christian man and I could never prove anything anyway."

"That's not at all suspicious."

"I know. He gave it away. I did get to talk to Robert Jones. Remember?"

Graham nodded. "The cleaning lady said she found those notes that Robert supposedly left for Soph lying around her wastebasket. They had the names of people that Robert had given insider information to, for Sophia to send follow-up information to."

"She said her testimony never changed."

"Bull. She was adamant that she found them at Soph's desk. Then she got to trial, and Keith tore her apart, making her admit that not only could those letters have been in the garbage of anyone near Sophia, but that she wasn't sure she remembered seeing all the notes that were presented in court. Suggesting that some were put in after the fact."

"She got real snippy with me. Then, I finally asked her if she was still working at Trotter. She said no. I asked her if she was fired. She wasn't. She quit on her own and isn't working right now. I played the pity game, feeling so sorry for her. Some people hate that more than anything. She was one. She told me, and I quote, 'Don't feel sorry for me, sister, because I don't need a job and I won't for a long, long time."

"She got money for giving her testimony the right way."

"I have a feeling if we look into the background of those witnesses that were supposed to be for the prosecution, we would find some recent financial gains like Terrence finding Robert's boat insurance. That's what I'm hoping the SEC will do."

"You contacted the SEC?"

Bree nodded, feeling proud as she saw the light return to Graham's eyes. "I called the prosecutor of this trial."

"I called Caroline Smith about a dozen times. She never agreed to speak with me."

"She wouldn't speak to me either, but her assistant did. She helped with some of the litigation for that trial. She wouldn't give me any specifics, but she said the whole team on that case was baffled by the testimony of witnesses who seemed so strong at first."

"Why didn't they do anything about it?"

"Trotter wasn't helping them out the way they said they would before it all got started. She told me she would talk to Caroline about it and see if she wanted to revisit it based on the information I gave her, which was basically all we know."

Graham grinned. "Little Bree the investigator."

Bree smiled. "That's not all. I went on the Internet to try and find out what this Century Forward bill is about. It's not even slated for Congress until next summer, but it has something to do with corporate philanthropy and members of Congress. That was all I could find out about it on the Web."

"How does that tie into Trotter, Robert Barber, CMA, and Cammermeyer and Storm?" Graham found one door opening every time another was closed.

"My brother Marcus can help us," Bree said. "I've called them at their house in D.C."

"You tried to contact your brother?" Graham couldn't believe she had risked so much for him. "Bree, where did you go to get this information?"

"Keith's offices."

"Did you run into him?"

She shook her head, surprised by the look on his face. "What's wrong?"

"You risked running into Keith and letting Marcus know where you were for me?"

She took his hands in hers. "I felt so guilty. But even after knowing it wasn't Nabb, I wouldn't change what I did. I told you when we met that I could help you. I wanted to. And the more I got to know you and Sophia, the more I wanted to help you. I did what I could, what I should have done."

"You could have taken the opportunity to skip town without me on your heels, being such a pain to you."

"No, I couldn't have," she said, feeling the emotion build within her. She looked deeply into his eyes. "I'm through running, Graham."

His lips came down on hers in a soft, sweet kiss. Bree was filled with a reaffirming calm at the touch of his mouth on hers. With every sensation, she was reminded that she didn't need to run anymore. Home was wherever Graham was.

Graham reluctantly separated himself from her. He wanted to tell her he loved her, but the look on her face suddenly changed. She was petrified. He turned to look where her eyes were focused. He saw the red jacket first. He saw the gun second. There was no mask this time, but a low-hanging hood on a baseball cap covered his face in the already dimly lit area.

Graham shot up from the chair, feeling Bree stand up behind him. He shielded her with his body.

"Stay back, Bree." Graham's surprise quickly turned to rage as he came face-to-face with the man who had attacked Sophia.

"I was waiting for you to leave the hospital." His voice sounded smooth and refined, vastly contrasting with his rough exterior. "Now give me that folder. I know what you have in there."

"I'm not giving you anything," Bree said, sticking her head out from behind Graham.

"Shut up," Graham whispered to Bree, never taking his eyes off the man. "You got a lot of nerve showing up here."

The man smiled. "Why wouldn't I come to General? Some of my best work is here."

Graham's hands formed into fists, trying to control his rage. He had to remind himself that he wasn't bulletproof and he had to protect Bree.

"Go to hell!" she screamed, stepping from behind Graham. She jerked away from him as he grabbed her, trying to pull her back behind him. "We know what you're up to, and there's no getting away with it now."

"Lady," he said, cautiously stepping closer to her, "I get away with everything. I'm going to get away with this. So, hand it over or I will shoot you. If you'll look, I have a silencer, so no one will come running. There's too much damn noise around this place to hear anything anyway."

"Give it to him, Bree." Graham nodded to her. She frowned at him, but he insisted with a stern tone. "Give it to him!"

"Listen to your boyfriend." The man snatched the folder from Bree, quickly stepping back. He stuffed the contents of the folder into his jacket, lifting the gun higher. "I'm going to kill you anyway. I just didn't want any blood on the merchandise.''

It happened so suddenly that Bree could barely keep track of the sequences. An ambulance driving by in silence chose the second it passed them to turn on its siren. It sounded an unworldly shriek at unheard-of decibel levels. She cringed and ducked. So did the man in the red jacket. Graham did not. He lunged at the man and grabbed his gun.

Bree knew she should run for help, but she couldn't move. She was frozen in place, scared to death that Graham would get hurt. The man was so much bigger than he. But the action took him off guard, and Graham had the opportunity to lay a few well-placed kicks and got the gun out of his hands. As if by instinct, the man hopped back, arms up.

"Hey, man.'' He laughed, but fear was in his voice. It was cracked, desperate. "Let's deal. I'll give you back the folder.''

Graham felt his breathing pick up as he moved toward the man. Sophia. "All you can do for me is to take back my sister's pain.''

"I . . . I can't do that, man. I'm sorry. But come on, she's fine. I only roughed her up a bit. No big deal, right?''

Bree screamed as she saw the butt of the gun make contact with the man's left cheek. He yelled in pain and hit the floor. She heard a groaning sound escape Graham as he leaped on top of the man. He raised the gun in the air.

She ran to him and grabbed his hand before it could come down on the man.

"No, Graham! This won't help Sophia.''

Graham felt the haze around him clear up. He had never been consumed with such hate and violence. He hated himself for even considering what he was about to do. "What have I become?''

Bree helped him stand up. "You're just a man that's been

pushed to the brink. There's nothing wrong with you. You're still Graham Lane, and Graham Lane would never beat anyone. Even if they deserved it. We need to get someone.''

He nodded, looking down at the gun in his hand. There was blood. He tossed the gun aside. ''I cut my hand on the gun when I hit him. He has blood on him.''

Bree looked down at the man. He was conscious, but didn't have his wits about him. She carefully reached into his jacket and got the folder back. She stuffed it back in her back pocket. ''You stay here and watch him. I'll get the cops.''

Bree looked at him, uncertain if he was still calm. She watched as his eyes widened.

''Bree! Run!''

The lights coming from her right blinded Bree. She felt Graham grab her by the arm and swing her around. She looked behind her as she followed Graham. It was a red sports car with tinted windows, and it was on the sidewalk. It bowled over the shrubbery that guarded the sitting area and darted right for them. She lost sight of it as they turned the corner and ran down the street. They ran for a few blocks before Bree felt winded.

''It's not coming after us anymore,'' she said, tugging at Graham. ''Stop. I can't run anymore. I'm out of breath.''

Graham looked behind them. No car. ''What in God's name was that?''

''I guess they didn't trust the red-jacket guy to get the job done all by himself, so they sent in backup.''

They walked into the entrance of a nearby building garage. To get out of sight, they went up the ramp and leaned against a large SUV.

''Damn!'' Graham yelled. ''The gun! We left the gun!''

Sirens. Not ambulance, but police sirens blared in the background. Both of them knew what those were about.

"Somebody might have seen us," Bree said.

"My fingerprints are on that gun," Graham said.

"The blood from your hand is on his face." Bree tried to quell her panic. "Look, he was fine. Just knocked out. Besides, it was self-defense. Let's just explain it to the cops."

"Let's hope they're in an explaining mood."

They walked back to the sitting area, now swarming with policemen. The red sports car wasn't anywhere in sight. Graham wiped his hand of the blood. Innocent or not, he was a black man. Blood on his hand, and a white man down. The last thing he needed was cops who reacted first and asked questions later.

"Graham. Stop." Bree grabbed at his shirt, pausing before they entered the fray. "Look."

His eyes followed her pointed finger in just enough time to see a policeman pull a white sheet over the man in the red jacket. Over his face. He was dead.

"He can't be," Graham said. "He was fine. He was . . ."

They looked at each other and spoke the same words at the same time. "The red car."

"Stay back, folks." A cop was coming toward them, hands up, motioning for them to back away. "This is a police scene. Back away."

Bree stepped forward. "What happened?"

"A man was shot to death, Miss. You don't need to see any of this."

Graham swallowed hard. "My sister is in this hospital. I need to make sure she is safe."

"Sir, she's safer than any of us. They got cops on every floor and they'll stay there until they feel the coast is clear. Don't worry about your sister."

"Let's go, Graham." Bree stepped away. "Sophia is perfectly safe."

"Yo, Hugh!" Another cop approached them. "I think we found the gun in the bushes here."

Bree gasped, squeezing at the bottoms of her shorts with her hands.

"Good," the other cop responded. "I think we have a witness, a nurse who saw a couple of people over here. Let's look at this gun."

"I should have picked up that gun," Graham said, an uneasy feeling settling within him. The stories he had heard.

"Let's just get out of here before that supposed witness identifies one of us."

"Good idea. This is a mess. We've come too far to get stopped now. We can't go back home. It's not safe. Whoever was in that red car is probably not going to stop coming after us."

"Let's get a hotel room." She hailed a cab as soon as they reached the corner. "Far away from here."

"I'll figure out what to do next then." He got into the cab next to her.

"Graham." Bree grabbed at his arm. "You don't have to save the world on your own. Don't treat me like a child. We're in this together."

He smiled, shutting the door behind him. "We'll figure out what to do next."

Bree nodded victoriously. She turned to the cab driver. "Take us to the Hilton."

"Which one?" he asked.

"At the airport." She turned back to Graham. "You said we'll figure out what to do next. I've just thought of something."

"Want to let me in on it?"

"After I get some food in my stomach, I'll tell you everything."

* * *

"I don't like it," Graham said, after placing his empty dinner plate on the stand next to the bed.

"What's not to like about it?" Bree asked, thinking her plan was perfect. "It solves all our problems."

"I like some of it." He turned, facing her on the bed. "But let's go about it another way."

"There is no other way, Graham. We need to get out of New York. We don't want the police on us about what happened tonight. Plus, whoever was in that red sports car was probably trying to kill us and will probably keep trying."

Graham thought of Sophia. He didn't want to leave her. But looking at Bree, he didn't want to be separated from her either. Nor did he want her in danger. "So, if we do go to D.C., what about Sophia?"

"After what happened tonight, Sophia will be fine for the next day or two," Bree answered. She was touched by his constant concern for his sister. She loved his loyalty to no end. "The doctor said she has to stay there for a few days for observation because of a possible concussion anyway. We'll catch the first train to D.C. tomorrow morning. In a couple of days, you can come back to New York to be with her. You can find a safe place for the two of you. Maybe her friend Alice's place? We'll figure that out.

"Once we tie this to the Century Forward bill, we'll have everything we'll need to convince the SEC to look further into this. You and Sophia will get all the security you need."

"That's the part I hate the most," Graham said. "Me coming back to New York alone. I'm worried about you."

Bree put her hand on Graham's knee. "It'll be okay. I have to do this."

Graham shook his head. "Bree, I can't have you going

back to Baltimore. It's going to be too painful for you. After everything you've told me.''

She smiled. ''You were the one who was telling me that I need to stand up to my mother. I need to face up to my family and get it over with so I can really live my life like I want to.''

''That was before . . .''

''Before what?'' Bree asked.

He looked into her eyes, feeling none of the fear he had expected to when he first said these words. ''Before I fell in love with you.''

Bree's entire body smiled. She had been told this by men before. Never had it meant this much. There was no going back now, and that was just fine with her. ''I love you too, Graham. I love you so much. But—''

''No buts, Bree.'' He placed his finger gently on her lips to silence her. ''Let's just enjoy this for a moment.''

Bree paused as long as she could, but she had to get back to the point. If not, her emotions were going to get the best of her and she would let him talk her out of it. She couldn't do that.

''This is for you, Graham,'' she said. ''If I go home, and say it's because of you, you don't owe Keith anything anymore. That huge weight is off your shoulders, and you can concentrate on what's really important.''

''I will figure out a way to handle my debt to Keith. There's got to be a way to fix that.'' Graham couldn't ignore the positives of her suggestion, but it didn't sit well with him at all. ''I just don't want you going home by yourself. Your mother is going to dig her claws into you and she'll put you through hell making you feel guilty.''

''You're so sweet to care, but, Graham, you know me. I'm a tough girl. I've dealt with worse. Especially in the last week. I can handle Victoria Hart. I'll let her rant and rave. I'll put up with it for a while. Just long enough to satisfy her. All that's important is that Keith gets off your back.''

Graham shook his head. ''I want to go with you when you go back to Baltimore. Once we get to the bottom of all of this and I know that Sophia is safe and back on track, you and I will go to Baltimore. I'll be there for you when you deal with your mother and—''

''No, Graham. I need to go home now. Keith is getting impatient and I know him. He doesn't leave things in the hands of others for long. He'll find out that I was in the office today investigating Sophia's case. He'll know what's up. If I wait longer, he'll take your deal off the table. And if you come home with me, Mother will resent me even more. Trust me, it will only make things worse. Let me do this for you. For us.''

Graham wrung his hands together, sighing impatiently. ''What about that other . . . issue? The other thing Victoria has in store for you?''

''The arranged marriage thing?'' She waved her hand. ''I'll handle her. This whole experience has renewed my strength. I love you. Nothing means more to me than coming home to you.''

''Home.'' He liked the sound of those words from her mouth. ''Are you sure you'll want that after returning to the Hart mansion? The Hart lifestyle? You'll be coming home to a college professor and his two-bedroom campus apartment.''

''I'll be coming home to where I belong,'' she answered.

He looked at her wicked little smile, wanting to make love to her over and over again. Forever. ''You're gonna shake everything in my life up, aren't you?''

Bree leaned back on the bed, a mischievous smile wetting her lips. ''You better believe it, Daddy.''

He lay next to her, bringing his face right to hers. "I can shake things up myself, you know."

She rolled her eyes. "I'll believe it when I see it."

Graham couldn't resist a challenge like that. His hand slowly slid under her shirt, reaching up as his lips came down on hers. They forgot the rest of the world as they shook things up for hours before falling asleep in each other's arms.

Chapter Nine

Graham stood patiently at the door of the lavish George-town home of Bree's brother and sister-in-law. It was nestled quietly on a private street lined with million-dollar colonial brick houses with white columns and black iron gates. The house itself was modest by standards of the block, but still large considering it was in the heart of a major city.

As soon as the door opened, Graham saw an attractive woman around his own age with caramel-colored skin, large brown eyes, and very light brown hair with sandy blond highlights that fell carelessly past her shoulders. She screamed with delight. Bree screamed at the same time and they fell into each other's arms, hopping around in a little circle.

He watched in silence, enjoying the opportunity to see Bree so happy and comfortable. No pretenses, no anger. Just happiness. She had been so quiet on the early morning train ride into Union Station. He knew it was fear of home, fear of her mother. He also knew there was no talking that woman out of doing something she was set on. All he could do was hold her hand and keep his mouth shut. So he had, the entire three-and-a-half-hour trip. But now he felt a little better, seeing her happy to be with someone that she obviously loved and who loved her back.

"What are you doing here?" The woman held Bree away, looking her over. "Are you all right?"

"As all right as I can be after the week I've had." Bree knew she would be happy to see her sister-in-law after such a long time, but hadn't anticipated feeling this strongly about it. She felt like crying. She really did miss her family, even though she had tried hard to tell herself she didn't.

The woman looked at Graham with a confused smile. "Hello."

Bree reached back, grabbing Graham by the arm and pulling him forward. "This is Graham Lane. Graham, this is my sister-in-law, Sydney Tanner-Hart."

Graham shook her hand, noticing an interesting hesitative look on her face. "Mrs. Hart. Nice to meet you. Bree has told me a lot about you."

"Graham is the professor that Mother and Keith tried to hire to kidnap me and bring me back home." Bree saw the look of skepticism on Sydney's face. "Well, maybe not kidnap me, but it's all the same. Keith represented his sister, Sophia, and Graham owed him legal fees in the thousands. Keith told him he would clear the bill if Graham snatched me for Mother."

"Sounds like my brother-in-law," Sydney said. "So, you both somehow end up here. Together. I would assume you would be enemies."

"I know this is confusing," Graham added. "It's a long story as to why I'm here with her."

"Everything with Bree is a long story." She stepped aside, widening the doorway. "Come inside."

"Where were you yesterday?" Bree asked, feeling comfort in the familiar settings of the house she had visited more than a few times in the past two years. She had come here to get away. It was really the farthest she could go without her mother releasing the hounds.

The inside of the house was country style, a big departure from Sydney's upbringing in the projects of Chicago. Reds, yellows, greens. Flowers and bright stripes everywhere. Pinewood and New England antiques created a comforting touch.

Sydney ushered them into the sitting room, where they were greeted by the happy screams of a baby in a playpen.

"Brandy!" Bree ran to the playpen, filled with affection and love for her niece. She picked the surprised baby up and hugged her tightly. She kissed her on the cheek several times, feeling the sweetest comfort of her face in those soft fat cheeks.

"I've missed you so much, Brandy." She hugged her tightly, turning to Sydney, who was watching the two of them with a look of love and pride on her face and in her posture. "I've missed all of you. It seems like forever."

"It's been too long," Sydney said. "Are you sure you're okay? You look very tired."

"I'm fine." After one last kiss, Bree returned Brandy to the playpen and sat down on the sofa. "Don't worry about me."

"How can I not worry, Bree?" Sydney sat next to her. "You're family. We love you. We didn't know what you were getting into or what was happening to you."

"Graham needs to use your phone," she answered, noticing the look of anticipation on his face. "He has to call his sister. She's in the hospital in New York."

Sydney looked back at Graham. "If you want some privacy, there's a phone down the hall. Just take a right outside of this room."

"Thanks." After a quick wink at Bree, Graham hurried to the phone, eager to check on Sophia.

"What is his sister doing in the hospital?" Sydney asked.

"She was attacked by this guy that tried to kill us last night." Bree sighed, feeling a pang of guilt at the thought of it. She didn't want to talk about Sophia right now. "Now that you think of it, I am kind of hungry."

Sydney let out an edgy laugh. "Now is when you tell me you were just joking and being your usual pain-in-the-butt self."

"No joke, Sydney. It's a long story though, and I don't want to get into it. Where is Marcus?"

"He's on the hill. Some special session meeting. What are you talking about? And I don't care if you don't want to get into it."

"When is he coming home?" Sydney was suddenly starving. "What did you make for breakfast? Any leftovers?"

"A few hours, waffles, and no." Sydney gently cupped Bree's chin and turned her wandering head to face her. She looked into her eyes. "Stop this."

"Stop what?" Bree asked, pulling away from her grip.

"This thing you always do when you have to explain yourself. You try to talk about a hundred different other things to distract me. It never works."

Bree rolled her eyes. "Fine, but I am starving."

"You'll eat after you talk." Sydney leaned back on the sofa, smoothing out the rose-colored rayon summer dress that fell loosely around her curvy, full figure. "Start with what in the world you are doing with the man that Victoria hired to get you back home."

"I'm in love with him, Sydney."

This time it was Sydney's turn to roll her eyes.

"I know what you're thinking," Bree said, "and you're wrong."

"You fall in love every three months, Bree."

"That was the old me. I swear to you, Sydney, I have never felt this way about anyone. He is the most amazing guy. Yeah, he's a college professor and he's kind of a nerd. But in the sweetest, cutest, sexiest way you'd ever want a guy to be. He is so loyal and caring. He knows who I am and he still wants me. He's what I need."

Sydney's expression said she wasn't buying this. "Did you get this guy to fall for you to keep him from sending you home?"

Bree shook her head. "We fell in love by accident. Neither of us expected it. We hated each other at first. It just happened. Sound familiar?"

Sydney smiled. "You leave me and your brother out of this."

Bree knew she had scored some brownie points. Sydney and Marcus couldn't stand each other when they first met. Well, at least Sydney couldn't stand Marcus. As attracted as they were to each other, they did nothing but fight and make each other miserable. Somehow through all of that, including the attempt on Sydney's life, they had fallen in love. Deeply in love. And here they were married with a child and happier than either of them had ever been.

"Fine," Bree answered, "but that's how it happened. But all of it is legit. He intended to get me to go back home, but we fell in love. And then there's the thing with Nabb trying to kill me and Robin. It only brought us closer—"

"Someone was trying to kill you?" Sydney leaned forward, her wide eyes opening even wider. "You and Robin? Is that the guy that Victoria said you were living with? Where does he fit in?"

Bree laughed. "It must have been driving Mother crazy to think I was shacking up with an ex-con boyfriend. Actually Robin is a girl and she's in the countryside of New York now. Nabb is in jail, so he can't get to me anymore."

"Why was he trying to kill you?"

"Go figure." Bree thought it best to stay out of that story. "Anyway, it just brought us closer since Nabb tried to kill him because he was with me. Then this whole thing with his sister and—"

"The sister who is in the hospital?"

"Yeah. The one who was attacked."

"By this guy Nabb who is now in jail?"

"No. She was attacked by the guy in the red jacket that attacked me and Graham in Terrence Stamps's apartment."

Sydney shook her head, looking utterly confused. "You were attacked?"

"Not really. He really only attacked Graham, but he was going to come after me, and Graham saved my life. He saved me from Nabb too. He also saved me from the guy in the red jacket the second time he tried to kill us, but I think I could have taken care of that one myself. And I did save him in Terrence's apartment when I hit the guy over the head with a pot."

"You have got to slow down." Sydney blinked, shaking her head. "Who is Terrence, and exactly how many times were you almost attacked by Nabb and the red-jacket guy?"

"Nabb tried to kill me probably twice, I think." Bree tried to remember, the last week was such a blur. "Then the red-jacket guy tried to kill me twice, but Graham almost killed him, because he attacked Graham's sister. But I got him to stop. That was pretty intense. And Terrence is Keith's intern. The red-jacket guy attacked him too."

"You wouldn't by any chance know why red jacket is attacking everybody, would you?"

"It started with Terrence, but it's another long story."

"What did Terrence do? And why is Keith involved in this?"

"He was helping Graham find out who framed his sister, Sophia." Bree really didn't want to go over this stuff anymore. "Can I eat something now?"

Sydney acted as if she didn't hear her. "Who was framing his sister? And why?"

"Why does anybody do anything?" Bree asked. "Everyone is nuts in New York. Marcus needs to get home. I have to ask him a very important question. Where were you two yesterday anyway? I tried calling a hundred times."

"We were in Great Falls for a few days," Sydney answered in a polite, conversational tone. "We would have stayed all weekend, except Marcus had to come in for this emergency session. Let's get back to you."

"I don't want to talk about it anymore."

"Just answer me one more question. You said Nabb was in jail, so he can't hurt you anymore. What about the red-jacket guy? Where is he?"

"He's dead."

Sydney paused. "Did you kill him?"

"Sydney!"

"I wouldn't put anything past you at this point. If I'm to believe all of this, I might as well ask everything."

"No, I didn't kill him."

"But Graham almost did."

"Yes, but I stopped him. Then the guy in the red car must have killed him."

"There's another killer here? That makes three so far."

"Yeah, he's the last one. He's still alive. I think. He tried to run me and Graham over, but we got away."

"Bree." Sydney took her sister-in-law's hands in her own. "You have seriously gone over the deep end."

"This wasn't about me," she said. "The red-jacket guy and the red-car guy are about Graham."

"I'm supposed to believe that these people are trying to kill a college professor?"

"Yes. It's a long—"

"Don't say that again." Sydney held up her hand to stop her. "I don't want to hear anymore. You've completely lost it and you've taken this innocent man down with you."

"I'm not so innocent."

Sydney turned to Graham as he returned to the room, sitting in the lounge chair across from them. She looked him over. "I have a feeling you've fallen under my sister-in-law's spell and you're trying to share the blame for her."

"Sydney." Bree pulled her hands away and got up to join Graham on the chair. She sat in his lap, wrapping her arm around him. "It's not like that. Graham loves me. I love him. We're in this together. We're not blaming anyone."

Sydney threw her hands in the air. "Fine. Fine with me. Far be it from me to pass judgment on the insane. I'm going to go to the kitchen and make you something to eat. I would just appreciate it if you could avoid any attempts on your lives while my baby is around."

After she left, Graham turned to Bree. "What did you tell her?"

Bree shrugged. "I just explained everything. She wasn't listening, but that's okay. How's Sophia?"

"She's fine. They're still looking for a killer, so the cops are all over. She's feeling better too. She just wants me to come home. The morning papers are going crazy with this. It's not good."

"At least she's okay. Anything about the two of us?"

He shook his head. "Sophia hadn't read the paper yet, but she watched the morning news and there was definitely a mention of a young man and woman in the area with the dead man. No concrete description. Just that we're black."

"Which for the cops is enough sometimes."

He nodded. "All the more reason for us to get the information we need as soon as possible and get back to New York. We have to clue the cops in on this before they start harassing every black couple in the area. Where's your brother?"

"He's on the hill, but he'll be back in a couple of hours." She kissed him on the forehead before jumping up. "I'll get Brandy. Let's go to the kitchen and get something to eat."

Over snacks, Graham gave Sydney a more clarified description of the week's past events. Although his version was less confusing, the overall effect only served to upset her more. Despite it all, she agreed with Bree's going home to clear the air. She wasn't familiar with the Century Forward bill, but Graham was hopeful that Marcus could help since she mentioned that senators usually heard about upcoming bills years ahead of time.

Wanting to change the subject, they engaged in small talk, the weather, Brandy's progress and misbehaviors, recent trips, current events. It was all a welcomed distraction for Graham. He knew he would like Sydney. He already did. She wasn't what he had expected in a "suitable" Hart spouse. Under that classic beauty was an edgy and streetwise young woman. She was no-nonsense with a defiant tone and a quick, dry wit.

He thought of the stories he had read when researching Keith. Stories about how she had started the whole family uproar two years ago that ended up with Anthony Hart in jail for attempted murder and Keith in the hospital. He could see her raising a little hell. Nothing like Bree, but a curious person who questioned the status quo. Somehow she had found a way to be happy, as she obviously seemed, as a Hart. It was encouraging for him.

It was after one in the afternoon when Marcus Hart finally came home. Graham admonished the cautious, unaccepting stare Marcus sent him as he hugged his sister. A joyful reunion quickly turned to an argument as Sydney updated him on what was going on and he took his anger out on Bree.

Graham wanted to stay out of it. He knew that Marcus was only speaking out of love and this was his house, after all, but he was forced to step in when Bree started to cry. He couldn't let anyone anger the woman he loved like that. Family or not.

"Lay off of her," he said, placing an arm on Bree's shoulder as they all sat in the kitchen. "She's been through enough this week not to have you yelling at her as if she's a child."

Marcus Hart was obviously not a man used to being challenged by another man. He gritted his teeth, staring Graham down. He looked as if he was about to charge the younger man until Sydney placed a soft hand on his shoulder. His head moved to the side only a few inches, his eyes setting on her hand for a moment. He took a deep breath, his entire body seeming to calm just at her touch. He turned to Graham, who hadn't backed down a bit.

"When my sister acts like a child, that's how I'll treat her." He sat on a stool at the kitchen island, looking from Graham to Bree. "She's in some serious trouble now, thanks in no small part to you."

Bree patted Graham on the thigh, appreciative of his defense. But she knew this would end up ugly if the men decided to challenge each other. Besides Sydney, no one was ever able to talk any sense into Marcus.

"Marcus," she said, "I know I've messed it up big time this go-around. I know I've said I've learned my lesson a hundred times, so there's no reason for you to believe me when I say I've learned it again this time. So I won't say it, even though I really mean it. The fact is, this is bigger than any of us could have imagined. And we need your help."

"My checkbook?" he asked.

"Marcus, stop it." Sydney jabbed him with her fist. "The Century Forward bill. It's tied into this craziness somehow. You know something about it, don't you?"

He nodded, turning to Graham. "What do you need to know?"

Brandy's crying in the distance broke some of the tension in the air. Sydney got off her stool and headed for her child.

"Sydney," Bree called after her. "You're coming right back, aren't you? We need you to keep the peace."

"No, you don't." She turned to Marcus with a stern squint in her eyes. "Marcus will behave. I'll be back soon."

"The Century Forward bill," Marcus went on, without prompting, "is a bill that should be coming up in the early part of the next summer session of Congress. Probably in June. It's a twenty-first-century initiative in response to the hot issues like campaign finance reform, members of Congress making so much money through lobbyists and such.

"This bill means that starting next year, all 535 members of Congress, as well as any appointed White House officials, meaning cabinet members, White House counsels, advisors, and top-notch folks, have to expose their entire portfolio of income. From their jobs, their speeches, any other boards they sit on. Basically anywhere they make a penny, it's got to be public."

"Isn't it already?" Bree asked.

"No," Graham added. "Not personal investments, not board salaries. Most people know what they make for speeches, but nothing specific. No record of how many speeches they actually give. They record the big ones, but not the little speeches, which can count up to a lot."

"How does this relate to firms like CMA?" Bree asked.

"What type of company is it?" Marcus asked.

"An investment type of banking firm," Graham answered.

"Does it have ties to philanthropy?"

"Not that we know of," Bree said. "But they are somehow tied to CMA, a firm that is deep into causes. I think a certain percentage of their client's profits have to go to charity to be connected with the firm."

Marcus nodded. "Then the tie is obvious. Part of this bill requires that those who fall under this bill, like me, have to . . . let's say, put a percentage of our money where our mouth is."

There was silence as Graham and Bree processed the information.

"Obviously," Bree said, "CMA profits from this bill. A company like theirs would already have the system in place to support this requirement."

"And I'm sure they have devised a way to make this as least costly to those involved," Graham said.

Marcus cleared his throat. "Hey, we aren't all like that."

Graham nodded in acknowledgment. "Yeah, but enough of the fat cats on Capitol Hill are that a firm like CMA would come in handy. So, a lot of congressmen and women will be giving them a call soon."

"They already have," Marcus said. "This bill is going to clear. Congressmen and women would get hell if they knocked it down. Next November, half of Congress is up for reelection. So, if they knock the bill down, they get bad pub and won't get reelected. If it passes, and it will, and their incomes are exposed at the obscene rate that so many of them are, with no evidence of charitable activities, they won't get reelected. So, they're calling CMA now to head this off."

"But where does my sister come in?" Graham asked as much to himself as anyone else. "She didn't know anything about CMA or this bill. Where does Cammermeyer and Storm fit in?"

Bree couldn't think of the answer. "And where does Robert Barber fit in? He's the connection with CMA, but he doesn't benefit from the Trotter-Cammermeyer merger. Trotter fired him, and Cammermeyer would never hire him."

"But CMA did." Graham shook his head in frustration. "Because he did something for them, and it's tied to all of this. And my sister was the one that would pay for it."

Marcus pushed away from the island, getting off his stool. "That's all I know about the bill. I haven't cared too much about it, because it won't change anything about me and what I do. Ten percent of all Sydney's income and mine goes to various charities and the community. There were a lot of men and women pretty ticked off about it all, but it's a no-win situation. I guess they would rather take this hit than campaign finance reform. With companies like CMA, who will make this as painless as possible, it's the only real solution."

Left alone in the kitchen, Bree and Graham were going backward in their minds to connect all of the information, trying to toss out the irrelevant tidbits that only made the already murky waters more difficult to navigate.

"What does CMA get out of framing your sister?" Bree asked herself as much as anyone. "Robert Barber? Is he that good?"

Graham shook his head. "Barber is good, but not that good. He had the tops in clients, but a lot of them deserted him when the scandal hit. They had to make it look as if they didn't have anything to do with it. He's not enough to make this happen."

The doorbell rang and Bree got up from her stool. "They're busy with the baby. I'll get it."

Graham smiled as she gently brushed her hand against his arm while passing by. Just a simple gesture, probably not noticeable to anyone who might see, but to him it brought a sense of comfort to his soul and clarity to his mind.

Considering all that had happened to her in the past couple of weeks, Bree should have developed a practice of caution when opening a door. But she hadn't. She didn't even look through the peephole. Like with her many other mistakes, she regretted her move the second after she opened the door. She knew all hell was about to break loose.

"What are you doing here?" She almost fell down as he practically pushed her out of his way, stepping into the house.

"Where is he?" Keith asked. The expression on his face as he looked down at his little sister was angry and impatient. "Where is Lane?"

"Calm down, okay?" She grabbed at his arm just before he darted down the hallway. She pulled tightly, almost getting dragged along by her much larger brother. "Just wait a second."

"What?" He jerked his arm away. "And don't try to give me one of your ridiculous explanations for what's going on. I know he's with you."

"How did you know we were here? Did Sydney or Marcus call you?"

An accomplished smile peeked out the edges of his mouth.

"You led me right to yourself, little one. When you showed up at my office. That showed a lot of nerve."

"I knew it could give me up. It just didn't matter at the time, Keith. You don't understand what's been happening. I had to—"

"Don't try the desperate heroine bit with me. I'm not in the mood."

"You just can't start anything, Keith. Graham didn't—"

"Graham and I had a deal, and he tried to play me for a fool. Do you have any idea how much money he owes me?"

"He was going to follow through on that deal. I am on my way home because of him. Can't you tell? Why else would I be in D.C.? We just had some things to figure out. You'd be interested to know—"

"No." He shook his head. "I'm not interested in anything, but the fact that he screwed me. This crap he pulled put Terrence in the hospital."

"And you care about that?" Her voice was laced with skepticism.

He smirked. "The firm has to cover all of his medical expenses. We've already spent more in hospital bills than we were going to pay him for the whole summer."

"Figures." She rolled her eyes. "You can't blame Graham for that. He didn't know this stuff with his sister was that deep."

"I can blame him and I will. When I found out you had been in the office, I got my own private investigator. I had known Graham was trying to screw me. I could just feel it. Mother didn't know. She would have had a fit if she knew I had hired a professional again. I know exactly what you've been up to since then."

"Then you know we've been trying desperately to get to the bottom of this. It's incredible."

"I said I don't care." He looked her over. "You look a mess. Get whatever crap you have and let's go."

"I can't go yet, Keith." Bree saw the anger brewing in his light eyes. "I will come home, I promise. It's just that we're so close."

"Mother knows now," he said.

Bree cringed, feeling a thump in the pit of her stomach. "Why did you tell her?"

"She heard me on the phone at my office in Baltimore. She stopped by to find out what was up, and she busted in on me. I had to tell her. I tracked your credit card on the Metroliner. She assumed you were coming home since it stops in Baltimore. But from the charge, I realized it was for two tickets all the way to D.C. She was pretty hysterical, Bree."

Bree couldn't help but feel guilty. "I know I have to deal with her. But Graham and I are so close."

"What is this Graham and I? Since when are you two partners in . . ." He leaned back, pressing his lips together with a nod. "What have you done, Bree?"

"It's not what you think!" Bree knew what he was suggesting. The same as Sydney. "We're in love."

"Great!" He threw his hands in the air. "Just great! No way, Bree. Mother will have a heart attack. Not a broke college professor."

"He's not completely broke, and it wouldn't matter either way."

"No way. It's not going to happen."

"It already has happened." Bree couldn't stand how Keith assumed a say in her life. Marcus used to be that way too. Victoria was always that way. Only a few hours back in her family's realm and they were already making decisions for her. "So, Mother will just have to deal with it."

"No, she won't." His arms folded across his chest.

"You're leaving this jerk behind, and you're leaving him behind for good."

Bree looked behind her, hopeful that Graham couldn't hear this. "No, Keith. Not this time. This is different."

"This is very different, Bree. You're right about that. Because, like I said, I know everything. Including the untimely death at the same hospital where Sophia is staying. The gun with fingerprints on it that don't belong to the dead man. The blood on the bad guy that's not his either. The eyewitness that saw you and Graham. I know it all."

Bree gasped. "What? How do you—"

"Not important," he answered. "I just do. It cost me a lot more money than I wanted to spend, but I got an ex-CIA guy this time around. He knows all the secrets. He probably knows more about what you and Graham have been doing than you do. He knows about the hotel room last night too. Want to hear what you ate for dinner? Because I can tell you."

"You're evil." Bree's hands formed in fist. She couldn't let him hurt Graham. "Graham didn't kill that man."

He rubbed at the bottom of his chin, eyes widening. "How do I know that? I don't know that? He very well could have. That man attacked his sister. His fingerprints are probably on the gun that shot him. That's his blood, I'll bet. The witness can ID him in a lineup. Gotta tell you, Gabrielle. I wouldn't want to defend him and I'm the best."

Without warning Bree's hand slapped Keith across the face so swiftly that he fell back against the wall.

"You little . . ." His hands reached for her, his eyes holding an embarrassed anger.

"Keith!"

Marcus grabbed his brother and pushed him back. Keith hit the wall again. He made eye contact with his older brother. As usual, it was a contest that Marcus immediately won. Keith backed down.

"Don't you dare," Marcus said.

"What in the hell is going on here?" Sydney showed up in the foyer of the house the same time as Graham.

Graham reached Bree. All he had heard was a slap and angry words. He heard Marcus clearly. Graham stared Keith down. He didn't care how he had gotten here. He just knew he would have hell to pay if he touched Bree.

Keith took a second to pull himself together, a wicked smile forming at his lips. "If it isn't the professor. The safe bet that turned out to be anything but."

"You shouldn't have assumed so much about me, Keith." Graham turned to Bree. "Are you all right? I heard—"

"You heard Bree slapping her brother," Marcus said, turning his ire to his baby sister. "What in God's name is your problem now?"

Bree tried to calm herself, but she was so upset just thinking of what Keith was threatening. "He deserved it. He deserves worse."

"Probably true," Sydney said. "Still, there's enough fighting in this family that we don't need to add beating the living tar out of each other. What are you doing here, Keith?"

"I've come to fetch my little sister."

Graham hated his tone, his choice of words. "You're not fetching anybody."

"Graham." Marcus nodded to him. "Let's keep it cool. What's up, Keith?"

Keith kept his eyes on Bree as he spoke to everyone. "Since our trusty professor here tried to cheat me and Mother, I had to hire someone new. I tracked them here. She used her credit card to buy the train tickets."

"It was a ridiculous deal in the first place," Sydney said. "So like Victoria. So like you, Keith."

"I'll take that as a compliment," he said with a smirk. He gently touched his cheek where he had been slapped. He squinted at Bree. "Little brat."

"That's it." Graham lunged for Keith, but Marcus and Sydney combined to hold him back.

"Stop it, Graham." Bree tugged tightly. "He's not worth it. He'll just turn it around and make you the bad guy. He's good at that."

Graham shrugged away from everyone. He couldn't stand to be away from Bree right now. "Bree isn't going with you tonight if that's what you thought."

"You want to bet?" Keith asked, apparently feeling accomplished that he made Graham lose his cool. "You're coming home with me, aren't you, sis?"

"Keith, stop." Sydney sighed. "There's a lot going on that's bigger than assuaging Mother's need for control."

"Wanna bet?" Keith asked. "You guys can sit here and be so matter-of-fact about it because you all ran away."

"Don't start that," Marcus said with a tired sigh.

"I have to handle the family now," Keith continued as if he hadn't heard Marcus. "Some things have to get done for Mother's sanity and sure as hell for mine. So get your stuff, Bree. And I'll deal with the good professor later."

"You'll deal with me now," Graham said. "Bree isn't going anywhere until she's good and ready. And I don't care about the money. I'll find another way to pay you. I shouldn't have taken this ridiculous deal in the first place."

"No one will argue with you there," Sydney said. "But he's right, Keith. Bree is planning on going home, but not right now. And you know she can't be forced to do anything she doesn't want to. So let's just get off that. Why don't we all just sit down and I'll get us something to drink. Besides, Keith, I'm sure you don't want to leave without seeing Brandy. Your niece, remember?"

"I don't have time today," Keith said in a quieter, milder tone. It was obvious to everyone that he hadn't even thought of the child and it seemed he felt a little guilty about that. "And I don't have time for a drink either. Bree is coming home with me now. And I don't have to force her. She's coming of her own free will."

Graham turned to Bree, after she gave no protest. Something was going on. He could feel it on the back of his neck. He could see it in her nervous blink. "Bree. Don't be afraid of him. I won't let anything happen to you."

Bree had to turn away from Graham. She threw Keith a venomous stare. "You are such a jackass."

"Let's just have a seat in the family room," Marcus said. "Sydney will make us—"

"Keith and I need a moment alone," Bree interrupted. She swallowed hard as Graham's expression changed quickly. He was sensing something was wrong. She couldn't let this happen to him. She could figure out a way to fix this. She just needed some time.

"No." Graham held on to Bree's arm. "Come on. Let's sit down. We're all a little too wound up."

"Well, do something," Marcus said with an impatient tone. As the phone rang, he moved through the group toward it. "I'm sick of this. I'm supposed to be at a romantic bed-and-breakfast in Great Falls with my beautiful wife right now. Not playing ringmaster to this circus."

Sydney rolled her eyes. "He's certainly not playing peace-maker. And you two don't need to be alone right now. Not with the way you're acting."

"I think Bree will behave herself now." Keith opened up the front door. "A step onto the beautiful front porch?"

Bree pulled away from Graham. It wasn't easy. He was gripping hard. She didn't look at him. She didn't look back as she spoke. "We'll be back in a minute, guys."

Graham watched as they walked out. Part of him wanted to grab her and shake her. But the other part wanted to trust her and the promises they had made to each other in every kiss, every touch. Every time they had made love.

"Come on," Sydney said, placing a hand on his shoulder. "I'll make you a drink. You look like you need one more than anyone."

Graham followed Sydney into the kitchen, leaving his heart in that foyer. He gritted his teeth, trying to control his anger and stave back his growing uncertainty.

"It's going to be okay," Sydney said with compassionate eyes as she passed him a glass of vintage cognac. "This usually does the trick for Marcus when he's really wound up or being his usual jerky self sometimes. It'll calm you."

"Thanks." Graham took a sip, feeling the good burn down his throat. "Good stuff."

"Only the best for my husband." She sat on the stool next to him. "It will be okay, you know."

Graham nodded, hoping his outward appearance was doing the job. Inside, he felt like pulling his hair out. He looked out the kitchen window. He couldn't see them from there. "It has to be."

Bree looked her brother in the eye. "Keith, even you aren't so cruel. Graham could never have . . . You know he didn't kill anyone."

"I don't care. I just want this all over with. I have a life of my own, a business to run. I have a relationship of my own that I would like to keep if at all possible. Unlike you, I don't fall in love every other week."

Bree chose to ignore the insult. "How can you talk about love at the same time you talk about blackmail? I love Graham."

"You love every guy you go out with." He waved his hand at her. "You'll get over it."

Bree knew that wasn't true. She would find a way to make this work. "I can make a deal with you, Keith."

"No. No more deals. I've made enough deals for the month, and I keep getting screwed. Here's the way it's going to go. You'll come home with me now and you will never see this jerk again."

"You just want to keep us apart because you're ticked that he got the best of you. You hate him and you just want to hurt him."

"That's the icing on the cake. The real reason you two aren't going to see each other is that Mother will have a fit if you try to bring a no-name college professor home, and I'm not going through that mess again. Because it'll be up to you-know-who to fix this for her."

"Coward." She kicked him in the shins. Bree knew it was an immature gesture, but she had nothing to gain or lose by it. "You just can't stand up to her."

"Then maybe I should run away to New York."

"Touché. Still, you can't keep us apart."

"Yes, I can. Because you love him."

"What do you mean?"

"You agree to cut this guy loose, I'll erase his debt."

"Screw your debt! I'll pay it for Graham."

"You know I won't accept your money. And more importantly, you know very well that Graham would rather slit his throat than let you pay his bill."

That much was true. His pride and feeling of responsibility for Sophia would make that a winless battle. Bree was starting to feel cornered. "He'll find another way to pay it over time."

Keith laughed. "I'm sure he would. But I want it now. I'll force him into bankruptcy. It'll be all your fault. And with all that money you have in your trust fund, that will make for fun dinner table conversation. How will you find a way to support the two of you without him knowing it? Nothing more emasculating for a proud man than being financially dependant on a woman because she ruined him. What a beautiful future you have. After he gets out of jail, of course.''

Bree felt her stomach tightening. She tried to calm her panic. She couldn't believe this was happening. ''Keith, you can't—''

''So,'' he continued, ignoring her. ''You come home with me now and I'll change my mind about payment in full upon demand. You cut him off completely, and I won't share anything with the cops. I mean, Bree, you have to admit that he's as good as guilty with the evidence the way it is. It's a small sacrifice.''

It was no small sacrifice, Bree knew. Only, it would be a waste of her time to try and explain that to Keith. She loved Graham. But she wouldn't give up. She would find a way to fix all of this. Her mind was already working, but she wasn't going to get any further right now.

She glanced back at the house, knowing that the man she loved was worried about what was going on outside. And she was about to purposefully make it worse for him. For now at least. She would explain to him that she would fix it all soon and it wouldn't be this way very long.

She turned to Keith. ''Let me just explain this to Graham. It'll take some time. He won't want to—''

''Nope.'' Keith cleared his throat, nodding to a woman passing by on the street with a Scottish terrier on a lease. ''You can't tell him. I left that part out. That part is for me. That bastard is going to get his.''

''You want me to make Graham think that I'm just

deserting him?'' Bree wouldn't. It was just what Graham was afraid she would do.

"You've done it plenty of times before. You can do it again.''

"Graham is different! How many times do I have to tell you?''

"I don't care. How many times do I have to tell you? Just let it go, Bree. You have no bargaining tools. You've made a mess of everything and you have to cut your losses and walk away.''

Bree paced the porch. What could she do? She looked at Keith. No, he wasn't bluffing, and she loved Graham too much to take the chance that he was. *Think, think,* she told herself. There wasn't enough time.

"Bree,'' Keith urged. "Let's do this now. If we leave now, I can get you home in time for dinner and—''

"Shut up, Keith.'' Bree didn't even want to think about facing Victoria so soon. Not this way. "Won't you even listen to what I have to say about Sophia and Trotter Securities? If you knew, you would understand why I need to stay.''

His expression was staid, unmoving, unaffected. He looked down at his watch, then back at her. "I've already spent enough time here.''

She bit her lip, knowing that she would find a way to fix this. She would find a way back to Graham and make Keith's threats worthless. It would just be a little harder than what she was used to. And meanwhile . . . her heart sank at what Graham would feel. But in a way, Keith was right. She had to walk away right now to put an end to part of this. There was always tomorrow. She hoped.

Graham couldn't hide his anticipation as Bree entered the kitchen. He swung around on his stool to face her, hoping to find something in her face that would erase his concerns.

His heart fell into his stomach as the exact opposite seemed to be true.

As she approached him, an apology was weaved into her walk, the look on her face, her eyes. Everything. An apology for what though? Graham decided this wasn't going to happen. He wouldn't let it.

"I'll be in the family room," Sydney said, hurrying out of the kitchen.

Bree avoided eye contact with her, knowing how keen Sydney was at reading people. This was hard enough. She had to be convincing, because as painful as it might be, if Graham doubted her right now, he would fight her and set Keith off. Then, who knew what would happen to him?

"Did Keith leave?" Graham asked, not at all welcoming this unfamiliar feeling in the pit of his stomach. It was pain. The look on her face was causing him physical pain.

"He's outside waiting for me," she said, forcing herself to look him in the face. She swallowed. She had to make this quick. She wasn't sure how long she could hold out.

He reached for her arm, pulling her closer. "No, Bree. You don't have to do this. We're going to go to Baltimore together after we figure all of this out about Sophia. Not now, not without me. I know you're worried about the money, but—"

"I don't care about the money, Graham." She sighed as if bored by the conversation. "I'm really tired of all of this."

Graham paused, choosing not to believe her. "Stop it, Bree. You're just trying to keep the peace. I'm sure Keith made you feel bad and—"

"There is nothing that jerk could do to make me feel bad." She ran fingers through her hair. *Make it seem as if you're annoyed just by being near him,* she told herself. "I'm going home, Graham. I'm just tired of all of it. Being chased, sleeping in a new place almost every night. This thing between us is losing its fire.''

"What are you talking about?" *No,* Graham thought. Something was wrong, but not this. She didn't mean it. "Listen, Bree. I know you're feeling pressure, but I'll take care of everything. We're so close to the truth."

"Just forget it, Graham. I mean, don't forget trying to find out what happened to Sophia. I wish you all the luck in the world with that. I'm just not interested anymore. I want something new. Besides, Keith said that Mother promises to stay off my back if I come home now."

Graham fought off this wave of panic that wanted to hit him. "What did he say to you? What did you threaten you with?"

"Nothing, Graham. It's just he told me everything is going to be better now, and I can't really say what's come over me. It's just . . . well, I'm tired. I can't say it enough. I just don't—"

"You won't have to deal with any more of it." Graham was talking fast, trying to think of what was going on at the same time. *Calm down. Calm down.* "If you want to go home, then fine. I just thought we agreed that we would—"

"I wasn't thinking straight. I was so caught up in what was going on. I've come down now and—"

"That's okay." Graham really didn't want to let her go on. He was afraid of what she would say if she kept talking. "We'll go to Baltimore tonight. We can deal with your mother."

"Not we, Graham." Bree thought she was going to be sick at Graham's behavior. He wouldn't make this easy. That only made her love him more. "You can't come with me. Mother is only going to be cool if I'm alone. She's too mad."

"I don't want you to go by yourself." Graham didn't

want to think about being separated from her. Not now, not ever. "Remember how upset you were just thinking about it?"

"Look, Graham." She rolled her eyes, trying to appear detached. "I don't know how you're going to settle your deal with my brother. It's not my problem. You shouldn't even have made this deal to begin with."

Graham was taken aback by her cold words. She seemed to be mad at him now. "I know, Bree. It was stupid of me, but I thought . . . I don't know what I thought. I don't care about the money, and I don't want you to either."

"I just wanted to say bye." She clenched her hands into fists, digging into the skin of her palms with her nails to keep herself from showing her true feelings. " 'Cause you were a nice guy and your sister is cool."

Graham heard her say the word bye, but he didn't believe it. "If you want to go home with your brother, that's okay. If you don't think you need me there, I'm fine with that. I wouldn't want to make it worse for you. I'll deal with things from New York. You can join me when you want to. Or just call me when you want me to come—"

"If I'm in New York again, I'll definitely look you up." *Please stop,* her heart begged him. *Please. I promise, I'll fix this. We'll be together, but you have to let me go for now.* "We had fun."

After a short silence, Graham let out a laugh that in no way hid his pain. "We had fun? Is that all you have to say? I don't believe it. I think you're tired like you say you are, and you're not thinking straight."

"I'm trying to be nice, Graham." Bree felt her knees getting weak. She placed a hand on the kitchen island to hold herself up. "I don't want to hurt you because you saved my life, but I don't want to do this anymore. This stuff with Sophia, with you, New York. Talking to Keith made me miss home. All of my friends are asking for me. And I really can't pass up this window to go home with a guarantee that Mother isn't going to jump on me. This is pretty precious. And I'm tired of being broke.''

Graham cringed at the laugh laced in her last words. ''I don't get it, Bree. You were as involved in finding out the truth about Sophia as I was. Are you trying to tell me that has all gone away?''

She shrugged, hoping his raised voice wouldn't bring Marcus back. She didn't want more trouble. ''No. I mean, I would love to hear how it turns out. I hope you're gonna be careful too. I just don't want to do it anymore.''

Graham's pride kicked in like clockwork. And he didn't fight it. It dulled out his pain and insecurities. ''This is great. This is just great!''

Bree jumped back as he got off his stool and kicked it. It was like instinct for her to reach out to him at seeing him so angry, but she stopped herself. She kept telling herself that this would all be resolved soon. Somehow. She was doing this for him.

''I feel bad, Graham. I know we worked together on this plan of action and I'm backing out. But you really don't need me anymore. You have everything on the Century Forward bill. You can figure it all out yourself.''

''And that's what is really important here, right? This whole plan we had. We had more than a plan, Bree!''

Bree groaned as she heard footsteps behind her. This was going to get worse before it was over, and Keith wasn't going to wait much longer.

''What's with all the racket?'' Sydney Tanner entered the kitchen, standing between them. ''You better keep it down or Marcus is going to come back in here.''

Bree pouted, trying her best to put on the show. If she couldn't get rid of him, she would have to make him want to be rid of her. "I'm going home and Graham is ticked off. I just don't want any more of this."

"I have to say I'm glad," Sydney said, "but I'm surprised. Just this morning you were excited about all this craziness."

"I was on a high still," Bree said, as if that were all there were to it. "I'm not anymore. I'm tired and I want to go home."

Graham threw his hands in the air. "I can't believe I fell for this."

"Really, Graham." Sydney turned to him. "This is best. If what you're saying is true, you need to take it to the cops and let them handle it. Bree doesn't need to be in this danger."

"I'm going to get to the truth before I let the cops take this away from me," he said. "But that's not all, Sydney. Little Ms. Hart has also changed her mind about something else since this morning. It appears she wants to just be friends."

Sydney turned to Bree, who turned away to maintain her composure before turning back. Sydney's face was skeptical and her eyes were full of disbelief.

"Don't be so dramatic, Sydney. He's exaggerating."

"Am I?" Graham asked. "Maybe we'll e-mail each other every day? That would be nice. I'll send you jokes and you can send me recipes!"

"Keep it down, Graham." Sydney sighed, looking at Bree as if she had been through this scene before. "I don't know what you've done, but you've had enough for one day. You need to go upstairs and take a nap. Graham, you—"

"We have to go," Bree said. "Keith and I have to go. He's outside waiting for me."

"Bree." Graham stepped closer to her, looking intently into her eyes. "I'm not going to put up with any more nonsense. I don't know what happened outside with Keith, but this is your last chance to stop this and start talking sense."

Bree was clenching her teeth together to keep the tears from coming. She looked at him as if she didn't understand why he was still trying. "I'm not deserting you, Graham. I promise I'll keep in touch, and whenever I'm in New York—"

"Don't say that again," he said. "I'll throw up if you feed me that line again."

"You said it yourself. When the adventure dies down, so would we. I realize what I'm doing is not cool at all, but at least I'm admitting you were right and I was wrong."

"How virtuous of you." Graham couldn't take this anymore. "It just would have been nicer for you to figure this out before you lied to me and told me you loved me."

Sydney was shaking her head in disappointment. "Bree. You told me you loved him."

"You made me," she answered. "You discredited everything that had happened in the last week. If I had just said he was a guy I was having fun with, you wouldn't have listened to me anymore."

"Did Keith cause this?" Sydney asked. "Did he threaten you, bribe you, or use Victoria to drag you back?"

Bree felt herself weakening with every second. "I'm leaving. I don't have to put up with this."

She looked at Graham. His empty eyes sent a shiver down her spine. Would she be able to fix this? He clearly hated her right now. "I'm sorry, Graham. I could have gone on with this a while longer, but it would only make it harder."

"How considerate of you," he said in a low, emotionless tone.

Bree couldn't even find the strength to say good-bye to anyone. She turned and ran out of the kitchen, grabbing her purse on the foyer table before heading out.

"It's about damn time," Keith said as she appeared on the porch.

She looked up at him. "You're going to be sorry for this, Keith. I'm going to see to it."

"Yeah, yeah. Just get in the car so I can get this mess over with and get on with my life."

Sydney watched quietly as Graham leaned over the sink. He was gripping the edges so tightly it looked as if he would rip the sink off the counter.

Graham knew Sydney was watching him. He didn't care. He was so full of anger, embarrassment, and heartache that he couldn't hold it all in any longer. He felt as if he had just been hit with a board in the face without warning.

"Graham." Sydney spoke with compassion and sympathy. "I'm sorry. I—"

"Don't apologize," he said, keeping his head down, staring at the sink. "This is my fault. I knew this would happen. I knew this from the first moment I met her. I can't even recall the moment when I lost track of my better judgment."

"Don't be so hard on yourself. It's easy to lose track with Bree. She's got a lot of charm. She means well, Graham. She really does. She's just . . . She's just Bree."

He shook his head, looking up in just enough time to see Keith's car drive by from the kitchen window. Just one nice last jab at his heart. *What a fool,* he thought. He turned to Sydney.

"She is just Bree. And that's the problem."

"You never know," Sydney said. "Keith probably lied to her to get her to go with him. She'll figure it out and come running back to you."

"Oh no!" He raised his hands in a surrender motion.

"No way am I going to be there. I'm not looking to get slapped around again. I'm through with Bree Hart. I have other things to get to anyway."

"Your sister?"

He nodded, finding it hard even to think about Sophia right now. He knew he was messed up inside. He just had to find a way to function despite it. Without Bree. "I'm so close."

"About Bree. I really—"

"Don't, Sydney." He held up his hand to stop her, trying to find a smile to show his appreciation for what she was doing. "I'll be okay. I'm a big boy. I knew what I was getting into when I met Bree."

"No one really knows what they're getting into with Bree," she corrected. "I sure didn't on that day she approached me at Howard. I just wouldn't give up on her yet. Something about what she said to me this morning, about the way she feels about you, was different than before."

He looked around the kitchen. "Then where is she? Why isn't she here? No, Sydney. I think the only thing different than before is me. I'm the one stomped on instead of some other sap."

"Where's Bree?" Marcus entered the kitchen. "Where's Keith?"

"While you were on the phone, everything kind of hit the fan," Sydney said. "Bree and Keith are gone. They went to Baltimore. He took her home."

"Good," he said, heading straight for the refrigerator. "Glad that mess is over."

"I think the mess is far from over," she said, looking at Graham.

Marcus closed the refrigerator door, having retrieved nothing from it. He looked at Graham, not appearing pleased to see him. "What are you still doing here?"

"Marcus!" Sydney's tone was harsh. She turned to Graham. "Ignore him. He uses up all his charm on the Hill. You can stay here tonight if you need to."

"He can?" Marcus asked, his tone showing that he didn't agree with the invitation. He looked at the island counter, noticing the open cognac. "Who's been drinking my good stuff?"

Graham ignored Marcus, showing Sydney an appreciative smile. "Thanks, but I'm fine. I have a lot of work to do, and my sister needs me in New York."

Sydney's brows centered, her eyes softening. "What are you going to do?"

"I'm going to try to connect all the information together and get some real answers from somebody. I'm hoping the SEC can—"

"No." She moved closer to him, touching his arm gently and looking tenderly at him. "About Bree. What are you going to do about her?"

Graham sighed, wishing he could fill the hole in his chest, knowing it wouldn't be okay for a long time, if ever. "There's nothing to be done but get over her. So, I guess I'll just get over her."

She followed him to the front door. "You know that phrase, easier said than done?"

"Yes, but I have the feeling that I'm going to know it in a much deeper way now." He looked at Sydney. He would have enjoyed getting to know her. "You know, Sydney, you're not bad for a Hart."

She smiled, flipping her hair back. "Thanks."

She opened the door, letting him walk through. He was halfway down the porch when she called after him. He turned back to her.

"By the way," she said. "Bree's not too bad for a Hart either. I promise."

He faked a smile before turning back. The sun was shining, but a breeze had picked up and the warm summer day was turning cold.

Or was it just him?

Chapter Ten

"No, Mother. It's out of the question." Bree was too angry and brokenhearted to deal with her mother so early in the morning. This argument had been going on since she arrived at the mansion last night.

Victoria Hart let out an exhausted sigh, throwing her arms helplessly in the air. The diamond and gold bracelets adorning her thin, fine wrists jingled about. She closed her eyes, letting out a deep breath. When she opened them, she smiled. Slowly, with all the class and demureness of a high-society woman, she sat down on the love seat stationed across from her youngest daughter.

There was a moment of silence as the two women stared at each other in the lavishly adorned greeting room of the Hart mansion that was tucked away in the wealthy suburbs of Baltimore. The room was massive, but the tension made it seem as if the women were pitted against each other in a tiny box.

At the corner of the room, Keith poured himself a drink from the bar. With Aunt May, the voice of peace and reason in the house, fast asleep when they had arrived, he had been the only witness to the endless debate over Bree's mistakes and mishaps and his mother's insanity and smothering that began last night. He had tried to escape, but it had become clear to everyone that he was the only thing keeping the two of them from killing each other. So he stayed, spending the night in his old bedroom.

"What is that I hear?" He tilted his head up and placed a hand behind his right ear. "Silence? Has the shrieking gotten so loud that humans can no longer hear it or have you both lost your voices?"

"Shut up, Keith." Victoria sent him a threatening glare. "What are you doing? It's not even noon yet."

"It's a mimosa," he said defensively. "Besides, if I've got to stick around here another day, I'm starting the buffer early."

Bree swallowed hard, making eye contact with her mother. She saw the judgment and disappointment as clear as day. There had been a second upon first glance that she had seen a hint of relief and emotion when she first saw her mother last night. Only a glance. It took less than a minute before the accusations and revelations of disappointment and suffering Bree had caused set in.

Victoria had won the first round. Bree had been too concerned about Graham, Sophia, her own future, and too plainly exhuasted to give her all to the argument. As tired as she was, she was more restless, so she wasn't able to sleep a wink last night in her room. It was so strange to be in the room she had spent her life in. So much had changed since she'd left it less than a year ago.

The only comfort she found was by sneaking into her Great Aunt May's bedroom and watching from a chair as the old woman slept peacefully. She didn't dare wake her. She just watched, making sure to get up and out before her aunt woke up. Bree felt too ashamed to face her.

But Victoria made sure to find her the moment she stepped out of her bedroom the next morning. She had placated her with a wonderful breakfast. Not having eaten since she was at Sydney's home, Bree was starving and took the bait. The energy that breakfast provided served to help her as round two in the Hart rumble commenced. Still, her mind was so focused on Graham, she didn't have the usual stubborn fight in her.

"Mother, I realize I have made an awful mess of things. I am aware that my devil-may-care attitude has caused a heap of trouble. It was selfish and insensitive of me to run away and let everyone worry about me. I am sorry. I can't apologize for it enough."

"No, you can't," Victoria said, her voice as smooth as her appearance. "The cover-up I have had to maneuver over this past year has been trying to my very soul. Especially after I told Alma Biden that you were traveling in South America the same time her daughter, Susan, called home and swore she saw you in Soho. The backtracking I have done. I can't begin to tell you."

"You seem to be telling me fine," Bree mumbled.

"What?"

"I'm sorry, Mother. Because I know, more importantly, you were worried about my safety and well-being."

Victoria nodded. "Of course I was. You're my child. I assumed it went without saying."

Bree shrugged, giving Keith the evil eye as he passed by her. "I just had to get out of here. You were getting so crazy, so controlling."

"That's ridiculous," Victoria said.

"Bree." Keith sent her a cautioning glance. "Mother has been through a lot these past two years."

"We all have," Bree said. "But things were getting better. Then all of a sudden—"

"I'm not here to be judged by you, Bree." Victoria slid a long, slim finger over her tightly done bun. Her glossy hair had several gray streaks running through it, but they only seemed to add glamour to her look. Victoria tried to fight them at first, but as sixty approached, the grays were winning, so she was letting them come.

"I'm not judging you," Bree said, trying not to. She didn't need more trouble. She wanted her mother out of her hair so she could figure out a way to get back to Graham and help him without Keith screwing it all up. "I will apologize to everyone you had to lie to for me."

"You will not," Victoria said. "I told Susan Biden she was sorely mistaken. I will not have anyone thinking you ran away and lived like a criminal for eight months in that cesspool of a city."

"I did not live like a . . ." Bree stopped herself. "Fine. You want to keep with the traveling overseas and backpacking around the world, that's okay with me. I realize I caused this to happen, so I will say whatever you want. But back to the subject at hand, no. No, Mother, I will not even consider marrying James Trapp. I can't believe you still think that's a feasible idea."

"I would assume you would reconsider. Considering the mess you've let your life get into these past few months. And don't play me for a fool. I know it's much worse than I've been told. You and your brother think you can keep things from me, but I've known you all your life and what you tell me is always only the tip of the iceberg."

"You got that right." Keith laughed.

"Shut up, Keith." Bree threw a pillow at him.

He ducked. "Look, Mother. We have our resident spoiled brat back. Throwing tantrums just like old times."

Bree's hands formed into fists. He was right. She was being a baby. "I'm sorry. Throwing pillows is immature."

Keith gasped mockingly. "What? Who are you and what have you done with Gabrielle Hart?"

"Enough." Victoria held up her hand to her youngest son. "Bree, considering what has happened, I would think you would take a second look at an opportunity for you to get your life back on track. James Trapp is a wonderful young man. He is well educated, stable, successful, at his age he has sown his wild oats. He is very eager to meet an appropriate mate."

"An appropriate mate?" Bree asked. "That sounds so cold, so snobby. I'm not buying in to these arranged marriages within the black elite nonsense. Whether James is a nice guy or not, I'm not marrying him."

"It'll get you out of this house," Keith said.

"This is not the 1700s. I don't have to have a husband to leave home."

"Don't talk about that right now." Victoria was visibly shaken by the turn the conversation had taken. "I realize you have to leave home one day, but that's not right now. What we need to focus on is you and James. In this past year, I have come to know his mother, Anabelle, so well. We've done so much on the Links together. She is—"

"Mother." Bree leaned forward. "I don't care about the Links, Jack and Jill, or Anabelle, or any of this other black elite stuff. I'm going to build a life for myself. And you're right. I've made a lot of mistakes because of immaturity, carelessness, and being a downright spoiled brat. It took almost costing me my life to get that, but it worked."

"Your life?" Victoria's hands went to her chest as it heaved. "What are you—"

"Not important, Mother." Keith placed a hand on her shoulder as he stood behind. "Quiet now. Bree is having another one of her 'I'll do things differently from now on' epiphanies. Maybe this one will last more than a month."

"I mean it," Bree said, aware she had promised to shape up a hundred times before. But that was before Graham. "I'm going to get a job, get an apartment, and—"

"That's all fine." Victoria waved her hand in the air as if dismissing her words. "But let's talk about James. I have arranged for a—"

"No luck with that, Mother." Keith winked at his sister. "Bree is in love with someone else. Again."

What was he doing? Bree wondered. Why would he bring her romance with Graham into the picture? "Keith, why don't you go home? Mother and I are fine."

"In love with who?" Victoria asked. "What family does he come from?"

Keith laughed. "None, Mother. He's our friend the professor. You know, the smart-ass we hired to find our princess. She seduced him to keep him from holding his end of the bargain. Almost worked."

"That is not true!" Bree was fuming.

"I had an idea that was going on." Victoria paused a moment, appearing completely in control. "But of course she doesn't love him. I saw him with my own eyes. He's not her type at all. Definitely not the type I want for her. Whatever happened, it was all a power play. Not a ladylike thing to do, but I'm sure it was beneficial."

"Our Bree is no lady."

Bree shot up from the sofa. She wanted to charge Keith. She couldn't. She had to control herself. He held Graham's future, his freedom in his hands. And until she could wrangle it from Keith, she could not get too much on his bad side.

He smiled wryly, apparently interested in egging her on. "Were you going to say something, Bree? Tell Mother about you and your lover perhaps? Or ex-lover, I should call him."

"The nerve of him," Victoria said. "We trusted him. I assumed he was a man of honor. I'm not pleased with this dalliance, but as long as it's over . . . It is over, right?"

Bree looked from her mother to Keith. *Play it cool. You still have work to do.* She turned again to Victoria. "Yes, it is. It's over. Graham was just a temporary indulgence. I won't be seeing him again. It was fun, but not what I want."

"Of course not." Victoria smiled a relieved smile. "He's a college professor. Ivy League or not, how much money could he possibly have?"

Bree felt as if she was going to be sick. How had she lived like this for so long? she asked herself. She sat back on the sofa, defeated. She knew her own situation didn't matter right now. She had to focus on Graham.

"Is that my baby?"

When everyone turned to see Aunt May in her wheelchair being escorted into the room by Sherilyn, the new maid, the mood of the room immediately lifted. The eighty-four-year-old woman was the joy of everyone's heart. She even found a way to soften Keith up.

Bree ran to her and wrapped her arms around her. "Aunt May! I'm so happy to see you."

She held the young girl away, gently touching her cheek with her dark brown hand. She spoke softly, so only Bree could hear. "Then why didn't you wake me last night?"

Bree blinked. "You knew I was there? I guess you were already awake. I just didn't want to—"

"I understand, baby. That's why I let you sit there. You had had enough explaining that night."

"Aunt May, I . . ." Bree shook her head, feeling the tears come. "I wish I could explain to you."

"And you will," she said, turning her attention to the motorized control of her chair. She maneuvered herself toward Keith and Victoria, with Bree following behind.

"I'm sure you were all fighting before I got here, so even though I didn't hear it, stop it now. It's Sunday. I just got back from church and I want to spend some time with my grandniece. First I'm going to let you know how much I love you and miss you. Then you're going to get it, girl. You better be glad I'm too old to take a switch to you."

"I'll do it," Keith added, with a laugh. He ignored the glares.

"No one is taking the switch to anyone here," Victoria said. She held her head up high, as if she had just won a battle. "You two spend all the time you want. I'm going to call Anabelle Trapp. I'm inviting them for dinner as soon as possible. James is very anxious to see Bree again."

Bree rolled her eyes, but didn't protest more. She knew if she harped on Graham, Keith would get angry. She couldn't have that right now. She would have to deal with this matchmaking nonsense to keep the waters calm while she tried to figure out a way to fix the mess her life was in.

All that mattered was protecting Graham from Keith's vengeful clutches, helping him solve the mystery behind Sophia's frame-up, and getting back in his arms where she could spend the rest of her life reassuring him that he owned her heart. Not a small task. But would he give her a chance to complete it? Would he believe her when she explained why she left him stranded in Georgetown? Would she ever feel his arms around her, his lips on hers, their bodies entwined again?

She had to. Bree knew this love was real. Being away from Graham only made her love him more. Her heart ached just thinking what he might be going through right now. Not just the hurt, anger, betrayal, and heartache, but the danger. He was all alone trying to find the truth to a dangerous secret and he could be anywhere. She couldn't stand it. She had to find her way back to him. But how would she do that without making his life worse off than it was now?

Bree eyed Keith as he went to the bar to make another mimosa. She wasn't about to let him destroy her one chance at true love.

"Graham." Sophia reached across her hospital bed and nudged her brother, who was looking away at nothing in particular. "Graham. Get it together. The nurse is calling you."

Graham snapped out of his daze, turning his attention to the nurse standing in the doorway of Sophia's hospital room. He sighed heavily. "What is it?"

"Sir, visiting hours are ending in fifteen minutes." She waited for his acknowledgment before exiting the room.

"Why don't you head out, Graham?" Sophia leaned back in her bed, using the remote control to turn the television on. "I'm fine really."

Graham nodded at his sister. It was hard to concentrate for more than one second. "Are you sure you're all right? Didn't you say you were in some pain?"

"I took an aspirin and I'm fine." Her eyes held an empathetic softness. "I wish I could give you something to help you with your pain."

Graham stood up, walking to the window. He looked outside at the setting sun. He felt emptier than he could ever remember feeling in his life. "I'm sorry, Soph. I wanted to hide this from you."

"I'm glad you told me. I would have made you tell me

anyway after the way you looked when you came back. Graham, I'm so sorry. I know you cared for Bree, but I wasn't aware you were so much in love with her.''

"Neither was I," he said. "I mean I knew I loved her, but not as much as I really did. I was in a sort of shock over it all when I got back Saturday night. But waking up yesterday morning, it hit me. I don't know how this happened."

"Love is like that," she said. "It never announces itself. Just sort of slaps you in the face and plops itself right in front of you."

He smiled, turning to her for a moment. "I'm sorry for being such a wuss about this."

"I think you're holding up pretty well. I know you remember when I broke up with Mitch a year ago, I was a bumbling idiot. I couldn't look at a can of soup without crying for two hours straight. But then again, he cheated on me. That's a real deal breaker, so I had no choice."

"What are you saying?" he asked.

"When you came here Sunday morning looking like a puppy that had been left out in the rain for a few hours, I listened to you. I didn't say a word. I just listened as you told me how she tossed you aside. But something just doesn't seem right."

"I know," Graham said. "I felt that way too. But I gave her chances and she refused to take them. In the end, she had the choice and she chose to leave. She turned and walked away."

"And I could kind of see her doing that, based on what little I know of her past. But I just thought something was different with you."

"Don't start that, Soph." Graham held up a hand to halt her. "It only makes me—"

"Want to try one last time?" she asked. "Then why don't you?"

"A man can only be stepped on so many times."

"Pride is the downfall of many a great man and a promising future, Graham."

He nodded, knowing his pride was at an all-time high. It was the only thing protecting his manhood. He was devastated by Bree's rejection. It had been almost two days, and the pain only seemed to grow as he came to face the fact that he might never touch her, hold her again. What had she done to him in such a short time? What had he let her do to him in such a short time?

"I can't go to her, Soph," he said. "If she rejected me another time, I would—"

"Then you'll have to get over her like you said you could do yesterday. But how are you going to do that? Every time I look at you, your mind is off wandering to thoughts of her. I can tell."

"I have you to think about. That's enough of a distraction."

"Distractions are always temporary. Nothing more. Besides, I'm getting out of here tomorrow and I'm going to stay with Alice Gibson."

"Now, Soph." Graham started for her bed.

"Don't start with me. I've already decided this. You were going to kill yourself worrying about my safety if I came back to your place. Alice lives in a secured-access high-rise and the security guard is sweet on her, so he'll watch out for me. I'll be safe there. I'm not going to let you worry about me."

"I went to the apartment this morning. It hasn't been touched. At least not in any way that I could notice."

"It's not safe being there, Graham."

"I just got a few things and got out quickly. I'm staying

with Justin Brenton, my friend at the university. The only
one that I've remotely kept in touch with. I was fine. Don't
worry.''

"I'm so frustrated," she said, tugging at the bedsheets.
"I wish I could help you more than I have. Did you get to
talk to that witch at the SEC who tried to send me to jail
today?''

He nodded. "I went there first thing in the morning. They
sent someone out to talk to me that looked like an intern,
but I stood my ground. I had to wait until two to talk to
her. I gave her everything and I told her everything. I don't
think she was too happy to hear me tell her for the one
millionth time that she was wrong to go after you, but I
think I eventually piqued her interest. I can't be sure if she's
going to follow up. She refused to make any promises.''

"You don't seem very optimistic.''

"I have to be. We need her help. I hate being this depen-
dent on someone else, but this is bigger than anything I
expected. People are getting murdered now. I guess one of
the only good things that came out of this disaster with Bree
is that she's not in danger now that she's not involved
anymore. I hope. I swear if anyone hurts you or her, I'll—''

"It's him," Sophia said, waving her hand toward the
television that was mounted on the wall across from her
bed. "It's him, Graham!''

Graham looked up to see a photo of the man in the red
jacket. He recognized him immediately, despite the fact that
the picture seemed several years old. "Turn it up.''

"Finally," the redheaded anchorwoman reported, "the
identity of the man shot and killed outside General Hospital
downtown this past Friday has been released. Jonathan King,
a thirty-two-year-old professional bodyguard to some of
New York's wealthiest residents, was brutally shot in the
courtyard in front of the hospital. Witnesses say King was

spotted in a heated exchange with a young man and woman just before he was murdered.''

Graham took a deep breath. This was another nightmare added on to the many others.

"No one saw him shot," she continued. "But several people heard it. One person reports a couple fleeing the scene. Another witness reports a red sports car fleeing the scene. The police have no suspects, but they do have a weapon with fingerprints and blood on the deceased that is not his own. So far, the prints have not turned up a suspect in the police system.''

"Good thing you don't have a record," Sophia said, looking down at the bandage on his hand. "I can't believe he was going to kill you and Bree. I can't believe you got his gun and were going to kill him.''

"I wasn't going to kill him.''

"Not even if Bree hadn't stopped you?''

Graham knew he had to tell Sophia about the incident. He didn't want anyone asking her questions that she couldn't carefully answer. He hated asking her to lie for him and Bree if necessary, but she had to until they found more evidence.

"I trust you didn't tell the prosecutor at the SEC about this.''

"I had to," he said. "It's what I debated over the most. I think I gained her trust when I brought out the coincidence in the breakdown of the witnesses for the prosecution during the trial. Then I told her what Bree ...'' He paused. Just saying her name pulled at his heart. "I told her what happened to Bree when she tried to contact those jurors. She was pretty intrigued.''

"But she's still a prosecutor, Graham.'' Sophia's eyes, her tone showed her concern. "Who obviously doesn't care whether or not someone is guilty before she tries to convict them. How can you trust she won't go after you?''

"First of all, she doesn't have anything to do with homicide cases. We made a deal. I have until Wednesday to present her with definitive proof that I didn't commit that murder. I think she trusts me. Why else would she agree to it? She must have done her research on me when she was preparing to prosecute you.''

"Trying to find some dirt on you that she could pin to a character assassination of me,'' Sophia said, rolling her eyes.

"That's her job,'' Graham said. "And it didn't matter, because she found nothing. I'm spotless and so are you. And together we'll get through this. We're family and that's all that matters. Soph, I . . .''

Graham's attention was brought back to the screen as they showed a video of Jonathan King. The reporter continued.

"Police are not certain that King's job as a bodyguard to the rich had anything to do with his death. At the time of his murder, he was not working for anyone. He had been a bodyguard for the heads of investment banking, financial services, and international monetary fund leaders. Such heads of major corporations are consistently threatened with murder and kidnapping, as are their families. He's recently protected board members and executives from Merrill Lynch, Citibank, CMA, and Cammermeyer and Storm.

Graham's eyes widened. He looked at Sophia. "That's my connection!''

"What does it prove?'' Sophia asked as Graham reached for the hospital phone.

"It proves he was working for Cammermeyer and CMA. They're linked. And with Barber at CMA, I can tie him back to Trotter now that Cammermeyer owns them. That's Robert Barber's new firm. Robert is the tie-in here. I can prove that he is still linked to this whole thing.''

He dialed the number of Caroline Smith with the SEC. "I've got to get her."

"She's gone, Graham. It's too late today. You'll have to wait until tomorrow."

"She gave me her direct line," Graham said, as he listened to the greeting of her voice mail. "Caroline, it's Graham Lane. I was wondering if you were watching the news. The man I described to you that attacked me, Bree Hart, and my sister is named Jonathan King. The one who was murdered at the hospital. He was a bodyguard and he used to work for CMA and Cammermeyer and Storm. It explains so much. These types of guys are almost always employed on trusted, close recommendations. Please call me the first chance you get. You have my number."

He hung up, feeling a certain sense of rejuvenation for the first time in what seemed like forever.

"Call her," Sophia said.

He looked at his sister. "What?"

"You know you want to. Call Bree right now. She'll be excited to hear this news. She's probably not getting any updates from Baltimore."

"I can't do that." Graham looked down at the phone. He realized his hand was still hovering over the receiver as if he was about to pick it up. He couldn't move it. In his heart, he realized that his first thought when he hung up the phone was to pick it right back up and call Bree. They had become partners in this quest at some point, and the joy at this new clue didn't seem quite complete without her being a part of it.

His hand finally jerked away as the phone rang abruptly. He stepped back, a feeling of longing coming over him. What if it was Bree? His heart wanted it to be as much as it wanted it not to be.

"Are you going to answer it?" Sophia asked, twisting

around so that she sat on the edge of the bed, only inches from the phone.

"No," Graham said. Something told him not to. "Just let it ring."

"It could be Alice," she said. "I need to know when she's coming to pick me up tomorrow."

Sophia picked up the phone. "Hello?"

Graham swallowed as Sophia looked at him, her eyes telling him exactly what he did and didn't want to know.

"Hi, Bree," she continued. "It's nice to hear from you."

Feelings of anger, resentment, and rejection swelled within him. None of them combined was more powerful than the feeling of longing that was still there. Graham nodded a good-bye to his sister and turned and left. He didn't want anyone to see the effect that Bree had on him.

Bree felt her entire body relax a bit. Only a bit. It had taken her a few hours to build up the nerve to call. She was so concerned about Sophia's progress, but scared to death that Graham would be there and pick up the phone. She missed him so much, she was certain she would not be able to hide it if she had heard his voice.

She wanted so much to tell him what she was doing to protect him and how her plan was in action right now. She still had some things to do, but she felt strongly that she would fix this in a matter of days. A matter of days.

"How are you, Sophia?" she asked in a whisper. She was in the room that used to be her father's office. It was a private line, and a room that no one in the family cared to acknowledge since his leaving for prison. She expected as much privacy as she needed.

"I'm doing much better, Bree. Still a little bruised, but I'll be going home tomorrow."

"Where will you be staying?" Bree couldn't ask about Graham although her heart begged her to. She couldn't do that.

"With a friend." There was a pause. "How are you, Bree?"

"I'm doing great," she lied, trying to sound happy. "I'm back home. It's not so bad at all. It's nice to be home. I get to see my friends."

"You sound miserable," Sophia said.

Bree swallowed. "I'm not really. I'm tired. It's been a long day. Have they found out about the ..."

"Yes. His name was Jonathan King. He used to work for CMA and Cammermeyer as a bodyguard."

"Are you kidding?" Bree's stomach tensed. "Did you tell Graham?"

"Graham knows," she answered. "He's talking with Caroline Smith at the SEC."

How is he? the voice inside her asked. "Is he making progress?"

"Do you care?"

"Of ... of course I care. That guy almost killed me. Look at what he did to you. I want everyone involved in this brought to justice."

"Are you going to tell me why you dumped my brother like a sack of potatoes or do I have to ask?"

Bree's heart sank into her stomach. "What did he tell you?"

"Everything. Let me correct myself. He told me everything he knew, but I have a feeling there's more. A woman thing, I guess. So, are you going to clear it up for me?"

"I can't tell you more, Sophia. I ... I didn't mean to hurt him."

"How could you have meant anything else?"

There was a moment of silence before Bree spoke again. "Are you both keeping safe?"

There was another pause. "Yes, we are. How can I keep in touch with you, Bree? I'm sure you'll want to know how it turns out."

Bree said nothing. *A matter of days,* she had to remind herself.

"Bree," Sophia repeated, "how can I keep in touch?"

After exchanging numbers, they said their awkward goodbyes and hung up. Bree sat in her father's old office for a long time. This had to work. She would never be complete again if she couldn't have Graham. No one else would do.

As she opened the door leading back into the side hallway of the first floor, Bree heard footsteps from around the corner. Quickly, she closed the door behind her and rushed toward the central hallway near the stairs. She didn't want anyone to know she had been back there.

Turning the corner, she almost ran right into Sherilyn.

"Ms. Bree," she said, stepping back, a little startled. "I've been looking for you."

"What for?"

"Ms. Walters is here. I assumed she was here to visit Keith, but he's not here. She said you asked her to come by."

"I did." Bree headed for the front of the large house. "She is Keith's girlfriend, so I assume we should be friends. I wanted to reach out to her. Everyone seems fond of her, right?"

Sherilyn followed quickly behind her. "Yes. Your mother seems to like her very much. She comes from a good family, but she isn't a snob."

"That's good." Bree was hoping for that. She needed Monica Walters to be a good-hearted person. If this was to work, she would have to be. "It's amazing how such a cold heart as Keith finds such good women to care for him."

"The only women that will tolerate him have to be good-hearted. Otherwise they would kill him. He seems to be very fond of this one."

"More than others?" Bree asked.

"I think so. From what I've witnessed, she's had quite an effect on him."

"Good," Bree said. "Then this should work perfectly."

"What should work perfectly?"

Bree turned to Sherilyn with a wink. "Nothing. Don't worry about it. Where is she waiting?"

"The greeting room." She pointed in the direction of the room where most visitors were directed.

Bree took a deep breath and headed for the room. A matter of days was starting right now.

Caroline Smith, junior prosecutor for the Securities and Exchange Commission, was just getting off the phone when Graham Lane welcomed himself into her office. She sighed, leaning back in her chair. Her oval blue eyes were red and tired. She pressed her small lips together.

"We don't have an appointment, Mr. Graham." She pressed the tips of her fingers against each other in a prayerful gesture. "It's been a long day for me and I would really like to go home."

"It's only five," he said, inviting himself to take the seat across from her. "We have to talk. You haven't called me back since I left that message for you yesterday about Jonathan King."

"I was going to call you in the morning," she said. "I'm just exhausted."

"I wish I could be doing more on my own," Graham

said. "I tried to find out more about him, but I can't garner too much attention from the police. I've tried to—"

"That's right. The whole murder suspect thing. I'm still not certain you didn't kill Mr. King. You're supposed to be scrounging up the proof by tomorrow or I have to call the cops."

"You don't think for one second I'm a murderer. Otherwise you wouldn't be threatening to call the police while I'm sitting alone in this room with you."

She paused for a second, looking him over. "I know your rep, Lane. Not even a parking ticket. But this harmless college professor thing could be a cover-up. If it is, it's one of the best I've seen."

"Besides," Graham said, "I have until Wednesday, right? That gives me twenty-four hours. And I've been working on it."

The truth is, he wasn't any closer to proving that he didn't murder Jonathan King than he was yesterday. He was counting on her to make that happen.

"So have I," she said. "Which is why I was going to call you tomorrow morning. I've decided to pursue this case."

"Thank God." He leaned forward. "Now we're talking. What made you decide to go forward?"

"We did some research on Mr. King and his connection with CMA and Cammermeyer. Nothing out of the ordinary. Hadn't worked for Cammermeyer for a while. He was let go about six months ago. I worked with my FBI friend to track his activity since. No record of employment, but he's been able to maintain a healthy lifestyle. He's made a fat cash deposit into his checking account every three weeks."

"Any hope of tracing where that's coming from?"

She shook her head. "I'm not hopeful. It would have to coincide with a withdrawal of similar amounts from one of the companies involved. But they're investment banking firms. They are always making out checks to clients and withdrawing cash. We'd have to have a valid investigation to dig into it."

"But we will now," Graham said. "Now that we'll have a case."

"I think so. But that's not what made me decide to go forward."

Graham would have fallen off his seat if he had moved forward another inch. It was all going to come together now. He knew it. So many questions, so many missing links and diversions. He was frustrated, and his mind was so busy fighting thoughts of Bree, that he couldn't concentrate. He would never have thought that Caroline, a person he had come to hate during Sophia's trial, would now be the answer to their prayers.

"The merger between Cammermeyer and Storm and Trotter got me thinking," she continued, wrapping a strand of blond hair behind her ear. "It's on the up-and-up really. But it still unnerved me, so I called my friend Najir at the firm that handled the merger. I worked out a plea bargain with his brother-in-law for an insider trading thing. I'm still not certain he didn't have anything to do with it, and I think he knows it. So, if I push hard enough, he'll tell me anything I want to know."

"He knows something about this?"

"He knows that after Cammermeyer merges with Trotter, they're going to swallow up CMA."

"I knew it!" Graham waved a fist in the air. "I thought it was a possibility, but it seemed like it was too obvious. They've been so careful to spread this stuff out."

"It won't happen for a long time. It'll take about six months for the Trotter name to disappear. Once all those papers have been signed and sealed, CMA is on the chopping block. It won't be like a regular merger of companies, so there won't be a lot of pub. What will happen is, one by one, the heads of CMA will defect and join Cammermeyer. This will automatically lead to attrition at the lower levels. Pretty soon, CMA will be worthless. No one of importance will work there, and no one of importance will want to join. They'll play this game that companies play and say, 'Oh well, we aren't in business anymore because it just isn't working.' Then it will just dissolve away. Meanwhile Cammermeyer will also be swallowing up a few other small companies, so CMA will hopefully get lost in the mix.''

"Son of a . . ." Graham knew exactly what this was all about now. He had to come up with a plan. "Hey, do you have a tape recorder I can borrow? One of those little ones you lawyers use to keep notes as you think of them?''

"Why?" She narrowed her brows. "What are you up to, Lane?''

"I just need to find some stuff out, and I want to take notes.''

"I'm not stupid. That Harvard law degree on the wall wasn't a gift from the store, you know. No, Lane. I've told you we're going to investigate this case. We'll use all the evidence you've found, but let us take it from here. I don't want you putting yourself in danger.''

"I wouldn't do that, Caroline. I have too much to live for now. There's no way I would put myself in danger. I have a couple of degrees myself. I know better. You can trust me.''

She sighed, reaching into her left drawer. She pulled out a minirecorder and tossed it at him. "I'm not going to be responsible for what happens to you, Lane. I can't control what you do. I know you can run to the store and get one of these anyway. I just want you to be careful. If that murder is tied into this case like you say it is, someone has taken this to the next level. Until we know who that is, anyone could have their very shaky finger on the trigger.''

"I know." He stood up, smiling at her. "Hey, and thanks a lot for hearing me out. You didn't have to.''

"Yes, I did," she said. "I do what I do because I believe it's what's right. I'm not always right. You know that first-hand. But my intentions are always good. When someone presents an injustice to me, I have to hear them out. We'll keep in touch.''

He nodded to her once before exiting the room. Inside, Graham was a sea of contradictions. He was so happy to have this clue that tied everything together, and at the same time furious beyond words at its confession.

Most of all, he wanted to share this with Bree. He could just imagine the look on her face at this news. The way her eyes lit up and her face came alive at the thought of something exciting.

Every second that went by without her only got worse. He hadn't slept more than an hour at a time since she walked out on him. Every second he was within ten feet of a phone, he had to focus all of his energy on keeping himself from picking it up and dialing. Sophia had given him the number that Bree left for her on Monday, making it unbearable.

And as he passed a line of pay phones on the way out of the building, the temptation was too strong. His emotions were at their highest pitch right now, and every road in his mind and heart led to Bree. He had to talk to her, hear her voice. He didn't care about the threat of another rejection. Or even worse, apathy. He loved her and couldn't go forward with any of this without making contact with her. Even if she wasn't here, he had to know there was a chance. Whatever it was that Keith said to her, he would erase it.

As he picked up the phone, Graham felt a sense of rejuvenation run through him. He felt reborn. Why had he tried so hard to fight this? He was fighting his soul by trying to get over Bree, because it simply wasn't going to happen. So what if she was a wild child? So what if he would have to work harder to make her happy, keep her interested and excited about them? He could do it. She was worth it. She had made him feel things he had never felt before, do things he would never have done before. Why couldn't he have the same effect on her? So, maybe she had never considered settling down. Well, she was about to.

Chapter Eleven

Bree tried to hold back her smile as she sat in the Great Room of her mother's home. Ignoring James Trapp and his self-absorbed conversation, she was focused on Keith, who was sitting on the sofa across from them with Monica Walters eating at his nerves. Her plan was working, and as she afforded James an occasional nod, just enough to keep him going, Bree's hope mounted. She would be with Graham soon.

"There's a bit of a competition between me and the other assistant district attorney, Alan Phills." James let out a laugh as if so amused by the story he was about to tell, he couldn't help himself.

Bree looked at him and laughed too. At what, she had no idea. James was a nice enough guy. He was definitely attractive, which was how she had noticed him at first. When she had found out he was a district attorney, she had assumed he would have stories of murderers and extortionists. All James wanted to talk about was himself.

"You see," he continued, "Alan is a Harvard man. Which is all fine and good. I believe in the Ivy League brotherhood, of course."

"Of course," Victoria added as she snapped at Sherilyn. She pointed to Anabelle Trapp's empty glass. The two women were seated only a few feet away in the love seat. "All of us with the Ivy's Seven Sisters must treat each other like family."

He nodded politely to her. "We must. But you see, I went to Yale law school. And although Harvard is the superior business school, everyone knows that Yale is the law school of choice. So we engage in barbs and harmless quips all day. I'm certain we get on District Attorney Matthew's nerve to no end."

Bree gritted her teeth together and laughed along with everyone else. Who talked like this? The man couldn't be a day over thirty-five. She looked toward Keith and Monica. Monica was still talking, her hands gesturing her frustration. Keith turned and looked at Bree. If looks could kill, Bree knew she'd be six feet under right now.

"You know," Victoria said, "Bree was accepted at my alma mater, Mt. Holyoke. But she didn't want to go to school out East. She wanted to get away from home and go down South for her undergrad. I regret that decision, and so does she."

Like hell I do, Bree said to only herself as she nodded in agreement. "I definitely do."

"Enough." Keith was speaking only to Monica, but everyone heard and turned to them. He and Monica turned to the rest of them. He ran his hands through his hair. "Sorry about that. Sorry."

Monica smiled and lowered her head. She was a beautiful woman in her early thirties, with chocolate-brown skin and wavy auburn hair that she wore in a braid down the back all the time. She was a lawyer as well. But Monica practiced charity law. She didn't make a penny. No harm done, she was from a well-off Atlanta family. Bree had taken a chance on her and that chance seemed to be working out well.

"Is there something wrong, Keith?" Bree asked as if surprised at his outburst. "I thought we were all having fun."

Keith's eyes were like darts at her. He looked around, trying to calm himself. "Nothing is wrong, Bree. Monica and I were just talking. Can I have a word with you?"

"Keith," Victoria said as she turned her head toward the hallway where the phone was ringing. "You leave your sister alone. She has James's attention and they're enjoying each other."

"Oh no," Bree said. "I'm sure James doesn't mind if I take a moment. It's nothing serious, right?"

Keith stood up. "Just a little thing. Five minutes tops. Private though."

"Oh, fine." Victoria stood up. "Where is Sherilyn? What's the point in having help if you have to pick up the phone yourself?"

Right at the edge of the hallway before the entrance into the Great Room, Victoria Hart picked up the phone.

"Hello?"

"Hello," Graham said. "May I speak to Bree?"

"Who is this?" Victoria asked suspiciously.

Graham recognized the voice. He could sense the mistrust and superior tone. "Mrs. Hart. It's Graham Lane. How are you?"

"What do you want?"

"I need to speak to Bree." Graham wouldn't let Victoria

get to him. He had made the call. That was the hardest part. Nothing could stop him now.

"We have company," she said. Her voice was quick and emotionless. "She can't speak to you right now."

"She'll want to speak to me. I have some information that she would be interested in."

"I don't think so, Mr. Graham. And as a matter of saying, I'm surprised that you would have the nerve to call my home. After your betrayal of our trust."

"Mrs. Hart." Graham didn't have time for this. "I'm sorry about everything that has transpired, but I really need to speak to Bree."

"Well, Bree has no interest in speaking to you. We were talking about you earlier in the week, and Keith told me that you took advantage of the situation and my daughter's affection."

"It was nothing like—"

"Regardless, Bree has made it clear that she had a good time with you, but she's over it now. As a matter of fact, her definition of you was a 'temporary indulgence.'"

Graham swallowed. He didn't want to believe it. "Can I just speak to her?"

"She is entertaining with her fiancé and his mother. It would be inappropriate for me to interrupt her with a call from a vacation affair."

"Fiancé? What are you talking about? You aren't still trying to marry her off to that . . . Look, Mrs. Hart, this is about serious business. I don't want to—"

"Hold on. I'll see if she wants to talk to you."

Victoria put the phone on the table and stepped away from it. She looked into the room, seeing Bree and Keith in the corner. She looked at James Trapp talking to his mother on the sofa. She looked at the phone again and paced the room a few steps each way. She took a deep breath and picked up the receiver.

"I'm sorry, Mr. Lane, but she doesn't want to come to the phone." Nor would she ever if it was up to Victoria. "She's having a good time. You know Bree. She doesn't like anything to mess up her flow. I can take a message."

Graham had a strong feeling that Bree had no idea he was on the phone. Or maybe he just didn't want to believe what Victoria was saying. "Mrs. Hart, I'm going to reach her eventually."

"I did all I could, Mr. Lane." She didn't even blink as she lied. "I asked her aside, so her fiancé wouldn't hear. She still said no thanks. You'll have to accept it, Mr. Lane. My daughter is over her fascination with you. It's for the best. You would never fit in with my family."

"But I will fit in, Mrs. Hart." Graham knew he wouldn't get to talk to Bree right now. He got over that disappointment and was determined to get the best of the moment. "You see, I'm going to be your son-in-law one day."

Victoria gasped as if the thought was too much. "You're mad. My daughter will never—"

"Yes, she will, Victoria. You see, whatever is happening right now, you weren't there when Bree and I connected. We have something special and I'm going to make it work. So all of your cover-ups and society threats are a waste of time. Because I love Bree Hart and she loves me."

Victoria's voice was uncertain and unsteady. "Then why, why would she walk away from you? Why would she—"

"She's overwhelmed," Graham said. "She's overwhelmed and she's scared. I know Bree has never been faced with someone like me. I understand, I feel the same. But I love her more than I have ever loved anyone. And I'm going to fight for her the same way I have fought for everyone and everything I love. Only this time, I'm going to fight harder.''

"Y-you don't know w-what—"

"We've been through life-and-death situations together. Those experiences form a bond, bring people close enough that nothing can come between them. Not permanently. I'm not sure what it was that your son did to get her to leave, but I'm never, ever going to give up on getting her back. So, you might want to be nicer to me than you have been, Victoria. Because despite what you think, that assistant DA sitting in your living room right now is history. I'm on my way and I'm going to be a part of the Hart family forever. So, please tell Bree I called. And you have a nice evening, Mother.''

Victoria's eyes were as wide as saucers. She was speechless as she set the phone down. Graham had already hung up. She stood in the doorway alone, a look of deep contemplation on her face.

"What do you think you're doing?" Keith asked as soon as he and Bree were out of earshot of the rest of the room.

"What do you mean?" Bree pushed his hand away from her shoulder.

"You know damn well what I mean." He leaned in closer. "You told Monica your sob story and now she's all over me about it.''

"I didn't know she'd be so against you," Bree said. "She's your girlfriend. I thought she'd be on your side.''

"You twisted the story. You twisted the situation.''

"No, I didn't. I told her everything exactly as it is. I told her how Graham and I fell in love braving the streets of New York together. How we faced death together and saw eternity in each other's eyes. And how we were ripped apart just as we were coming to find the truth that would allow us to be safe and together forever. Finally. By you. You and your pride and evil streak."

"Your version," he said. "You knew she would nag me to death about it. You little witch. All I've been listening to since yesterday is how horrible I am and how wrong I am. How I'm the enemy of love and all that crap."

Bree shrugged. "Sorry. I could never have expected it to be that bad. But come on. What's the big deal? She's just a girl. You've had plenty before. You'll have more after."

"You know that's not true. That's why you did this. You conniving little . . . You know that I care about Monica. I want to share my life with her. There's no way I'm going to let you or that stupid professor come between us."

"Then be the savior, Keith. Drop this threat of implicating Graham for murder. The truth is going to come out soon anyway. Then, not only will you not be able to keep Graham and me apart, but you'll look like a fool. And you might lose Monica, because I certainly won't give up. If you don't lose her completely, you'll at least lose some of her respect and affection. However, if you take this opportunity to correct your mistake at the request of your love, you've got some serious brownie points."

Keith shook his head. "I'm not letting you and that professor beat me. I don't lose, Bree."

Bree had expected this. Now for the icing on the cake. "You're smart, Keith. You're a strategist. You would lose one battle if it meant you won the war. The big one? Wouldn't you want to be a part of that?"

"I have a feeling I'm going to regret this, but what are you talking about?"

"Graham is getting the SEC involved again. That's what I've been trying to tell you, but you keep shutting me up. We've uncovered the truth behind Sophia's frame-up. Graham is working on it right now. We can connect CMA to Cammermeyer and Storm and, most of all, Trotter Securities.''

Keith's brows narrowed. He looked as if he was struggling with whether or not to believe her. Bree knew he hated Trotter and would love the opportunity to stick it to them. "You say the SEC is involved? A legitimate case?''

"Yes.'' Bree hoped that Graham convinced them to get involved. She didn't know for sure yet, but she had to risk it. Any misstep and she could lose her momentum. "It's a huge cover-up and Trotter and Robert Barber are at the center of it. It's Wall Street, politics, and some serious money.''

"Where do politics come in?''

Bree knew she was sliding into home plate. Nothing could beat Keith's desire for power and influence. Not even his pride. "That's why we were at Marcus and Sydney's. This whole thing is tied to a bill that's coming. There are a lot of people in powerful places involved here. And it all turns into a sweet little frame-up of Sophia Lane. Now, wouldn't you like to be the lawyer that represents her in her lawsuit against Trotter? Criminal defense, corporate lawsuit. Not too big a specialty jump for as skilled a lawyer as you. You would get ten times more than Graham ever owed you. And as for Trotter, you could stick it to them twice. But this time, with the SEC bringing them down, it's a slam-dunk case. And it could be yours.''

He rubbed at his cheeks, his eyes shifting quickly as he thought. He looked at Bree. "If you're trying to pull one over on me, I'll make you regret it, Bree. I swear, sister or not, you'll be sorrier than you ever have been.''

"I know that.'' She did. It was only that she was certain she could make this happen. If she could get back to Graham, she could make anything happen. "Do we have a deal?''

"What do you get out of this? To continue your fling with a nobody, have-nothing college professor? I don't believe that for a second."

"I don't need you to, Keith. I love Graham. I don't care if anyone believes it. And I need to be with him. He needs me right now more than ever."

"You're stupid. He's never going to make you happy. He's not exciting, dangerous, or rich. He's not anything you like in a man."

"Yet, I love him. Go figure. Look at you. You can't possibly be anything that Monica assumed she wanted in a man."

"You're pushing your luck," he said. "Fine. You get your loser back and I get some peace in my love life and a chance to destroy Trotter. They're going to regret firing me as their lawyer."

Bree was already headed for the door when Keith grabbed her and pulled her back.

"What?" she asked. He couldn't possibly have changed his mind.

"You said politicians are involved, right?"

"Yes."

"I wouldn't by any chance get the opportunity to bring down Marcus?"

She socked him in the stomach. "Keith. You're horrid. He's your brother. You take that back right now."

He rubbed his stomach, letting her arm go. "Just kidding."

"I'm gonna pray for you, Keith Hart. You really need it."

He nodded with a conciliatory gesture. His voice was humbled. "I do. I know."

With that, Bree passed by Monica, slipping her a victorious wink. Monica nodded back. She stopped a moment to tell the visitors an emergency called her away. Although their faces showed the opposite, they both gave the impression they were perfectly all right with her impromptu departure.

As she headed out of the room, all Bree could see was the door to the front of the house. She had no time to pack anything. Nothing mattered to her at that moment, but Graham and getting to New York. She knew there were still Metroliners running both ways. She could get there in a little over two hours.

"Where do you think you're going?"

Bree jumped and turned to see her mother standing in the hallway. She was leaning against the wall, arms crossed at her chest. The look on her face was something that Bree could not decipher. The cool, smooth posture was gone. The poker face was gone. Replaced by . . . what, a look of resign, defeat? It was hard to tell.

"Mother." Bree grabbed her keys and purse sitting on the console table. "I have to go to New York."

"To him?" she asked, her words created by more of a sigh than any tone.

Bree nodded slowly, not yet sure what to expect, but knowing it wouldn't be pretty. "Graham. Yes, I am. He needs me, Mother. I have to go. I love him and—"

"When will you come back?" She came closer, tenderly holding her hands together. She wasn't smiling or frowning.

Bree had expected an argument, an objection, an order for her to stay, or a demand for an explanation. None of that. The calmness on her mother's face made her worry. "Do you have something you want to say to me, Mother? You look—"

"I do love you, Bree," she interrupted. "You seem to hate that about me, but I do love you."

Bree felt the emotion swelling in her throat. She had come

home against her will, but she had a purpose for being here and knew she shouldn't leave without dealing with it.

"I know you love me, Mother. I love you too. And I don't hate that you love me. I hate that you try to control me and make your hopes and dreams come true through me."

"I'm your mother," she said. "It's not wrong for me to want the best for you."

"Based on what? Most of the time what you want for me is nowhere near anything I would want for myself. Even if I'm wrong, you can't right me by forcing me into something I don't want to be in."

Victoria turned around, appearing reluctant to face those in the Great Room. She turned back to her daughter. "You're going to run out and leave everyone behind again?"

"I'm not running away this time, Mother." Bree wasn't used to seeing humility in her mother's posture and in her tone. She loved her mother despite everything, and no matter what she told others, she did not enjoy hurting her. "But I have to go. Graham and I, what we have, what we're doing right now can't wait. What's in that room is never going to happen. You understand that, right?"

Victoria took a deep breath. "When will you be back?"

"Mother." Bree reached out and took her mother's hand in hers. She looked into her eyes. "You understand that, right?"

Victoria nodded. "I just want . . . It would have been so perfect. These past two years have been so hard at times and so joyous at others. But lately, you've all been leaving, coming back less often. It's brought it all back to me. And I was trying to stop it."

Bree wrapped her arms around her mother, who was crying now. Her tears came quickly. Victoria Hart rarely cried.

Even when she found out her husband was an attempted murderer, she did not let any of her children see her cry.

Bree held her tight. "I was wrong to run away, Mother. I got so caught up in my own frustrations that I didn't care to see your pain. I was being selfish and childish. I just wanted to make you the bad guy so I wouldn't feel guilty about running away from my own problems. I'm so sorry."

After a while, the women separated, both wiping their tears. There were faint smiles on their faces. Victoria placed a hand on Bree's cheek, tilting her face up. She smiled lovingly into her face. Bree felt overwhelmed by a display of emotion from her mother that she could barely recognize.

"He's all wrong for you," she said. "He's a professor, Bree. He'll never be rich."

Bree laughed. "You never give up, do you?"

"I guess I'll be a cross you must bear forever."

"Mother, what Graham offers me is more valuable than all the money and social standing in the world. He's the calm to my storm. He's the mind to my heart. He loves me, and I can't bear to be away from him for another minute."

Victoria backed away, shaking her head. "I'm not going to approve of this. I know that's what you want, but I won't give it to you. Even if you don't marry James Trapp, I won't approve of you marrying a lowly professor."

"You're going to love him, Mother." Bree winked at her as she flipped her purse over her shoulder. She didn't expect Victoria to change overnight. There had been enough progress for one day. "Just like you love Sydney and you thought you never would. Besides, you still have Keith to work on. Maybe he'll marry right."

Victoria's eyes widened as she lifted her head high again. "Of course he will. And so will you after you get this Mr. Lane out of your system. Now, for the last time, when will you be back?"

"I can't say. I'm sorry, Mother. But I hope it's soon. And I'll keep in touch every day this time. I have to stay with Graham as long as he needs me."

"You have to be careful, Bree. I know what is going on and it's dangerous. Your devil-may-care attitude will get you hurt."

"I'll be fine, Mother." Bree opened the door, looking back once at the woman that gave birth to her and would never stop loving her no matter what. "I love you, Mother. And no matter what happens, I will not leave you behind. You won't ever be alone. I promise."

Victoria smiled with a shrug of her shoulders. "At least he's Ivy League."

With that, she turned and headed back for the Great Room. Bree watched her leave, hoping that her mother would be okay. It must be hard to let your children go. As they get their own lives and their own families, it gets harder and harder. She had to make a commitment to keep her mother in her life, whether she lived in Baltimore or New York. Victoria deserved that much. Not just because of what she had been through in the last two years, but because she was her mother.

As she hopped off the porch of the large home, Bree didn't know what lay ahead of her. It didn't matter. All she cared about was finding Graham and being with him. There was so much more ahead of them, and it was dangerous. But she knew if they were together, everything would eventually be okay.

Chapter Twelve

Graham stepped out of the way of a convertible Saab that was driving down the ramp of the corporate garage way too fast. He didn't bother to give the driver a look. He didn't care. He had found what he came for and nothing else mattered right now.

He stood across from it, the red sports car. It was a brand-new Japanese model. The detail was impressive, although Graham hadn't gotten the chance to eye that detail when the car almost ran him and Bree over only a few nights ago. But it was the same car. Graham was sure of it. And it was exactly where he expected it to be.

Making his way into the building through the parking lot entrance, Graham treaded lightly. The security guards were probably warned about him, and would escort him right out upon sight. But Graham was more determined than all those guards combined. He knew they slowed down at the end of the day. That, plus the advantage of an office building full of people eager to get out and start their commute home, helped him get into the elevator and up the stairs to the thirteenth floor.

Robert Barber was filling his briefcase with the papers he intended to take home with him that evening when Graham stormed into his office. With a look of alarm on his face, Robert started to get up from his chair.

"Please." Graham motioned for him to sit back down. "Don't get up on my account. You never have before."

Robert looked around as if expecting help to come from somewhere. He calmed down and relaxed in his chair. "So you slipped by security again, huh? You're getting good, Lane. What ridiculous claims do you have to throw at me today? And please hurry up with them. I'd like to get home at a reasonable time tonight."

"You'll get home in no time in that fancy sports car of yours." Graham wanted to reach across the table and grab his neck, but he kept his calm. He had waited a long time for this. Might as well enjoy it. "I'm just surprised that you still have it."

Robert smirked. "What do you mean?"

"I would expect you to ditch it after hearing that a witnesses saw it leaving the scene of that murder you committed."

Robert swallowed noticeably. "Not funny, Graham. Trying to pin murder on me now?"

He nodded. "I thought you were too chicken myself, but I guess things have changed. I know it's gotten more desperate lately. But murder? Had Jonathan King messed things up so bad?"

Robert shifted in his seat. "I'm going to call security if

you don't get the hell out of my office. I don't know what you're talking about and you're wasting my time."

"You were so much more careful with the boat. You spread that out well. That was a good move. Almost got past us. I guess when we confronted Cheryl Ripley, that was taking it a step too far."

Robert slammed the top of his briefcase down. "You've become obsessed with this, Graham. You're really out of hand. You need to let it go."

"I've let it go, actually," Graham said. "The SEC has it now."

Robert's jaw dropped. All attempts at cover-up were gone. "What the hell did you do?"

Graham smiled.

"Please tell me you're bluffing, Lane. You've got to be bluffing. Graham . . . Graham. You don't understand what could happen."

"Compiling evidence, forming alliances, interviewing witnesses. You guys tried really hard to make this look smooth. It was all coming together, but then we found out about the future. The truth always lies in the future. The future of CMA becoming a part of Cammermeyer and Storm, and by that fact, Trotter. Or should I say the Century Forward bill? Those prosecutors at the SEC were very interested. They love this kind of stuff."

Robert sat there staring at Graham as if he couldn't believe a word he was hearing. His face went blank for a moment. Then he closed his eyes and slowly opened them again. "You better—"

"I better nothing." Graham leaned over the desk and grabbed Robert's tie, pulling him toward him. "It was bad enough you tried to frame my sister for this, but you went and attacked her. You also tried to attack the woman I love. You had blinders on to this college professor. You forgot that just because I'm not on Wall Street doesn't mean I can't be a shark. Well now, Robert, I'm not just a shark. I'm a freakin' great white. And you and all your boys are in my water.''

He let Robert go and took a seat across from the desk. Robert fell back into his chair and smoothed out his tie in a gesture to busy his nervously shaking hands. He was noticeably shaken.

''I want answers. Start now, and I'll let you get out of here alive.''

Robert shook his head. ''You think this is about me and Trotter? This is about more than that. When Trotter was going to merge with McLaughlin Silverman, I was happier than anyone in the world. It was my doing. I had pushed this merger for over a year, and it was going to make me a director at the firm. But the boys at Trotter are very tied into the boys on Capitol Hill. And when they found out about the Century Forward bill, I all of a sudden became the redheaded stepchild.

''This merger was going to take us in the exact opposite direction of the future of finance in this country. You see, the guys at Capitol Hill said that if they were going to move this way, they would push bills to make this the way all leaders in the U.S. would invest. Not just senators, governors, and presidents, but CEOs and CFOs. You see, they figure the more powerful people that have to do it this way, the more incentive for someone to come up with a quick way of getting around it. McLaughlin wasn't about that at all. Trotter wanted Cammermeyer and Storm, the most powerful firm, serving the leaders of government and corporate America.''

''But you were too deep in the merger to get out without losing a ton of money and a ton of face. So, instead of the company looking bad, they would have a miniscandal that could be believed to be unknown by management, but enough to call off a merger without sending out too many red flags."

"And I had to be the scapegoat." Robert nodded. "You got it. Because the merger was my idea, I had to take it for the team. I would create an insider trading scandal and be very careful not to let it touch senior management. That way, McLaughlin would pull away from us for the time being. Trotter would clean up the little mess I single-handedly made, and be back on the block again. Only next time, Cammermeyer would step in before McLaughlin got the chance to come back. It would look like a simple highest bidder contest."

"Single-handedly?" Graham asked. "So, where did pulling my sister into this come about?"

"I couldn't look like I did this all by myself. I wouldn't be able to strike a deal when I was . . . caught. And I wasn't allowed to involve anyone of . . . importance . . . at the firm. It would look like too much of a corporatewide situation. So, I would get an admin of no importance and not enough money to afford a lawyer that could sniff anything out or make a deal before I could—"

"You didn't count on Keith Hart," Graham said. "You didn't count on my sister and me believing she was of importance. You didn't count on us making sure that the truth came out."

"It was all laid out. It seemed so simple. I would plea bargain and get a light sentence. Sophia would get the trial that took attention away from me. Her trial would be weak. They promised me she would get off. They told me they had the witnesses and a couple of jurors."

Graham touched gently at his sport jacket pocket. He felt the minirecorder moving along.

"I would stay out of the fray for a while and this job at

CMA was set up for me. Then Trotter and Cammermeyer and Storm could handle their business. I would be taken care of as discreetly as possible, and quietly brought back into the fold when CMA became part of Cammermeyer."

"But why start attacking and murdering people?" Graham asked. "I thought you white-collar criminals didn't touch that stuff."

"You made this happen." He pointed at Graham as if to accuse him of it all. "You had that idiot kid look into our directors' backgrounds. We just wanted the files he had compiled. You and that rich spoiled brat weren't supposed to be at the apartment. Then you threatened Cheryl Ripley. We had to let you know how serious we were by going after Sophia. These are powerful people, Graham. And they had had enough of you two. You obviously knew too much. King was sent to the hospital to retrieve those files because he knew you would show for Sophia. He was supposed to finish it. But he only made it worse. When I showed up, I saw you on top of him and panicked. When King came to, he lost it. I had to handle it. Everyone was on my back, blaming me. I had to fix it."

"You decided if you couldn't get me to shut up about it, you could at least make me look like a murderer, so nothing I would say would be credible."

"When you were caught, we were going to make a deal with you to keep you quiet. For your freedom."

Graham laughed. "It would never have happened. You would have had to kill me."

"That was an option we considered. There's a lot of money to be made, and a lot of careers to be destroyed."

"Well, the latter is going to happen now," Graham said. "It's all over."

In a quick second, Robert reached into his top drawer and pulled out a nickel-plated pistol. He pointed it at Graham.

Graham gripped the edges of the chair. He felt panic set in. He thought of Bree, Sophia, then Bree again. It couldn't end like this.

Suddenly, Robert turned the gun on himself, putting it to his right temple. His hand was shaking. He was looking at Graham with confusion, fear, and hatred. He squeezed his eyes shut and pressed his lips together tightly. Graham stayed still and watched. It was happening in seconds, but seemed like several unbearably slow minutes.

Robert opened his eyes and groaned. Biting his lower lip, he pointed the gun at the wall behind Graham and shot. Graham felt the breeze of the bullet as it passed only a foot away from his left ear. His stomach tightened, but he never closed his eyes. He watched Robert. He watched as Robert threw the gun to the ground and fell over on his desk. The man knew it was all over, and the worst, the unimaginable was about to come.

"Consequences are a bitch, aren't they?" Graham asked.

He reached for the phone to call the police, but was startled as Robert's head lifted up suddenly. He grabbed Graham's wrist, squeezing tightly around his wrist.

"You don't know what you've done, Lane." Resignation laced his words. "My life is over, but there are more people that will go down with this than you could even imagine."

Graham jerked his hand away. "You can plea bargain. You have names the SEC wants to know about. People they want to get more than you. You'll get a deal."

"What would a deal be? I'd be crossing some of the richest businessmen and most powerful politicians in the country. How long do you expect me to live?"

Graham looked at him, amazed at the man's self-pity.

"I don't care."

Graham was dialing 911 just as two security guards busted into the room.

* * *

"Where have you been?" Sophia stepped aside to let her brother into her friend Alice's apartment. "It's after nine. I called your friend's apartment and he said he hadn't seen you. I thought you'd gotten into something you shouldn't and . . . I don't even want to say it."

"I'm sorry," Graham said. He sat down on the sofa in the living room of the very small, very artistic Soho apartment. Alice was a not so starving artist, and her paintings littered the walls. "I should have called. Too much was going on."

"It can't have been good," she said, sitting across from him. "You look like you've been through a gauntlet."

"Just the opposite, Soph. It was fantastic. We've done it. Your name is finally going to be cleared."

Sophia's lips parted, but only a whimper came out. Her expression said she didn't believe it. It was too good. "Don't say that, Graham. Don't say it if you don't . . ."

He leaned closer to her on the sofa, taking her hands in his. They were shaking. He gripped them tightly. "It's going to happen, Soph. Caroline Smith is going to take the case. Trotter, Robert Barber, and all the rest of them are going down. Best of all, I have it on tape. I've spent the last few hours at the police station."

Sophia gasped. "I can't believe it. How . . . why?"

"Barber's own words, sweety. You were supposed to be a distraction from him and Trotter. They never wanted the McLaughlin merger, but they had gotten too far in to back out without losing their reputation and clients. Barber was in on it. He was going to be rewarded in the end, but you had to be sacrificed. He was provided with the job at CMA, which is going to be swallowed up by Cammermeyer once Trotter's name has disappeared."

"Why didn't I think of that?" Sophia asked, hitting her forehead. "They just seemed too excited about the McLaughlin merger. They seemed so upset when this all came out and the merger was canceled."

"All a front. They had to make it look that way, so McLaughlin wouldn't suspect anything when it came time to try again, and they were beat to the punch by Cammermeyer."

"And of course I was dispensible." Sophia shook her head, a smile forming at her lips. "I'm so angry, but I'm so happy. You have to tell me everything. How did you get Robert to confess?"

"Scared out of his mind. I don't even know where to begin. But, Soph, I can't start right now. I have to go. I just stopped by to tell you that everything is going to be okay. Barber is in jail now, and that's where a lot of other people will be before the end of the night. The police are going to protect you wherever you go. They're outside right now."

"Where are you going? You can't go yet. I have to tell you something."

"No time. I have to catch the next train or flight to Baltimore. Whichever I can get. I came face-to-face with a gun tonight and what I remember the most was Bree's face, her smile, and how much I wanted to live so I could be with her. I love her, Soph. I don't care how hard it is, or what chance I have. We have to be together. I promise, I won't be too long, but I have to go. My life can't move forward one inch without her."

"Then, you're in luck."

That voice. Graham turned around, blinking with amazement. Yes, it was she! Bree was walking toward him from the dining room. It was that face, that smile that he had seen when his life flashed before him earlier tonight. He jumped up from the sofa and raced around it to reach her. Her arms were spread out to receive him. He saw the loving smile on her face, and a perfect tear dropping from her left eye.

"Oh, Graham!" When he embraced her, Bree felt relief and love sweep through her. It felt as if he hadn't held her in years instead of days. "When I heard you come in, I was scared to death you'd throw me out the second you saw me. Then I heard you . . . Oh, Graham!"

He kissed her tear-stained cheek, leaning back to look into her eyes. "What are you doing here?"

"I came to find you. I didn't know where you would be, so I called Sophia and she told me to come here. I've been waiting for you. I thought you hated me."

"I could never hate you, Bree." His hand went to her cheek, touching it gently. He could smell the lavender, and it was like a drug to him. Had she come back because she loved him or because she still found him interesting? "I just thought . . ."

"It was Keith," she said, trying to focus against her unbridled joy. "He threatened to pin Jonathan King's murder on you if I didn't leave you behind. I had to go. Somehow he knew about the gun and the blood. We didn't have enough evidence to prove you didn't do it yet. I couldn't have that happen to you. Not for anything, especially because of me. It tore me apart to walk away from you. And even though I'm glad I faced up to Mother on my own, I never wanted to leave you. I love you. You have to understand that I didn't mean any of what I said in Sydney's kitchen. It was all lies."

"I believe you." And he did. He would believe anything she told him. "And none of that matters anymore. Neither Keith nor anyone else can hurt us now. It's almost over. And I couldn't have done it without you. We did this together."

"We did, didn't we?" She turned to Sophia, who had

tears coming down her face as she beamed proudly at the two of them. "We all did it. I can't believe it."

"Well, believe it," Graham said. "We make a good pair. I had to get you back. I thought I was going to have to kidnap you, drag you back to New York, and make you fall in love with me again. And I was prepared to. I was prepared to do whatever it took to make you want to be with me again. Again and forever."

"You don't have to do anything, baby." She buried her face in his chest, holding him tighter. Bree was almost choking on her words, she was so emotional. "I was going to do the same. I was going to do whatever it took to convince you that you are what I want no matter how different we are. We're going to take the phrase 'opposites attract' to another level."

He placed his hand on her chin, lifting her face to his. He looked down at her, swimming in her large, loving eyes. "Bree, I can promise to love you with all my heart, and I will. But I'm a professor. That's who I am and I'll never be anything but that."

"That's more than enough for me. As long as you understand that I have a wild streak and a tendency to create havoc. I can't turn that part of me off. It's who I am. But I can promise you that I will never let it harm our love. That will always come first."

"Always?"

"Or as long as you think you'll be interested in me."

He smiled, understanding the meaning of her words. "Then always."

When his lips touched hers, Bree knew that her penchant for drama would never satisfy her yearnings as much as this man's lips would. Her search for a passion so great she felt weak at the thought of it was over. She had been on a never-ending quest for adventure and excitement for so long. She would never have guessed she would find it in the arms of a college professor.

Bree loved a challenge. And for the first time in her life, she realized that nothing in the world was more challenging than making a relationship last forever. She could do this. She would do this.

"Graham," she whispered breathlessly, "don't ever let me go."

"I don't intend to. You hold on tight too. We're in for a wild ride."

Epilogue

"Keith," Bree yelled at her brother. "Turn it off! We're trying to toast."

"Just a second," he said, not looking back. "I just want to hear one thing."

"They're dropping like flies," the courtroom television reporter said with almost a smile on his face. The video of executives being led out of the New York State Supreme Court building was streaming behind him on the left.

"Four more plea bargains today in the case that is galvanizing Wall Street. Bigger than anyone expected, the trial started almost a year ago as a one-man insider trading scandal. That man was Robert Barber. That one man has turned into a matrix of people, all involved in a conspiracy to deceive the SEC, countless ethics violations, aggravated assault, and even murder."

"Keith." This time it was Victoria who called after her son. "Turn the television off."

He held up his hand to the group sitting in the living room of Graham and Bree's New York apartment. "Just one more second."

The reporter continued. "The reason so many powerful men are choosing to plea bargain instead of taking their chances with their high-priced lawyers in court? Somebody's talking and the evidence is mounting. But it's not over. After the SEC finishes with them, they have to deal with Keith Hart. The man whose innocent and unfairly prosecuted client is at the center of this. The lawsuit has been filed and Mr. Hart, probably the most famous lawyer in New York these days, has rolled up his sleeves for his client, Sophia Lane."

"That's enough." Monica Walters grabbed the remote from Keith and turned the television off. "Don't you get tired of hearing your name mentioned every day?"

"Never." He let her lead him to the dining room area where everyone was waiting. "Now what are you all bugging me for?"

Bree was sitting comfortably on Graham's lap at the mission-style cherry-wood table. Her arm was wrapped around his shoulders. "Our toast, idiot. Everyone, get a glass."

Bree was happy now that everyone was at the table. Sophia, a radiant and redeemed woman, sat across from them. Standing behind her, Victoria held that eternal reluctant look on her face. Keith wrapped his arms around Monica. Sydney did the same with Marcus. Even Kelly, the Hart child that seemed at times to disappear from the face of the earth, was there with her husband Mike and her son Jordan, who was playing on the floor with Brandy. Her protruding belly was reason enough to bring the family together.

"I can't believe everyone is here," Bree said, brimming with happiness. "Everyone."

Sydney spoke up. "I think I speak for everyone when I say that we all had to see it to believe it."

"Yeah," Marcus added. "Bree getting married. Actually settling down. Unbelievable."

Victoria rolled her eyes, making a smacking sound with her lips. "Can we get on with this?"

"Now, Mother," Graham said. He knew it drove her crazy when he called her Mother. He was warming to Victoria despite her continued attempts at breaking him and Bree up. He knew her game, and played it up. Soon, she would love him despite herself.

"Don't start." Bree leaned down, kissing Graham on the forehead. She held up her glass. "This toast is for a lot of things. It's for Mother, who has found a way to be only somewhat meddling in my life instead of completely meddling."

Victoria rolled her eyes and shrugged as chuckles and smirks traveled the room.

"You're my mama," Bree continued. "And I love you. Graham is even taking a liking to you even though you haven't given him any reason to."

Graham blew a kiss at his future mother-in-law. "Let's toast."

"Wait," Bree said. "This toast is also for Sophia, who is getting a well-deserved justice and more job offers than any person could ever want."

Keith smirked. "She won't need a job after I'm through. She'll have enough money to buy most of the companies that are offering her a job."

"Which leads me to Keith," Bree said. "My demonic, but well-intentioned brother."

"Well intentioned?" Marcus huffed with a smile.

"Let's hope so," Bree said. "This is also to Keith for absolving Graham and Sophia of their debt to him in exchange for letting him represent Sophia in her lawsuit against Trotter. The lawyer's fee on the settlement she'll get will be ten times more than what he was owed in the first place. So he's making out real good."

"Can we toast now?" Victoria asked impatiently. "I have a plane to catch back to Baltimore."

"Okay, I'll hurry up." Bree spoke quickly. She wanted to get it all out. "Most of all, this toast is to Graham Lane. The love of my life. These last few months have been the best I've ever lived. Everything we've been through has only brought us closer together. Living together has been more of an adventure than I could have dreamed of. But it's all made us more and more certain that we belong together forever. Took him long enough to propose though."

Graham smiled with a nod. "Trust me, I wanted to propose to you that day you came back from Baltimore and I saw you in Alice's apartment. I just waited three months because I didn't want to offend your sense of independence."

"Whatever." Bree tilted her head carelessly to the side.

"Bree!" Keith sighed, gesturing a threat to put his glass down.

"I'm happy!" she yelled out. "I'm deliriously happy and my life couldn't be more perfect."

She leaned down, kissing Graham on the lips. Her toes twinkled.

"You could have a job," Sydney added.

Bree stuck her tongue out. "So much you know. I'm going to work full-time at the Dusty Rose Center for kids. I start Monday."

"Bree." Victoria's voice held exasperation. "What is that? Some homeless shelter or orphanage or something? That's not an appropriate job for a—"

"Toast!" Graham held his cup up and everyone followed suit.

Victoria stubbornly shut up and drank from her glass.

"To my money!" Keith took another sip as Monica jabbed him in the ribs.

"To family and love," Bree said. "And having so much of it that you can barely stand it. But you'll find a way to manage."

ABOUT THE AUTHOR

Angela was born in Chicago, Illinois, the youngest of six children. She began writing short stories and poems at the age of eleven. After high school, she received her Bachelor's in Communications at the University of Illinois at Urbana-Champaign, where she worked on the school paper *The Daily Illini*. From there, Angela went on to work in investor relations and executive research. She is currently a consultant with a Fortune 500 financial services company in the DC metro area.

Angela Winters's first romance novel, ONLY YOU, was published by Arabesque Books in January 1997. It was followed in May 1997 by "Never Say Never," one of three stories in the Mother's Day anthology entitled MAMA DEAR. Angela's first romantic suspense for Arabesque came in 1998 with SWEET SURRENDER, followed by ISLAND PROMISE, SUDDEN LOVE, A FOREVER PASSION, THE BUSINESS OF LOVE, and KNOW BY HEART. Her next novel, REMEMBER YOU LOVE ME, will be released next year, followed by a third installment of the Hart Family romantic suspense series.

Own the Entire ANGELA WINTERS
Arabesque Collection Today

__The Business of Love
                1-58314-150-2 $5.99US/$7.99CAN

__Forever Passion
                1-58314-077-8 $5.99US/$7.99CAN

__Island Promise
                0-7860-0574-2 $4.99US/$6.50CAN

__Only You
                0-7860-0352-9 $4.99US/$6.50CAN

__Sudden Love
                1-58314-023-9 $4.99US/$6.50CAN

__Sweet Surrender
                0-7860-0497-5 $4.99US/$6.50CAN

Call toll free **1-888-345-BOOK** to order by phone or use this coupon to order by mail.

Name_____

Address_____

City_____ State_____ Zip_____

Please send me the books that I checked above.

I am enclosing $_____

Plus postage and handling* $_____

Sales tax (in NY, TN, and DC) $_____

Total amount enclosed $_____

*Add $2.50 for the first book and $.50 for each additional book.

Send check or money order (no cash or CODs) to: **Arabesque Romances, Dept. C.O., 850 Third Avenue 16th Floor, New York, NY 10022**

Prices and numbers subject to change without notice.

All orders subject to availability. **NO ADVANCE ORDERS.**

Visit our website at **www.arabesquebooks.com.**